Long Shadows

Also by Thorne Moore

Shadows (Llysygarn I)
A Time For Silence (Cwmderwen I)
The Covenant (Cwmderwen II)
Motherlove
The Unravelling
Fatal Collision
Bethulia

Science Fiction
Inside Out
Making Waves

LONG SHADOWS

Thorne Moore

Llysygarn II

Old sins cast long shadows

Published in 2018 by FeedARead.com Publishing
Copyright © Thorne Moore.

2nd edition 2023

A CIP catalogue record for this title is available from the
British Library.

Acknowledgements

Many thanks to Rebekah Moore, Judith Barrow and Alex Martin for their judgement and opinions.
And thanks to Gerald of Wales, George Owen and Richard Fenton for their unwitting inspiration.

CONTENTS

Prelude

Llys y Garn, a rambling Victorian-Gothic mansion, with vestiges of older glories, lies on the steep slopes of the Arian stream, under the Preseli heights, in the isolated parish of Rhyd y Groes in North Pembrokeshire. It is *the* house of the parish, even in its decline, deeply conscious of its importance, its pedigree and its permanence.

Others see it differently.

Rooks wheel over the deep valley of the Arian and see it in its entirety. Below them, tangled oak forests cloak the slopes, from the high crags to the glinting flash of the river as it swells, gathering the gullies that pour down from the hills, heading for the thundering ocean.

The rooks are the real owners of these forests. Their nests cluster in the trees and have done so from time beyond time. To them, the great house, Llys y Garn, is a transitory thing, intrusive, shape-shifting, of value for the occasional perch it offers, the food it discards. But it isn't permanent, like them.

They see it from above, a mess of slate and cobbles, gable ends and chimney pots and mossy urns on terraces, clinging to the hillside.

But they saw it too when there was nothing here but round houses, women squatting over querns and wolves howling in the deep woods.

They saw it when, below the Devil's stones of Bedd y Blaidd, a nobleman held court for poets, in a timber hall under sooty thatch, and men quarrelled over family feuds.

They saw it when gatehouse, stables, kitchen and stores

clustered around a great stone hall and tower, and kings fought for sovereignty.

They saw it when Tudor wings embraced the hall and people battled over the sanctity of bread and wine.

They saw the dismantling and remodelling as Queen Anne breathed her last.

They saw the slow decay, the arrival of Victorian affluence and the building of a house that dreamed of King Arthur and croquet on the lawn. The rooks were not, and never will be, greatly concerned with documents, but it might be of interest to note that in the 1881 census, Llys y Garn, with its associated dwellings, was listed as the home of Edward Merrick-Jones, gentleman, aged thirty-six, his wife Agnes, son James, aged five, aunt Eleanor Pendrick (visitor), and twenty-seven servants, indoors and out. The Arthurian croquet lifestyle required a great deal of maintenance.

The Good Servant

1

1884

The unwonted darkness of the afternoon flashed brilliant for a moment, painting the landscape livid, as a carriage rolled up to the entrance of the great house. A flight of rooks screamed in unearthly panic.

The mistress of the house, Agnes Merrick-Jones, was standing motionless, refusing to flinch. A lady did not succumb to small terrors like thunderstorms, but the housemaid could see her knuckles were white as her fists clenched in the shadow of her skirts. At her side, her son James, eight-year-old heir to Llys y Garn, was steady as a rock. He hadn't shown fear of anything, since he was two.

Out of the shelter of the porch's grand leaded canopy, on the gravel terrace, Skeel the housemaid stood with Mrs. Markham the housekeeper and Charles the footman, to add proper dignity to the occasion.

Skeel watched the inky clouds churning overhead, silently counting until the expectant hush erupted into the vibrating growl of thunder. It was miles away still, beyond the hills, but closing in. Lightning flashes didn't terrify her but she had no wish to stand there getting soaked. She willed the footman on, as he stepped forward to open the carriage door.

Mr. Edward Merrick-Jones, esquire, master of Llys y Garn, tight-buttoned and nobly whiskered, peered out, scowling his displeasure at the roiling clouds, as the first fat raindrops began to splatter. He climbed down.

4

'Well then, don't keep me waiting, boy. Look sharp about it. Out, before we both get a soaking.'

In his wake, a child appeared at the coach door. Six years old, with girlish curls and tear-streaked face. He was too small to tackle the drop to the drive easily, and stood staring down with tragic eyes.

'Hand him out, East,' snapped the master, and his valet plucked up the boy under the armpits and dropped him unceremoniously on the gravel, where the boy stumbled, the chippings biting into his hands and knees. The valet stepped out, ostentatiously wiping his hands.

'Come on, up, boy.' The master plucked him by the collar and thrust him at the slate steps, where his wife was waiting. 'So here he is. And just as sorry a piece of work as you'd expect of Alfred Lawson's son. Take him, Agnes, and make what you can of him.'

The boy peered up at the figures looming over him. His lip quivered and then stilled, as his eyes darted from one face to another, assessing the enemy.

Another lightning flash.

Young Master James studied the newcomer with silent contempt, the lift of his lip already the image of his father's.

The mistress folded her hands hastily over her belly, fending contamination off the baby within. 'Well, Cyril. So you are to live with us. I trust you'll be a good boy and a credit to your uncle, who has so kindly taken you in.' She half-turned to the housekeeper. 'Mrs Markham. See to it that he's…' She waved a hand vaguely. 'Washed and fed.'

And that was that. The mistress guided James into the house, her belly bulging out in counterbalance to the purple swathes of her bustle, so that she seemed twisted out of womanhood, into a grotesque, pantomime creature. The master shrugged up his collar and hurried up the steps, handing his hat to the housekeeper, leaving footman and valet to see to the luggage.

Mrs. Markham beckoned the housemaid, irritably. 'Skeel, take the boy. See to the mistress's wishes.'

Valet, to master, to mistress, to housekeeper, to maid. There was no one else for the child to be passed on to. Skeel surveyed the scrap of child at her feet.

'Master Cyril Lawson.'

He sniffed, face in balance, waiting to swing from submission to belligerence, whichever seemed appropriate.

She pitied him.

She didn't know why she wasted pity on him. He had no natural claim to any compassion she might be capable of feeling. He belonged, if he belonged anywhere, with Them, her "betters," the masters and mistresses who paid her small wages and commanded her unstinting service, who addressed her as if she were some sub-human species. That was their prerogative. She understood what was required of her: respect and loyalty. Affection was not in the equation. It was neither expected nor given. She fully intended to care for Master James, as the heir who would one day be her employer, but it never occurred to her to think fondly of him. He was simply the Heir.

This child, though, this unprepossessing and unwanted nephew of the house, tugged at something within her that she didn't know was there. His brows knit. Belligerence was winning out and she admired it. Admired that a six-year-old orphan, thrust unwillingly on disapproving strangers, could find a spirit of resistance somewhere deep within him.

She smiled.

Skeel smiled. It was a rare event that would have brought the rest of the household up short. For twenty-six years, since the age of seven, she had studied so assiduously to keep a mien of respectful subservience that she'd almost forgotten how to smile. She could feel untried muscles twitching.

The boy's frown froze, softened, ready to surrender. He watched her cautiously through those long lashes.

'Come.' She held out her hand. He slipped his sticky paw into her grasp and let her lead him in, as another lightning bolt seared the sky and almost instantly, thunder roared, rolling, rumbling up and down the valley, and the rain came down in torrents.

She bathed him before the fire in the servant's hall. It was a task she should have passed to Mary Ann, the nursemaid, who was doubtless sitting idle in the nursery, warming her toes, with little enough to do until the arrival of the new baby. But hadn't Mrs Markham instructed her to see it done? Skeel perversely chose to take the instruction literally.

The task conjured up all but forgotten memories, of a dimly lit cottage and her, a child no bigger than this one, tending to a sister while her mother, limp with fever and malnutrition, nursed a baby. Had she bathed the child then? She could not recall a tin bath in the cottage, but she could remember little arms around her neck, and a head of soft hair nestled into her shoulder...

But that was all quarter of a century ago. Another world. Here at Llys y Garn, she had never expected to care for any child. With her looks, they'd have said, she's have caused nightmares in the nursery. But little Cyril didn't seem to mind about her pock-marked, knife-sharp features. Was she too rough? It seemed not. He enjoyed the exercise. She supposed the warm water was welcome after the long, tiring train journey and the jolting, draughty coach-ride.

'There. You'll do. Fit enough, I think.' She wrapped him in the towel she'd set warming before the flames, tousling his hair dry.

He laughed.

She felt an odd knot in her stomach at the sound of that laugh.

'So then. Supper for you. What would you like? Bread and jam?'

'Yes please.' He was eying her through folds of the towel, any initial shyness dispelled. 'What's your name?' He had an impish grin.

'Skeel.'

'That's not a name. Just Skeel?'

'I'm a housemaid. I'm Skeel, just as you are Master Lawson.'

'No I'm not. I'm Cyril. What's your proper name?'

What was she expected to do? Chide him for his familiarity and help to bolster in him a proper gentleman's contempt for the lower orders? She chose not to chide. But she still didn't know how to answer. Mostly, here, they called her Skeel. It had become her name when she was judged a mature and steady member of the household. When she'd been young, a raw and undernourished shrimp, tossed back and forth between the upper servants, they used to call her Nelly. A servant's name. Nelly, take this. Nelly, do that. Nelly, what's keeping you, girl?

'My mother called me…' Eluned. She couldn't say it. It was a foreign language, a name that hadn't been spoken for years. Eluned Skeel. It belonged to someone else. Someone who had been rubbed out when she'd come to this house to start a second life as servant. 'I'm just Skeel.'

'My mother's dead.'

'Yes, child. I know. As is mine. We are both orphans, you and I.'

'I'm not an orphan!' the boy insisted. 'My father is not dead!'

'No. But he has his fortune to make and cannot care for you just now.'

8

'One day, he'll come back for me.'

'Never doubt it,' she said. Just as she had never doubted her father's return, when he left wife and children to seek work in the mines. She had never doubted until the day they brought word of his death and burial far away. Crushed by a runaway truck. That would not be Alfred Lawson's fate, so let the child believe, however false the hope.

She cut bread, buttered it, spooned out a dollop of raspberry jam and watched him wolf it down with gusto. Again, that twist of undefined pleasure.

'More?'

'Please!'

'Didn't you eat on the journey, with your uncle?'

He was silent, looking at her with suddenly swimming eyes in which she could see the reflections of all the misery of the journey. He managed a nod.

She squeezed his hand, crouching beside him. 'If you ever need—'

'Skeel!' Mrs. Markham, the housekeeper, bustled into the hall, frowning at the boy. 'Whatever are you doing? You were to pass him on to the nursery. His bed is prepared. You have no business giving him bread and jam down here. Empty that bath, silly woman, then take him up to Nurse.'

'Yes, Mrs. Markham.'

'Don't know what she'll make of him. A milksop with all his father's vices, Mr. Merrick-Jones says. And he should know. A bad lot. It's in the blood. Well, at least Master James will set him a good example. Let's hope he chooses to follow it. I haven't got time for naughty, whining children running around this house, with all that I've got to do. The shoot starts tomorrow. Warn Nurse to keep him well out of reach of the guns. Though truth be told, it might solve everyone's problems…'

'I'll take him up, Mrs. Markham.'

9

The boy allowed himself to be led up to the top of the house. He was silent after the housekeeper's tirade, face blank.

Skeel didn't want to relinquish him, but it was not her place to challenge commands. Her function in life was to serve, to obey and keep silent. But she would at least win one more smile from him, before she handed him over.

'You'll like it here, at Llys y Garn.' She held his hand as they turned for the second flight of stairs.

'No I won't.'

'Then we shall be very disappointed.'

'No you won't. Nobody wants me. I want Mama, but she's dead.' Tears squeezed from his eyes. 'Nobody wants me here.'

'I do.'

He surveyed her, doubtfully. 'You don't, really, though.'

'Yes, I do. I like you best of anyone here.'

He hugged her, impulsively, as she opened the nursery door.

It was a quiet knocking, but it roused her. She'd been sleeping fitfully ever since she'd had the garret room to herself. Betty James, who had shared with her for seven years, had left to get married and Skeel missed the lulling rhythm of Betty's snores. These days she often woke, even at a mouse's scratching.

'Skeel!'

She was already out of bed, pulling a shawl around her as she opened the door. Mary Ann Morris, the nursery maid, stood there, rumpled hair writhing like snakes in the flickering light of her candle. Muffled in the gloom beyond her, Skeel could hear a faint, choking wail.

'He won't hush,' said Mary Ann, pleading, looking over her shoulder, for fear that Mrs. Markham would descend on them. 'We've tried everything. We've given him sugar, we've given him the strap, but he won't lie quiet. He says he wants you. Nothing else. Nurse has no laudanum, and the master and mistress will be woken up and I don't know what to do.'

'I'll come.' Skeel pushed her back into the corridor, urging her on, in the chill, flickering candle light, to the night nursery. As she opened the door, Master James flung himself flat down, into his covers, as if no one could possibly accuse him of anything at all. Nurse, big-bosomed and scowling, loomed over the second little cot, threatening Hell-fire and damnation, but her threats had no effect on Cyril. The boy was huddled, howling, in his nightgown, the blankets swept to the floor.

'He's in a state, nothing will beat it out of him,' declared Nurse, tossing her switch to one side in exasperation.

But the boy had seen Skeel. His sobbing couldn't stop at once. It had become too convulsive for easy control, but his panic began to fade. He gulped, choking himself as he reached out to her.

'Skeel. I want Skeel.'

'Hush now, child.' She looked down on him as his sobs turned to hiccoughs, his face flushed scarlet. Experimentally, she lay her hands on his shoulders, and instantly he shot forward, into her embrace, his arms round her neck, clinging.

Behind her, from the other bed, she caught a snigger.

'Well!' said Nurse. 'I don't know. He was well enough when I put them down, meek as a lamb, I thought. Snivelled a bit at Master James's teasing, but no more than that. Asleep the both of them, before I knew it. And then, out of the blue, would you believe, this silly racket. What a to-do!'

'I expect he had a nightmare. He's just lost his mother.'

Nurse lacked too much in imagination and empathy to comprehend his situation. She harrumphed. 'Is he to go

11

waking the whole house, every time he has a bad dream? Look at Master James, poor lamb. How is he to sleep?'

'I'll take the boy.' Skeel lifted him, expecting her suggestion to be contradicted, but no one complained that she had taken charge. He was still clinging, heavy in her arms, but she didn't care. She could carry him to world's end and back. 'Let him sleep in my room, till his dreams quieten.'

She nodded to Mary Ann to shut the door behind her, and just caught Nurse's grumble. 'Molly-coddling never did any child good, but anything for a quiet night.'

Let the fat woman complain, if that was all the trouble she made. Skeel marched on, in triumph and a gush of love. The boy's grip tightened round her, and hers around him.

'Don't worry, boy. Skeel will look after you. Always.'

2

They were hay-making down by the river. Skeel could hear the voices, carried up on the faintest of breezes. Shouts. Occasionally a high-pitched laugh. The day was hot, sweltering for the toiling men, stripped to their shirt sleeves. It was equally sweltering for Skeel, even without the exertion, swathed in unforgiving black from head to toe, bombazine stretched tight across her unforgiving stays.

She was housekeeper now. By default, perhaps, but what did that matter? Mrs Markham had died, quite suddenly, choking on a fishbone that wouldn't dislodge, despite the footman's heroic efforts, and Skeel had stepped in, while they advertised for a replacement. The replacement had let them down, offered a better position in a titled household at the last minute, so Skeel had stayed on, running the household with painstaking efficiency, making herself indispensable, until everyone took her for granted. She became "Mrs Skeel." She had her housekeeper's salary, her dignity and her black bombazine.

For a moment, in the sweltering sun, she almost let a fantasy of light cotton and cool water creep in, but she thrust it aside. Her costume, from high collar to tight stays, was the price of promotion, and in fairness she could usually retreat in such weather to the relative cool of her housekeeper's parlour at the shaded rear of the house, letting her staff do the running around. But this day it was her choice to stand, in the full sun, on the wide slate step, even if she were baked alive. She would be there to greet her boy.

She patted the perspiration from her neck as she heard the

trotting hoofs and the jingle of the trap, before it came into sight along the drive. Phillips, the elderly coachman, was hunched over the reins. She could see the heaped portmanteau, still miraculously strapped in place, despite the jolting of the road from Rosebush station.

Then she saw the boy, her boy. He was huddled beside the big man, a forlorn waif still, though he was twelve now.

She paced across the gravel, to follow his progress up the drive, sure that he would be on the look-out for her. Was he sitting straighter, suddenly? Had he caught sight of her? He'd know she would be there, waiting for him.

No one else. No reception committee this time, to welcome him home, but Skeel would always there, to offer one swift gesture of affection, before the roaring and the flogging got underway.

And there was, always, invariably, roaring and flogging when Master Cyril Lawson came home from school. Years had not lessened, by one jot, the dislike he had for the distant boy-breaking, man-making establishment he attended with his cousin, and the school returned the compliment. Master James came home triumphant at the end of each term, crowned in glory, ever more swaggering and confident, and, just as inevitably, Cyril came home in disgrace.

The knife still twisted within Skeel, whenever she remembered the first time he was bundled into the coach and sent into scholarly exile. The mistress had been on the step to give a carefully measured, maternal hug to James. She was a woman for whom motherhood, like dressing, or dining, or praying, was an endless string of words and deeds, dictated by convention and performed by duty rather than instinct. She had given a polite pat on the arm to Cyril, her sole gesture of consolation as he sobbed his heart out. The boy wasn't wanted at Llys y Garn, but still he didn't want to leave. He'd been distraught, hysterical. Only his uncle's

14

arresting arm had prevented him from running back to Skeel.

'Skeel, you'd best take yourself off inside,' the master had barked. 'The boy will play the milksop while you are watching.'

So she'd had no option but to turn and walk away, with his pleading whimpers following her down the hall.

But she was always there to welcome him back. Always.

Yes! He had seen her. He was bouncing up and waving with childish glee. She raised a hand, and lowered it again, one finger touching her lips to blow a kiss that she hoped Phillips didn't see, as the trap swept round onto the gravel of the terrace.

Cyril's gaze moved from her to the forbidding portal of the house, looming over them both, and his grin of joyful liberty faded. He climbed down soberly, and stood before her, while Phillips grumbled and unloaded his luggage.

'Good day, Skeel. Here I am again, you see.'

'Indeed I do see.' She tutted, looking stern. There was never a housekeeper quite so stern as Mrs. Skeel. The housemaids would have quaked, but Cyril knew better. He was careful not to smile just yet, though.

'So what has brought you back this time, a week ahead of your cousin?' She maintained her grim expression, only a slight pulse in her lips giving her away.

'Must there be a cause?' asked Cyril. 'Isn't it just custom to send me home early?'

'And who established that custom, eh?'

'Not me, Skeel. I had no hand in it.' There was a shadow of hurt defiance underlying his jaunty tone. Defiance and resignation to the inevitable. He had never yet come home from school without a multitude of school-masters' complaints at his heels, and his uncle waiting for him, rising up and down on his toes, riding crop clasped behind his back.

School reports were a sad, hopeless litany. He was late, stupid, unmanly, he moped, he ran away, he was careless and lost things – books, clothes, anything and everything. But Skeel believed his claim that he had no hand in any of it. She was certain he was bullied, though he would die rather than admit it. He was tormented, locked up, tripped up, set up, by his fellow pupils, who tore his clothes and stole his books, leaving him to take the blame. He wouldn't speak of it, ever, because he had learned that this was the way his life was doomed to be. He came home, each time, to endure his uncle's bawling and thrashing, and then he came to Skeel, for the hugs, the whispers of reassurance, and the bread and jam that made Llys y Garn the nearest thing to home he had. Her embrace, without fail, swept the shadows away and restored his mischievous grin and impudence.

But her embrace would have to be postponed for a while longer.

'Well, you may be whiter than the driven snow, my boy, but there's still a letter come from the school, so you'd best have your excuses ready. Your aunt is waiting for you.'

'Aunt Agnes? Where's my uncle.'

'He's away on business. He won't be back until Saturday.'

Like clouds parting, any vestige of wariness vanished and the grin broadened, his eyes sparkling. Mrs. Merrick-Jones would doubtless reel off the usual pained comments about disappointment and shame and ingratitude, but she didn't know how to roar like an angry bear, or even raise her voice if she could help it, and she certainly wouldn't be standing by, ready to wallop him. Uncle Edward might intend to give him the full treatment when he returned, but that was another day. For this one, at least, he was safe.

'Wipe off that grin, now.' Skeel smoothed down his fair hair, the curls shorn off long ago. 'Look contrite. Apologise to your aunt for all the distress you've caused.'

Cyril composed his features into sorrowful repentance. As she knew full well, he could be a cunning actor when he chose. And why not? How else was he to survive?

The mistress was waiting in the drawing room, stiff as a poker, on edge, because this was a situation that required her attention. Skeel understood that the mistress would rather not have to deal with any situation, ever.

'Ma'am, here is Master Cyril.' Skeel pushed the boy forward. He was hunched in seemly humility.

Mrs. Merrick-Jones turned, her face a picture of distaste. 'Thank you, Mrs. Skeel.'

The housekeeper was dismissed, but held herself in readiness, instead of occupying herself with other business. Mr. Merrick-Jones's dressing downs, verbal and physical, could take an hour or more, but the mistress would want to be out of this as soon as possible. So Skeel was ready for the summons when it came, minutes later.

'Mrs. Skeel.' Mrs. Merrick-Jones looked round in relief, as Skeel entered, as if she were looking to the housekeeper to save her from a savage mob, but there was never anything savage about Cyril. The boy stood in resigned boredom, his pretence of contrition wearing thin as he waited for the business to be over.

'Take him, please, and flog him.'

'Madam?'

'As my husband would do. It is the best thing, I believe. Spare the rod and spoil the child, they say. He must be flogged. Here.' She handed Skeel a riding crop. She must have had it ready.

'Yes, ma'am.'

Cyril looked stunned, as well he might. Neither he nor Skeel had expected this from Mrs. Merrick-Jones. Pained rebukes, yes, before she had to retire to her laudanum haze,

17

but not a flogging. The tears in his eyes were more genuine than his sorrow had been.

Skeel took him by the wrist and led him out. What she would have done if there had been no one to see and hear, she didn't know. Settled him down with bread and jam, probably, and hide the crop in a corner. But Llys y Garn was a busy world. The footman, Charles, was in the hall, gazing into thin air, pretending he hadn't heard a word. A big man, Charles, with muscles of iron in his arms as well as his calves. Cyril could be grateful Mrs Merrick-Jones hadn't employed the footman's strong arm to administer chastisement.

'Please don't,' said Cyril, as she led him on.

'Hush, boy.'

Beyond the green baize door, Jane Bowen, Skeel's replacement as senior housemaid, was standing witness. Why must the woman always be in the way?

'About your business, Jane. Haven't you work to do?'

'Yes, Mrs. Skeel.'

The girl hurried on down the corridor, but Skeel could feel other eyes watching, waiting to see what she would do. She guided the boy to her parlour, pushed him in and shut the door.

'You won't, will you? Not really?'

'Your aunt has ordered. I can hardly disobey. Come along now, boy. Take your punishment like a man.' Skeel pulled him about, to face away from her, one hand gripping his collar. Cyril was quaking. She could feel him clench in readiness.

With a swish, she brought down the crop on the horse-hair armchair.

Thwack.

The boy's shriek was quite genuine. He was in such a state of frightened anticipation that the surprise was enough

18

to make him cry out. He peered round, over his shoulder, caught her eye, then understood and stuffed his hand in his mouth to silence his laughter.

Each time she thwacked the padded arm of the chair, his shrieks and moans doubled.

'Oh please, Skeel, have mercy.'

'That'll do,' she whispered. 'You'll have them thinking I'm skinning you alive.' Then she added, louder, 'That will do. Stand up.'

As soon as she released him, he turned, whipped the crop from her hand and hurled it across the room. Then he hugged her, his face buried in her apron to stifle his giggles.

'Hush,' she warned.

But the giggles gave way to laughter, loud, unrestrained, deep and wicked. For a fleeting moment she wondered how such laughter could escape from a child. Was there truly such a thing as demonic possession? Then she realised.

It wasn't Cyril's laughter.

Cyril met her eye, then they both turned to the window, where Davy Thomas, the groom, was peering in, watching the scene with an evil grin.

Davy Thomas. Demonic indeed. He was a nauseating creature, perpetually leering, but favoured by the master because of his expertise with horses. Good with beasts he might be, but vile with people, especially girls. Not one of the maids who worked at Llys y Garn had escaped his lewd comments and groping hands. Skeel would have had him out of Llys y Garn, if she had any command over the outside servants. All she could do was glare at him and sweep her skirts clear of any contact with him, if he came too close. But she had never cowed him, as she could cow the other servants. His response was always a leer and a snide muttering that would have the stable lads hooting with laughter.

19

And now he was leering through the window, shaking a finger at her, and winking at the boy.

Cyril looked relieved, but she felt nothing but dread. She gathered herself to reprimand the man, but he was gone, laughing still.

What would he do? What would he say? It wasn't like her to feel so flustered.

Cyril looked up at her, questioning. 'It's all right, isn't it?'

'Yes, of course it is. Now, upstairs with you. And stay there. Your aunt won't wish to see more of you, today.'

3

It was the end of her idyll. Since Cyril's arrival, six years before, Skeel had been his only friend in the house, the only focus of his affection, but now, she knew in her innards, that was over. Perhaps it was a subconscious awareness of the end that had her thrown into such internal confusion, when she caught Davy Thomas smirking at them, but it was three more days before the realisation turned concrete, and something within her died.

Cyril was with Davy. She watched the grinning man beckon to him and the boy, at a loose end and anxious to keep out of his uncle's eye, had gone to him eagerly enough, disappearing into the secretive darkness of the stables. She wanted to summon him back, but what excuse did she have? His pony was kept there. It was only natural that he would want to visit the stables.

But there was no call for this long a visit. He could have had his pony saddled by now and be out cantering up on the hills. What was keeping him? She knew what. The Devil incarnate had him in his clutches. Tempting him. Soiling him. Teaching him filth.

She couldn't concentrate. The bills and ledgers arranged before her were a blur, refusing to make sense until she had resolved this thing. It was eating her.

Would the fine weather hold? She stepped outside, into the courtyard, glancing up at the sky as if concerned about the build-up of clouds, but all her attention was focused on the stable block. She wanted to run to it, racing across the cobbles, to storm in, screeching, demanding to know what

Davy was doing with the boy, but if she did, the entire household would witness her obsessive concern. How many were watching from the windows of the servants' quarters, ready to snigger at the housekeeper's pathetic discomfort?

She stepped back inside, fingers clenching, refusing to be defeated. She couldn't storm across the yard in full view perhaps, but she would not leave the boy in Davy's clutches. She had to see. She had to witness.

She turned, head high, jaw set, and marched down the passages, through the offices, nodding to Jane Bowen at her mending, chiding Elsie Richards for her careless ironing, snapping at the boot boy for his daydreaming. She bustled into the old hall, under the echoing rafters, lifting her skirts to stop them trailing in the dust and straw, as if she had an urgent mission and must not be delayed.

When she'd been a seven-year-old innocent, she'd dreaded the old hall, vestige of the house's distant history, creaking with the whispers of ghosts and the squeak of rats. She had been told that back in the early years after Mr Thomas Merrick-Jones had purchased Llys y Garn, a grand Mediaeval ball had been held in the hall, all torch light and colour, at which one elderly guest had caught a fatal chill, but, since the family preferred their fashionable Gothic pretences to come with well-fitted sash windows and Rumford fireplaces, the place had been abandoned ever since to the gardeners and farm managers for storage of tools and hay and roots. It was easy, in its neglected ruin, to imagine ghosts in the dark shadows. But she had no thought for ghosts now. She was after a more substantial demon. She glanced dismissively at Jones the carpenter, who was working on some damaged shuttering, or would be, if Charles were not diverting him with gossip and a bottle that he whisked out of sight as she appeared. The two men sprang up as if caught in the act of murder.

22

'What are you doing here, Charles?'

'Mr. Griggs asked me to check on the work, m'm.'

'Well you have done so, so back to your duties.' She sailed past them, too busy to linger, out into the kitchen garden, where Smale and his boys were hoeing endless rows of salads, beans, cabbages, beets, asparagus and artichokes. The heat of the sun was doubled here, the air still and thick within the high walls of the garden.

She nodded to Smale, who straightened and looked up expectantly. What now? This far, no one would have questioned her purposeful march, but how would she explain her escape through the back gate, plunging into the shade of the trees. A housekeeper had no business out there.

But a housekeeper need not explain herself to gardeners or their like. Chin up, she strode up, through the gate and out. Let them watch and wonder, if they must. She no longer cared. She'd gone too far to stop herself.

It was a foreign world in the woods, full of alien sounds and smells, rampaging greenery instead of the dust-free order she kept in the house. Visitors, approaching the house along the drive, would observe the rising acres of trees and perceive a valuable asset, for timber and game, but creeping out through the back gate, into the green depths, Skeel saw it differently. It was illicit, untamed, taunting her with rampant, thrusting wilderness. An axe rang out. The rank smell of leaf mould and rot was warm and damp. Unseen creatures rustled in the moist darkness of the undergrowth.

She felt threatened, by what she didn't know. But the shade at least was welcome, cooling her body if not her fevered brain. She skirted the rear of the house, the crumbling buttresses of the old hall, the ivy-clawed stump of the ancient tower, the coach house…

The rear of the stables. She took a deep breath, torn between a desperate anxiety and a consciousness of her own

23

absurdity. She found a tiny casement window propped ajar – all the windows were flung open in the summer heat. She could smell horses, dung, sweet hay. She could see pools of brilliant sunlight painting white patterns on cobbles and stalls.

She couldn't see the men, but she could hear them, over the soft snuffling and whinnies, the clank of metal links, the swish of water gushing from pails. She heard Davy's evil cackle, that leering, suggestive laugh he directed at any maid who showed her face in the courtyard. She heard the yelps of agreement and encouragement from the stable boys. She heard Cyril's high laughter. A child's laugh, still.

Her stomach was gripped with jealousy, bending her double with its violence. She straightened with an effort, to catch the man's words.

'…make a proper man of you. That's what they're there for, boy. You think your cousin Jamie hasn't dipped his wick into every little tart in Llys y Garn? Women are there for us, boy. All they're good for. Most of them. Not that withered old maid, Skeel. Time you stopped hanging on her skirts, boy, or she'll shrivel your balls off.'

More laughter and Cyril laughed with them.

'Here, boy. Have another swig.'

So that was where he was getting the spirits. She'd smelt them on his breath the day before, though he swore he hadn't been near his uncle's decanters.

She would get him back. She would not let that beast, Davy Thomas, prise Cyril from her. Did he imagine she'd stand by and do nothing, just because he'd caught her defying the mistress's orders? She'd have him out, she'd destroy him. Cyril was hers.

No longer caring what the other servants saw, or deduced, or muttered behind their hands, she hurried back to the coach house, striding past the carriage, the cart and the gig and out into the courtyard, to the open doors of the stables. She swept inside.

'Master Cyril, come please. Your aunt has summoned you.'

The boy was perched on a bale of straw, while Davy stood over him, bottle in hand, one boot up on the bale, loins wide and priapic.

She averted her gaze hastily. The stable boys giggled.

'You shouldn't be lingering in here with these people, Cyril.'

'Just giving him some man talk, missis,' said Davy. 'Don't want him growing up a nancy, do we? Not Mr. Merrick-Jones's nephew. Oh no.'

She ignored him, holding out her hand.

Grinning, Cyril jumped down to join her, content to obey, but he refused her hand. She shepherded him from the stables.

'Pity the man who ever had to…' She didn't hear the rest of Davy's mocking words to his lads.

'I have something special for you,' she whispered.

'What?' Cyril demanded, instantly focussed again on her. If he had a care for his self interest, what of it? He would have to seek his own advantage, for no one else would do it for him.

'Wait and see. But only if you're a good boy. No messing around with brutes like Davy Thomas.'

'But—'

'Mrs. Skeel, the missis has been ringing for you,' said Jane, waiting for them on the doorstep. 'I said I'd fetch you.'

'All right, no need to stand there gawping. I'm here, aren't I?' Skeel flicked her skirt free of the dust and leaves of the woods, then whispered once more to the boy. 'Something special, if you're good.'

What it would be, she didn't know. She would think of

something. She'd cut her own heart out, if it kept him from the clutches of the groom.

Brandy. The master's best brandy. Griggs, the elderly butler, hadn't noticed what she'd purloined. With his failing eyesight, he wouldn't notice if she snatched the whole decanter from under his nose.

Cyril tried it, pulling a face, as she would expect a child to do, but it wasn't a grimace of shock at the burning assault of strong liquor. It was the grimace of a connoisseur, savouring. Or of a child remembering something he'd tasted before.

'Davy Thomas didn't give you brandy?' It was gin in that bottle the groom had been offering Cyril, Skeel was certain. She'd smelt it.

Cyril shook his head, grinning, holding out his glass. She'd only given him the smallest sip. 'No, but my father drinks brandy. Sometimes I'd sit with him after dinner and he'd let me try it.'

'Did he, indeed!' No surprise in that. A father who, in the last six years, had visited his son only twice, and not at all in the last three.

Alfred Lawson had been a city man, with fine prospects, when the master's sister, Harriet, had married him. Harriet, a cold and ambitious young woman, had hoped for a title, but as the years had passed and titles slipped away, she had finally settled for smart and cosmopolitan. Skeel, the under-housemaid, had helped to carry her bags, trunks, hat boxes and portmanteaux to the cart that was to follow her carriage, as the young bride-to-be departed for London, anticipating a life of fashionable luxury and elegant extravagance.

The extravagance had been real enough, for the first year or two, while Alfred Lawson spent and gambled his way through his wife's fortune. Cyril had passed his early years in a fine city house, with fine city gentlemen going out through one door and bailiffs coming in at another.

If Alfred Lawson's idea of parental care had been to debauch his infant son for the amusement of his rakish colleagues, at their rowdy dinners, it was no wonder that Harriet was rumoured to be permanently at war with her husband over the child's upbringing. She had won the last battle, though. Her final wish, as pneumonia and disappointment carried her off, was to give the boy into her brother's reluctant care, and Alfred had acquiesced. Perhaps he had lost interest in his son, the moment there were no more small victories to score over his disapproving wife. Since Harriet's death, he'd been bankrupted, recovered, failed again, gone to India and found another wife.

Some people might consider it a sad business for the boy. Skeel thought otherwise. Providence, by whatever cruel means, had delivered him into her care, and she would keep caring for him, as long as she drew breath. She gave him another thimbleful of brandy. If this was what it took to keep him from a beast every bit as corrupting as Alfred Lawson, so be it.

'More?' Cyril held out his glass again.

She shut the bottle away in a cupboard. 'That's more than enough. Do you want to be breathing it all over your little cousin Gertrude? You must remember, you're not an ill-bred stable boy, you're a young gentleman. Like Master James.'

'James drinks brandy with my uncle.'

'James is fourteen. You are only twelve.'

'When I'm fourteen, he'll be sixteen. And when I'm sixteen, he'll be eighteen.'

'Silly boy. Do you think I'm too dull-witted to know that?' She knew exactly what he meant though. He would always be behind his cousin. James was the magnificent young cock of the walk, all that his family hoped and expected, flawless in swaggering looks, manners, arrogance and daring, destined to be the glorious champion of his family, of the county, of the Empire. And Cyril was the irritatingly inadequate nephew.

When the boys were home at Llys y Garn, James treated his cousin like a younger brother, with apparently good-humoured disdain – a younger brother to be commanded and patronised with no more rivalry and tussles than would be found in any family. His behaviour, perhaps, was dictated by the lack of any alternative company. Cyril would do for a companion if none other were to be had. But it was always James who was summoned by the master to be presented to guests, James who now dined with the family, and passed the port with his father, while Cyril remained in the nursery with six-year-old Gertrude.

'James returns tomorrow. You can ride out together. No need to waste your time with the likes of Davy Thomas.'

'Davy says he'll teach me to fight.' Cyril was eying the cupboard as she locked it, trying to note which of her many keys did the trick.

'He'll not teach you anything!' She jangled the keys back into confusion. 'Do you want to brawl like a guttersnipe?'

'I'd like to give James a black eye.'

'No you would not.'

'I would, though.'

Of course he would. She guessed the cause of his misery at school, the reason for his frequent disgrace. The bullying, humiliation and ill-treatment were almost certainly at James's instigation. In the hierarchical battleground of the school dormitory and the playing field, James's superior contempt for his younger cousin was at liberty to display a more malignant side.

But there was no help for it. 'You should never brawl,' she insisted. 'It will get you nowhere.'

'Except that I'll have the satisfaction of knocking James down. You don't understand. You don't have cousins.'

'No, I don't.' A brother, maybe, if he still lived, but John had gone to sea at thirteen and never returned. The baby William hadn't lived three months and sister Mary, the child who had nestled on Skeel's shoulder, had coughed up her lungs in the workhouse at the age of six, a year after their mother. 'I have no one.'

'You're lucky,' said Cyril.

'Except I have you.'

He laughed. 'Yes, but you're not there, at school. James is. You can't help me, you're just a servant.'

And so she was. Never had been, never would be, anything else. All she had really known of life was this life at Llys y Garn, where she was Nelly the scullery maid, Skeel the housemaid, Mrs. Skeel the housekeeper, her function and status serving the needs and honour of the Merrick-Jones name. She had her housekeeper's parlour, her keys, her ledgers... and Cyril, her boy.

Her boy must grow into a gentleman, and this school torture was deemed to be an essential part of the process. How else would he learn his place in society, whatever that future position might be?

Sometimes, when she lay alone, at night, counting the owl calls and fox barks, a fantasy would infiltrate her drowsing thoughts. A fantasy of some catastrophe – an epidemic perhaps, or a train crash – that carried off Master James and Miss Gertrude, and left her boy heir to this estate. A wicked fantasy that had no hope of fulfilment, because the Merrick-Jones children were as well-nourished and nurtured and healthy as any alive. It wasn't a dream she'd ever acknowledge in daylight, even to herself. Just a moonlight fancy.

.

The master and mistress retired. Skeel toured the house, candle in hand, ensuring all the windows were locked, the lamps out. No fires to be damped in this heat. The house was silent.

Or should be. She caught the opening of the baize door, the pad of feet on thick carpet, hesitant, turning one way, then another.

Skeel quit the dining parlour to find Jane, the housemaid, in cap and nightgown, shawl wrapped round her, white-faced with shock that exploded into relief when she saw the housekeeper.

'Yes, what is it?'

'Nurse, Mrs. Skeel. She said to call you.' Jane took a deep breath. 'It's a terrible thing. Master Cyril. He's…' She stopped, unable to complete the words.

Skeel tutted, shepherding the girl back to the servant's quarters. The boy must be intoxicated. Not on the little sip of brandy she'd allowed him, which meant he must have slipped out again, after dark, to be plied with more gin by Davy Thomas. Skeel's limbs stiffened at the outrage, the possibility that the groom still had his claws in the boy.

But, of course, it wasn't thoughts of Davy Thomas that had Jane on the point of hysteria. It was the thought of intoxication. Jane the pious Methodist, the God-fearing tea-drinker. Chapel oozed out of every one of Jane Bowen's pores and seasoned her every word.

Many of the servants claimed allegiance to one or other of the chapels that perched in odd corners of the countryside around, but most of them were content, on Sundays, to take the short walk, or cart ride if the weather were foul, to St. Brynach's church in Rhyd y Groes, to say their ritual prayers, in orderly, sober parade behind the Merrick-Jones family. But Jane Bowen had to spend her free Sabbath hours plodding up the valley to Bethel Chapel. Plain Jane, an easy catch of the last revival. Doubtless she knew the arms of Jesus were the only arms that would ever embrace her. She said Amen, loudly, to the garbled grace Griggs recited at a run at the servants' table. She never missed her night-time prayers.

Skeel found her earnest piety irritating beyond endurance, but the woman was far too diligent and superficially respectful, despite her air of sanctimonious disapproval when witnessing loose behaviour or lewd language, for the housekeeper to have any good reason to be rid of her. She's probably been on her knees, haranguing the Lord, when Nurse had called for her.

'A terrible, wicked thing,' Jane repeated.

Skeel prodded her up the narrow stairs. 'Hush, girl. I shall speak to Nurse. Go back to your bed now.'

But just for once, considering the case to be so very serious, Jane disobeyed, following as Skeel headed for the open door of the night nursery.

Nurse was waiting in a state of guilt and panic.

Stupid girl, what was a little gin and merriment? Betsy, the unrelentingly stern old nurse, would have coped with such a little matter as a tipsy child. She'd never have let Cyril slip past her in the first place. But she'd taken sick and retired, with a miserly pension, to her sister's cottage in the valley, leaving Mary Ann Morris, endlessly flapping, to take her place.

'What is all this nonsense?' Skeel pushed past her, into the nursery, expecting to see Cyril rolling on the floor and giggling, but he was standing in a corner, in his nightgown, hands clasped behind his back, his lip aquiver with tearful guilt.

'I didn't mean—' he began, gulping, but she lifted a finger to her lips.

'Hush, child. Speak when you're spoken to.'

'A wicked child, he is!' burst in Mary Ann, wringing her hands.

'What has happened? Calm yourself, Nurse.' Skeel noted the two empty beds. 'Where is Miss Gertrude?'

'I've got her safe, Mrs. Skeel, where he can't get at her. In my bed, through there. Filthy beast. I heard her whimper and I found him. Had her nightgown up and he was touching her. Wicked, wicked!'

'Be quiet!' Skeel looked through to Mary Ann's bed. Miss Gertrude, daughter of the house, all ringlets and roses, was showing sleepy signs of distress, but she was barely awake, probably more upset by Nurse's palaver than by the thing, whatever it was, the boy was supposed to have done. 'He was probably just tickling her. Children do.'

'No, he was not! I saw him with my own eyes. His fingers—'

'That's enough, Nurse! You'll have the girl in tears. Please, keep calm.'

'Mrs. Merrick-Jones must be told. She's got to be told, but I daren't. You can do it, can't you, Mrs. Skeel? And take the boy. I can't deal with him. You've flogged him, haven't you, Mrs. Skeel? That's what he needs. A flogging, dirty little monster!'

'Hush!' Did she have to slap the woman to calm her down? 'Control yourself and tend to the girl. I'll take Master Cyril. I'll deal with it.'

That was what Mary Ann needed to hear. She calmed, though she was still snorting like an over-taxed horse.

'Cyril. Come with me.'

He looked at her, all doe eyes, ready to weep – if it would do the job. He was playing her. She knew he did it, but what of it? He was a boy, her boy, who would have to make his own way in the world. He had to play people if he were to survive. Let him play her.

She led him past Jane, who was watching the scene, shawl clasped round her, lips tight.

'That will do, Bowen. Go back to bed.'

In her parlour, she lit a lamp and sat Cyril down.

'What did you think you were doing?'

'Nothing! I wasn't doing anything, honestly.'

She stood over him. 'Don't lie to me. Not here, while we're alone. Tell me the truth. You were touching her. Your cousin, Gertrude.'

'No! Not really. I just…'

'Well?'

'I just wanted to see. Davy says girls—'

'I don't want to hear what Davy Thomas says! He is a filthy brute and you should shut your ears when he is by!'

'I just wanted to see.' He looked down, apparently ashamed, but she caught that quick sideways glance through his lashes. Hadn't she always admired that naughty spirit of defiance?

'You're too young to be thinking of women, let alone girls. Little girls, and your own cousin, too. Do you understand, your aunt and uncle would do more than flog you if they heard of this? They'd throw you out of this house, and where would you be then?'

'I don't know.' He looked up, eyes shining. 'You'd take me in.'

Oh, what she would give for that. As if it could ever happen.

'Where? This is my home. I have no other. I am like you, boy. Dependent on your aunt and uncle for my very existence. We must both bend to their wishes if we don't want to starve. So I want you to promise me, yes? You'll not touch your cousin.'

'I promise.'

'Or try to look where you have no business looking.'

33

'Yes. Davy says he'll—'

'I will not have you speak that beast's name in here. Would you have him drag you down to his filthy gutter? You are a gentleman, Cyril. Not a beast.'

'I only wanted to see,' he pleaded again.

'It's a wicked thing, such curiosity. You should put such thoughts out of your mind. If you cannot, if you must be wicked...' She busied herself, mending the lamp. 'Play your naughty games with Annie Lewis. Not with your little cousin.'

She spoke to Mrs. Merrick-Jones. It was something she had to do, before Jane and the nurse decided to take matters into their own hands. Besides, it was for the best that something should be done.

'Ma'am, I think it's time for Master Cyril to have his own room.'

Mrs. Merrick-Jones sighed. She didn't like being bothered, with this or anything else. 'Oh. You think so? Perhaps you are right. A room, yes. Is there a room?'

'The one next to Master James, ma'am?'

'Yes, yes.'

'Best for Miss Gertrude to have the nursery to herself.'

Mrs. Merrick-Jones took her attention from the roses in their Chinese vase, and looked, not at Skeel, but over her shoulder, somewhere in Skeel's vicinity. It was a habit she had, which made her look languidly detached, lost in her own world, but Skeel had come to recognise it as a sign that the mistress was thinking – had caught the implication of something said and was letting it flutter around the perimeter of her mind. Best not to let her think too much.

'With Master James coming home, ma'am, it will be a good thing for the young men to be together. Master James is quite the young gentleman now. Cyril will learn so much from—'

'Yes, yes. You're right. See to it.'

Mrs. Merrick-Jones was not an over-effusive mother. She wasn't effusive in any of her emotions, if she had them at all. But she shows a dutiful affection for her children. When James arrived, she would allow him to kiss her on the cheek. She would pat Gertrude on the head when Nurse brought her down in the evening, and she'd sit patiently while the child delivered a song or poem or whatever little exercise she has been schooled in today. She would bestow a nod and a half-smile on Cyril, now that the obligatory reprimands on his early return had been executed. She was confident that the staff she employed would do whatever was required in feeding, washing, chivvying, instructing and nurturing the children of the house. There was nothing to be gained in inquiring too diligently into the whys and wherefores of any decisions taken by the utterly dependable Mrs. Skeel.

Skeel looked in on the laundry. The room was full of steam, and the moist fumes of soap and starch and scorched linen. Mrs. Phillips, from the village, brawny arms stripped bare and running with sweat and hot water, was heaving sheets from the boiler. Annie Lewis, Llys y Garn's youngest maid, was folding damp unmentionables into a wicker basket. She was a small thing, eleven or twelve, but looked younger. Though her hands were raw and her shoulders bony, her dark eyes were huge, dimples creased her cheeks and curls of chestnut hair escaped from her cap. She had the makings of a good-looking girl – the sort who could, one day, when her red fingers were softened, and her figure filled out, be appointed parlour maid, to wait on the family at breakfast, in lace cap and apron, and greet guests at the door. Skeel had missed that rung of the ladder. She'd been too plain, too scarred, too angular and heavy-footed, for the family to wish

35

to look at her over their kedgeree and devilled kidneys, but Annie Lewis would be far more pleasing on the eye.

'Leave that,' Skeel commanded. 'Master Cyril has been moved into the room next to Master James. His clean linen can be taken there.'

'Yes, m'm. I'll give them to Jane, m'm.'

'No. No, don't bother Jane. Take them yourself.'

'Me, Mrs. Skeel?'

'Yes, Annie. You. Hurry along now and take them up to Master Cyril's room. He's waiting.'

4

'Cyril!' Skeel started, dropping her pen. There were times, in her idle moments, when she conjured up his face to quieten her private longing, but never quite this vividly. Lounging in her parlour doorway, he looked disreputable, unabashed and very real. 'What are you doing here? You're at Oxford.'

'And yet I'm here. An indisputable riddle. How do you suppose I come to be in two places at once?'

'Silly boy, you know what I mean.' She'd risen, wanting to hug him, but fine young gentlemen were not to be hugged. 'Why aren't you at Oxford?'

'Rusticated.' He said it with a defiant pride. 'Don't tell me you're surprised. I have to maintain the tradition, don't I? At least I don't get a flogging from Uncle Edward, these days. Though I'll take one of yours without complaint.'

'Hush, boy. What have you done, this time?'

'Nothing. Nothing of any importance. So how is my Skillers? Missing me?'

'Not at all.' She brushed a speck of dust from his fashionable jacket. 'Do you think I don't have better things to do than dream of having you under my feet?'

'Which is where I'm most at home.' He threw himself into her armchair, crossing his legs, his polished boots perfectly placed to trip her up. 'How about a celebratory sip? You still keep the brandy stashed away in that cabinet of yours? I need a restorative and the old man seems to have been pre-warned of my arrival, yet again. He's ordered Charles to lock up the decanters when I'm around. And Charles has grown to be a pompous bore. He's not for bribing.'

'So I should think. Your uncle is quite right. You drink far too much.'

'Now, now, Skillers. I don't expect that sort of dreary nagging from you. I'm a young gentleman and I have a young gentleman's tastes. I must be allowed my little pleasures. But speaking of pompous Charles, when is my uncle going to find a proper replacement for Griggs? Charley's no butler. Too much of a sour-faced bear, and his boots squeak.'

'Perhaps your uncle thinks a footman is quite sufficient for this household. No need to go to the expense of having a butler too.'

'Not like Uncle Teddy to be so tight.'

No, Skeel knew that was true, well enough. It was not like Edward Merrick-Jones to spare expense. Or it would not have been, in the past. Mr. Edward's father, who had purchased the estate, was a man of undistinguished family who, though canny investments in coal, iron, railways and African ventures, had turned a modest fortune into a very large one. His son had inherited property, shares, connections with peers and the surrounding gentry, so he had embraced, as his birth right, a certain style of living – a house in London, his clubs, the mistress's fashionable wardrobe, county-wide entertaining, guns, a stable full of hunters, a pack of hounds, an army of servants, mostly unseen, catering to his every whim. All this maintained on a fortune that was no longer expanding but gradually, inexorably contracting, thanks to depression and some mismanaged investments. Even the landed gentry couldn't exceed their income forever. Especially not if they were blessed with a nephew who invariably exceeded his allowance and landed his outrageous debts on his irate uncle.

It would never do to advertise the need for retrenchment,

but Skeel, in charge of the household bills, knew the painful truth. Nothing had been spelled out – no need – but she was the one who supervised the discreet savings behind the elegant façade. Butcher's orders shaved, a carriage disposed of, new vintages not laid down, repairs on the old hall roof not attended to. Even the household staff had diminished, though a reduction in servants' wages was hardly going to register on the accounts. An under-gardener had gone, along with two maids and a boy. The steward had retired without being replaced, leaving much of his work to Skeel, and now that old Griggs has finally shuffled off, the appointment of a new butler was being perpetually postponed.

But there was no purpose served in pointing out any of this to Cyril. Thrift and economy were words he'd weeded out of his vocabulary, the moment he'd escaped to the liberty of Oxford. All his restraints were loosed. In time, it was proposed that he should take up the law, or some such profession suited to a young man whose connections were good but whose personal fortune was non-existent. But that time of dreary responsibility and hard grind was still a long way off. Why should he not have his pleasures now? He'd been denied them long enough.

For all her tolerant understanding, Skeel still shook her head over him, as she passed him a glass of cognac. 'Don't speak disrespectfully of your uncle. You owe him far too much for that. So he knows you're here. Have you seen James, too?'

'Have I seen James? Is it possible to miss him, do you suppose? My eyes are fairly blinded by his splendour. Off to join his regiment in a week, I hear. How shall we survive without him?'

'Your poor aunt will be distraught.'

'Fiddle-faddle, Skillers. My aunt doesn't know how to be distraught. Mildly discomforted, perhaps. Give her a sip of

39

her laudanum and she'll have forgotten him in half an hour. My uncle will miss the chance to parade him round the county, of course. Never mind. He can parade me instead. Do you think he'll take satisfaction in that?'

'I don't think he'd be at all happy with that arrangement.'

He laughed. 'No. I believe he'd rather cut his throat. He hopes not to set eyes on me at all, and I return the compliment. The less I see of him, the better. I shall, however, endure my aunt's company, and James's, while he's here. Gertie too. Where is she? I haven't clapped eyes on her yet.'

'Miss Gertrude is visiting your aunt Rowland, with her governess.'

'Ah. Visiting. That sounds far too energetic for the little piggy. Still the same governess?'

'Yes, still Miss Richards. You cousin is not a naughty wretch like you.'

'A pity. Richards is an old crone. I was hoping there might be someone a little tastier...' Cyril rose and strolled to the window, looking out on the courtyard, head on one side.

Skeel stepped across to follow his gaze.

Netty Price, a new acquisition for some of the grubbier work around the house, was heaving an over-filled coal scuttle to the laundry, skirt hoisted half-way up her skinny calves, red hair spilling in damp snakes down her back.

'Is she new?'

The girl was scarcely twelve.

'Never mind Netty. I suppose you'll be running after our parlour-maid before the day is out. Or have you already searched out that hussy, Annie?' She maintained the right to disapprove of the girl, even if her faults were of Skeel's own making. At eighteen, Annie Lewis was as bonnie and buxom as Skeel had predicted, but also careless, lazy, disrespectful, and worst of all, flirtatious – with the male servants, with guests, with random strangers, but most especially with Cyril. She paid no heed to Skeel's reprimands – she'd learned licence and its rewards long ago. If any other female servant had proved as insolent and wanton as Annie Lewis, Skeel would have dismissed her on the spot, but as long as it pleased Cyril to play the fool with her, the girl would remain. A young gentleman had to be allowed to sow his wild oats.

Cyril continued to gaze out of the window for another minute, before responding to her words.

'Oh, Annie Lewis. Is she still here? I'd have thought she'd be off to some whorehouse by now. Why haven't you dismissed her, Skillers? She's a thorough slut.'

'Cyril! I thought you were taken with her.'

'But she's old, Skillers. Old and stale. I can't being doing with that. Can't I look at a new pretty face?'

He was taunting her, she knew it. Knew that he could push her, mock her, tease her and always be forgiven. He brushed a kiss on her cheek, then stretched. 'Well, I'm off to check on the horses. Davy still has the care of them, I suppose?'

'Don't!' She knew he was playing with her, but she couldn't help herself. 'Don't go to Davy Thomas.'

'But I must, Skillers. James and I are riding out, tomorrow. Can't stay in with the women all day, can we?'

Laughing, he swaggered away, leaving her aching with love and fury. She watched him head for the stables and, like an evil demon, sensing his approach, Davy Thomas appeared in the doorway, grinning, a finger raised to his forelock in satirical respect.

She couldn't stop herself glancing up, repeatedly, watching for Cyril to emerge, her pulse racing every time a shadow crossed the arch.

When he did finally appear, she feasted on him, willing

him back towards her. Only her. But as he strolled across the yard, the girl, Netty Price, came into view again, trotting across to the stores on another mission.

The child nervously averted her eyes, as she did with all members of the family, with the senior servants even, dropping a curtsey as she tried to edge round the courtyard.

Cyril was chewing a straw, watching her, his grin broadening, then he sauntered towards her.

Skeel half-rose, hesitated – then she heard a door open, the click of rapid footsteps on the cobbles. Jane Bowen. Housemaid. Pious busybody, hurrying to join the girl, dropping a minimal curtsey in Cyril's direction, her face instantly turned from him in righteous disgust, as she took Netty's arm.

Netty looked up at her in questioning relief.

Cyril spared the girl one more glance, then turned back towards Skeel's parlour.

Skeel bit her lip. So she wasn't the only one watching him. He had gained a reputation in the servant's hall that was never voiced when she was around, but she'd caught the whispers. Chapel Jane was doubtless behind it, flapping in shock and horror at the mere thought of any young man in company with a pretty young woman. Plain, prim, ungraceful Jane, who had never turned any young man's head and never would.

Just like Skeel.

Quietly fishing out the correct key, Skeel unlocked her cupboard, and brought out the brandy bottle.

5

'She's none too pleased to be sent packing in the middle of the season, that's the truth of it.' Mary Brownlow, parlour maid, recently returned from London, might be pert and a little too supercilious for Llys y Garn, but she was as eager for a gossip as any of them.

'She must be very distressed by this terrible tragedy,' said Jane, solemnly working through a pile of cuffs.

'Distressed? Oh well, yes, naturally. Although there's this very nice young gentleman, third son of an earl, who was more than ready to console her. Mrs. Jackson says his valet says...'

Skeel never participated in gossip in the servant's hall, but that didn't mean she wasn't willing to listen, from a seemingly detached distance. She was the housekeeper. It was her duty to know what was going on.

Finely balanced, where she stood, she could also catch the solemn murmurings of the visitor in the hall, although his voice was so low she couldn't distinguish the words. Charles's reply was reverently hushed, too, but she caught the drawing room door open, and his respectful voice raised just enough. 'The Reverend Selby, Madam.'

Ah. So it was the vicar. The mistress had expressed a wish to see him. She'd never shown religious inclinations in the past. The social ritual of church attendance had been enough for her, but in a situation like this, she was probably in need of some spiritual consolation – if the Reverend Selby's wheezing platitudes could be called consolation.

So the vicar was ushered in, while other visitors merely

left their cards and tiptoed away across the straw laid across the terrace.

The anticipated bell rang a minute later.

'You'd best take the mistress's tea, Mary.'

'Yes, Mrs. Skeel.'

The house had been run with a skeleton staff while the family was in London – just Cook, Jane, Netty and the boy, Bob Smale, under Skeel's command, keeping quiet order in a quiet house. But now the ladies had return and her battalion has increased – Mrs. Merrick-Jones's personal maid, Chantwell; Mary, come to tend on Miss Gertrude, and Charles to add the necessary masculine dignity. There had been a time in the past when her predecessor, Mrs. Markham, had commanded an army four times as large, but if Skeel had to make do with less, she'd still see to it that all was exactly as it should be. Every detail of the mourning formalities would be strictly observed. In the same way, she'd made sure that they'd been strictly observed at the start of the year, with the passing of the Queen Empress, even though the family hadn't been in residence to notice, and Cook had been all for lifting the obligatory gloom. None of the surrounding great families could point a finger at Llys y Garn and suggest it had failed to demonstrate the proper patriotic grief.

Skeel did all things properly and efficiently. She took a private pride in it, but she trusted blindly that the mistress would notice how all ran so smoothly here, even with a reduced household.

Alone in the dark, that trust was less secure. Anxieties prodded her. The family's fortune was still slithering precariously towards a threatening abyss, and the maintenance of appearances couldn't carry on forever. Two households were a severe drain. A Mrs Jackson presided over the house in London, while Mrs. Skeel ruled Llys y

Garn. How long would it be before the master concluded that two housekeepers were an unnecessary expense? Which one would he let go? Skeel had never met Mrs Jackson, she knew her only by repute and gossip, and she's heard mention of a daughter. Skeel has no daughter, no family, nowhere to go. Sometimes, she dared not look ahead.

A clatter of hoofs in the courtyard brought her to the window.

The rattle and jangle, the shout, 'Ho there, Davy. Off your arse, man.'

Her automatic icy disapproval of this disregard for the occasion was swept away in an instant by the sight of Cyril, springing from the hack he'd hired. What was he doing there? And in such a cheerfully nonchalant mood, so inappropriate that it almost seemed designed to offend. As she rushed to the door, she wasn't sure whether to chide him or kiss him.

So she merely stood waiting. No sign of Davy Thomas, thank God. The groom must be round on the terrace, tending to the Reverend's horses. The stableboy, Jack, ran out to take his horse, as Cyril strode across the courtyard, lifted Skeel off her feet and whirled her round.

'Put me down, you silly boy! Stop it at once! There. Now. Let me look at you. Is that the best you can manage?' She slapped the mourning band on his arm. 'What will your aunt say, when she sees you like this?'

'She'll say what she always says, that I've let the family down and I'm a sad disgrace and please to leave her now as she has a dreadful headache. I suppose she's in the full veil and all that. Perhaps you can dig one out for me. I always thought a veil would suit me well. But I don't suppose anything I wear will appease her. Uncle Teddy's not here then?'

'No, just your aunt and Miss Gertrude. They arrived on

45

Tuesday. Don't distress them, Cyril. Think of their loss, if you can't feel any of your own.'

'Very well, so I shall. You can give me a glass of my uncle's excellent brandy, and one of his best cigars, and then you can rustle up a good black suit for me, before I go in to be hauled over the coals. My box is being sent up from the station.'

'All right. Come in – and keep your voice down. How can I instruct the servants to whisper and tiptoe round the house, with you hollering across the yard? What are you doing here, anyway?'

'Visiting you, Skillers.'

'No, you're not. Come on. Tell me the truth.'

But he wouldn't. Not until he had his glass and cigar and was sprawled in her armchair.

'Truth is, I can't be doing with old man Huddlestone. It's just not for me.'

She sighed. 'You mean, Mr. Huddlestone can't be doing with you. He's sent you packing, hasn't he?'

'That will surely be the gloss he'll put on it, when he speaks to my uncle.'

'Cyril, could you not have found a better moment to get yourself dismissed again? Think of your family. They are grief-stricken over your poor cousin.'

'They'll survive. Rather a delicious joke, don't you think? James, the great warrior, the knight in shining armour, itching to charge the foe with sword drawn, in a hail of smoke and bullets, and it's typhoid that carries him off. Wanted to be a lion and finished up a poor mongrel dog in the gutter.'

'Hush! Show a little respect. However he met his end, your cousin was serving his Queen – King and country.'

'Whereas wicked Cyril has no noble ambitions to go and take pot shots at the dratted Boers. Just wants a quiet life.'

46

'It's never a quiet life you're after, Cyril. And don't you grin at me. Finish that filthy cigar while I find you some more fitting clothes, then you can go and commiserate with your aunt.'

When he'd dutifully changed and adjusted his chameleon features into an air of mournful condolence, she attended him personally to the drawing room. 'Your nephew, Mr. Cyril, madam.'

Mrs. Merrick-Jones, swathed in black and veiled, turned from the mantelpiece on which she'd been leaning, with a convulsion of genuine grief.

'Aunt Agnes!' said Cyril, bounding forward. 'What can I say?'

But young Miss Merrick-Jones, curled up on a sofa by the window, replied first, her face wet with tears, contorted with anguish. 'Oh Cyril, isn't it dreadful? They say I might not be allowed to return to London for the coronation. It's so horrid!'

Skeel bowed out, shutting the door behind her.

She turned to face the portrait of James, in full dress uniform, scarlet jacket, sword, magnificent moustache. The master commissioned it before James embarked for South Africa, to embody all the noble hopes and aspirations of the Merrick-Jones family on the world stage. Now it stood, swathed in black crepe, banked by white lilies, a symbol of all those hopes dashed.

His mother would grieve, letting slip occasional glimpses of those feelings she'd been so successful in concealing for the last quarter of a century. His father would undoubtedly feel the loss, too – his investment in the future. Miss Gertrude would flutter and sob prettily on the arms of suitors, for a brother she scarcely knew. And Skeel...

She didn't know what she felt. She'd mended linen by candlelight for the mistress, a young bride, new to Llys y

47

Garn and fretful in confinement. She'd carried hot water up to the nursery when Master James was a bawling infant, receiving the adulation of the neighbourhood. She'd seen him ride his first pony, set off for school, dress up for his first dinner with guests, shoot his first pheasant, ride off to his first ball, grow his moustache, demonstrate his elegant sword skills... She'd been there, on the fringe, all his life, until the end, always imagining that she would die in his service, but it had never been love that she'd felt for him. After all, he'd never shown her anything other than that patronising contempt a young gentleman was expected to show to his inferiors. Even as housekeeper, she was there to be taken for granted. No, she never missed him in his absences. Nor his sister or his parents. There was only one she ever missed.

And now he was home.

'Netty Price! What are you doing, silly girl?'

'Nothing, m'm. Sorry, m'm.' The girl was snivelling.

Skeel looked round the store room, preserves in jars, dried fruits, sugar loaves. There was no obvious reason for a servant to be cowering in the corner. 'Did Cook send you to fetch something?'

Netty nodded.

'Then take it and go.'

'From the garden, m'm.'

'Well then, go to the garden! If you don't intend to reach it by climbing through the window, out of here, now!'

The girl sidled out, into the passage, towards the door that opened into the old hall. She took two paces, then shrank back.

'What is it, you foolish child?'

'It's haunted, m'm.'

'Stuff and nonsense. Go on, now!'

She waited until the girl, trembling, pushed the door, and stepped through, into the echoing cavern beyond. Then she turned and marched away.

Silly tales for silly girls. When she'd been Netty's age, she'd believed them too. There were the ghosts of dead men lurking behind those old blackened panels, waiting to grab at her ankles. But she'd put such nonsense behind her, and sympathy with it. Of course the place was old and dark and full of chill shadows, when it wasn't being used by the gardeners, but Netty has never been scared of it before. Who had been putting ideas in her head?

There were no ghosts. No spirits in the old hall, except, perhaps, the brandy in the bottle that Cyril had taken in there, half an hour since. It was a place where he could be sure to escape attention. If he chose to doze on the straw bales, smoking his cigars, out of the family's sight, what of it?

She was tending to her own duties when she heard Cook bawl.

'Where's that girl!'

She confronted the woman in the corridor. 'Hush, Mrs Evans. Remember the family is in mourning.'

'And is the family still expecting to eat? There's chops to be grilled and I sent that Netty for peas half an hour since.'

'That'll do. I'll speak to her.'

'I'll find her.' Jane appeared out of nowhere.

'You'll do no such thing. Get on with your own work,' said Skeel.

But Jane was already off, striding in the direction of the old hall, fists clenched.

Skeel hesitated.

'When will I have a proper kitchen maid again, that's what I want to know,' said Cook, smacking flour from her fat arms. 'With the mistress and Miss Gertrude and now

Master Cyril and all.'

'You have the use of Netty, don't you?'

'That little shrimp of a thing. I need a girl with strong arms and a strong back. I tell you, Mrs. Skeel—'

'I'll see what can be done.' Skeel turned away. She couldn't stand around listening to the fat woman's complaints. She set off, in pursuit of Jane.

She found them already returning, the two maids, coming up the passage leading from the hall – Jane in fearsome support, like some female warrior, the fire of righteousness in her eyes, and a distraught Netty. The girl was sobbing, her clothing dishevelled and torn, her hair loose and tangled, her mouth swollen, her cheek bruised.

She was incapable of speaking, only choking and spluttering in wordless distress.

But Jane could speak, and was ready to do so. 'She was ass—'

Skeel was ready too, speaking promptly and authoritatively, taking charge. 'Clumsy child, you've fallen over again. Why must you always be tripping over things? You're not safe to be left on your own.'

'No, because she cannot—'

'Go to your room, Netty. Compose yourself. Change your dress. Come on, now!'

Netty was only too willing to be sent packing. She had neither courage nor strength for accusations. She broke from Jane's protective grip and ran past Skeel.

'That'll do, Jane. Get back to your work. I'll fetch the peas, myself.'

'It was Cyril Lawson.' The woman would not shut up. 'Ever since he arrived—'

'That's enough! Don't you start feeding me that child's silly fantasies. And show respect to your betters. Mr. Lawson to you. Mind your tongue or you can pack your box, you hear me?'

They faced each other. Both armed – Jane Bowen could go to the mistress. She looked capable of denouncing Cyril and the housekeeper and all the wickedness in the world. But Skeel knew her own power. It was her word that carried authority in this house, with Mrs Merrick-Jones at least, the mistress who has no wish to hear or see anything. And she had the dread power of dismissal, without references. Jane Bowen had an idiot sister, down in the village, who relied on her. She wouldn't dare risk her employment, miserably paid though it was.

'To your work,' said Skeel.

She won. Jane raised her shoulders in martyred resentment, then turned and stomped away. To the attics, no doubt, to fuss over the silly little child, who couldn't help tripping over her own feet.

Skeel went to fetch the peas from the gardener, since no one else was there to do it. Cyril was sprawled on the straw in the hall, drunk as a lord and half asleep, but he stirred and propped himself on his elbow as she bustled past.

'Hello, Skillers. Come to join me?'

'No I have not. Sober up before your aunt catches you.' She nudged his foot out of her way, bending to pick a torn maid's cap out of the straw. 'And do yourself up.'

6

Skeel watched Jane on her hands and knees, cleaning the brasswork of the morning-room grate, before laying the fire. The London house was shut up, the master was back in residence, and though there would be no large gatherings and shooting parties while the family was officially in mourning, the household was restored. There were servants for all things, and cleaning the grate before breakfast was a job for the under-housemaid.

'Where is Netty?'

Jane's head rose, but she didn't look round, or slacken, her arm working like a steam piston. 'Netty is sick, Mrs. Skeel.'

'Nonsense. She's always moping, that girl.'

Jane said nothing. She gathered her cloths and brush and the ash pan, and rose to her feet, shoulders flexing.

'I'll see if she requires a tonic,' said Skeel.

'Yes, Mrs. Skeel.'

There was nothing definably insolent in Bowen's tone. Nothing deferential either. It was flat – and yet somehow challenging. They were at war, but no war had been declared. If the woman would only show her intent, Skeel could unleash her big guns. But Jane did nothing.

Skeel turned away. She had better things to do – although the house ran so smoothly, she really had nothing to do than confirm, for her own satisfaction, that all was in order. Water had been carried up, Cook had breakfast in hand, and the parlour maid was standing by to serve it. The housekeeper could spare a moment to see what ailed moping maids.

She gave one knock on the door of Netty's garret room, then opened it. She was, after all, the one with all the keys to the house. Nowhere was out of bounds to her.

The chill room smelled of damp and vomit. The girl was huddled under her thin coverlet, her face white and tear-stained. She sat up, though, as Skeel came in, not from obedience or willingness, but from terror. The house could do without a hysterical girl, imagining all manner of absurd things. Best to calm her.

'So what have you been eating, Netty Price, to make you so ill this morning?'

The girl shook her head, mumbling.

'It's not the first time, is it? This sickness.'

Another shake. Tears began to gush. Best to resolve this quickly, before other things began to gush. Such as words.

'I suppose you'll deny you've let some young scoundrel take liberties with you.'

Netty looked up at her, not in shame but in disbelief, quite lost, sensing in an instant the futility of resistance.

'Silly girl. You know the mistress would have you out on your ear, if she so much as suspected you of loose behaviour. Do you want to keep your place?'

The girl gaped, uncomprehending. Was she disgraced or not? Was she to be punished or offered salvation? There was only one possible answer to Skeel's question. To stay in service at Llys y Garn meant continuing a life of fear and misery, but to be dismissed was to face the workhouse, or worse. She nodded.

'Dry your tears and blow your nose,' said Skeel. 'Here, have a sip of water. Get yourself dressed when you can, and get on with your work. I'll see that something is sorted.'

The girl's terror, in a gulp, became pathetic gratitude. So it was to be salvation. At least all threat of hysteria has gone. The dragon whose fire she most dreaded was going to sort it

53

out.

It wasn't something that she was happy to do, but needs must. The Cooper's Inn was four miles along the valley, a dingy ale house under dark trees. Not the sort of place that any respectable woman would frequent, although there were one or two disreputable ones loitering outside, and vulgar labouring men in plenty, with their coarse comments and raucous laughter. Skeel's entrance caused one or two to look abashed and guard their tongues, but most let loose a flood of ribaldry.

The barmaid, plump and flourishing, leaned on the bar, bosom near to spilling from her low-cut gown, as she grinned in ironic welcome. 'Well, well. Nelly Skeel, from Llys y Garn. Come to beg me to come back, have you?'

Skeel pulled her coat more tightly around her bony form, gripping her umbrella like a priest holding a crucifix to ward off a vampire. 'I hope to speak with you, Annie, if I may.'

'No!' The former parlour maid held up a finger. 'Not Annie, to you, Nelly Skeel. Not any more. Not Lewis. I'm Mrs. Jenkins now.'

Howel Jenkins, the landlord, a huge, lowering man, scowled at her from across the low, smoky room. If Annie Lewis has become Mrs. Jenkins, she'd done it without benefit of banns and wedding vows, that was for sure. But what of it? It didn't matter.

'Mrs. Jenkins, then.'

Annie sniffed, wiped her mouth, considering. Then she grinned again, in acquiescence. 'Very well, you'd best come through to the back.'

'Eh!' roared Howel Jenkins. 'What about the customers?'

'See to them yourself!' Annie nodded the way to a back parlour that was as grubby and untidy as Skeel would have expected from one as slovenly as Annie Lewis. Grubby and untidy, but not poverty-stricken. There was good china on the dresser, a fine carpet, a suspiciously expensive clock on the mantel. Not hard to guess how Annie has earned herself such luxuries. She was one cat who knew how to fall on her feet. Her dismissal, by Skeel, the moment it was clear she no longer commanded Cyril's interest, hadn't dismayed her in the least. She'd marched straight into a new life and new loves at the Cooper's Inn.

'So, Nelly Skeel. What brings you traipsing down here? Mistress thrown you out? Caught fiddling the accounts, were you? Sorry, but I can't offer you work. You haven't the face or figure for my customers.'

'Netty Price.'

'The little one? What of her? I'll not have her here, if you're thinking of throwing her out too. Pretty enough, but she's too soft for this lark.'

'I wasn't proposing to dismiss her. But she's got herself in a spot of trouble.'

Annie roared with coarse laughter. 'Got herself? Someone got her, more like.' Her eyes narrowed. 'Cyril Lawson, I'll be bound.'

'You know nothing about it, Annie Lewis. No doubt it was some passing tinker or one of the gardener's lads. What does it matter? Whoever it is, she's not looking to marry.'

'Cyril won't marry her, that's for sure.'

'How would you even suggest such a thing? An utterly ridiculous idea. No one could possibly expect Mr Merrick-Jones's nephew to think of marrying a servant slut!'

'She could be the Queen of Sheba and he wouldn't marry her. You know why? Of course you do. Because one day, sooner or later, she'd get to be a woman, all bosomy and hairy, and he can't be doing with that. Not our Cyril.'

'He is not your Cyril!'

'Nor yours, Nelly Skeel, though you'd love to think it. I

suppose you made a present of her, like you did with me, and the silly innocent is too gormless to know what's what or how to make profit of it. So what do you want of me?'

'What I want.' Skeel produced a purse and laid out three guineas, one by one, on the table. 'I've no doubt you know some old woman who deals with these things.'

'Maybe I do.'

'Well then.'

'And maybe, if you put down another two guineas, I'll be generous and take your trouble off your hands.'

In silence, Skeel shelled out two more coins.

Annie smiled, the easiest money she's ever earned. 'I'll come for her then. Tell her to be ready. This evening.'

From the landing window, Skeel watched Annie Lewis, bold as brass, march across the courtyard to the servants' entrance and fling the door open without knocking. Jane was occupied upstairs – Skeel had seen to that. No one to observe and file away the information in a suspicious mind. No one to witness meek little Netty Price being hustled along by brazen Annie Lewis, out of the back door, across the cobbles of the courtyard.

No one but Davy Thomas, lounging in the arch of the stables, watching the women pass, throwing some lewd comment at Annie as she passed, and receiving as good in return. Netty kept her head down.

He looked after them for a moment and then, unerringly, as if he could hear her thoughts, he looked straight up at the landing window. He grinned, taunting Skeel with obscene gestures, winked and tapped his nose. As if he knew everything. He, the beast who had brought all this about.

Skeel stepped back out of sight. She could still see through the window though. She could see the evening gloom deepening, even as she watched. In a moment, all that was visible was the glow of Netty's white bonnet, bobbing into the dark.

Cyril bent over the billiard table, lining up a shot. 'In my light, Skillers.'

'Never mind that, Cyril. Put the cue down.'

'But I can't. I've started. Never interrupt a gentleman at billiards, Skillers. It's not the done thing.'

'Stop it, you little fool!' She hissed, enough to bring him upright.

He took the cigar from his mouth. 'Skillers is in a temper. What's this? Servant problems? Where's that tasty little Netty? I haven't seen her around for a few—'

She slapped him. It was so unexpected, he was stunned into silence.

'Don't!' she said. 'Don't you mention her name. You hear me? I'm serious. You don't know Netty, you have no idea which one she is. Do you understand?'

He'd recovered. He began to shrug and raise the cigar back to his lips. She snatched it away, feeling it burn her hand.

'Netty is dead. There were – unfortunate circumstances. She attempted to deal with her difficulty. She died. Blood poisoning.'

He sobered, fractionally. 'That's sad. She was—'

'Never mind what she was. She was a foolish girl, a slut and she's paid the price, but now there's a scandal. Do you understand? There's a coroner's hearing. The police are involved.'

'I had nothing to do with it.'

'Don't play innocent, Cyril! Not with me. The police! You understand? They will ask questions. How do you suppose your aunt and uncle will respond, if they come to question you? While they're still in mourning? Do you think they'll put up with that sort of disgrace? Cyril, you are dependent on them, for every penny, since you're so determined not to stick to any career they offer you.'

'Perhaps I won't need to, now that James is out of the running.'

'Don't be a fool. Gertrude is their heiress now, and she'll be married, with children of her own, soon enough. You'll not inherit Llys y Garn, Cyril. Dispel any thought of that from your mind. You are a dependant, and if you don't take care, you'll not even be that. You'll be out without a penny to your name, and a reputation in the gutter. If your uncle chooses to ruin you, he'll ensure the whole world blackballs you. Do you understand?'

He was truly sober now. 'What should I do?'

She hated the only prescription she had to offer. 'Take yourself out of your uncle's sight for a while. Go back to London. Speak to your uncle's agent. Ask him to find you a position. Oh, I know, you won't keep it – I think you're not capable of holding down anything he offers – but at least make a show of your willingness. And whatever you do, don't you dare, ever, speak Netty Price's name.'

Skeel ran into Jane Bowen, in coat and hat, heading for the door. The woman couldn't leave. Couldn't just walk away, spreading her rumours and lies.

'Where do you think you are going, Bowen? This isn't your half day.'

Jane met her eye defiantly. Yes, it was defiance, bald and undisguised. 'I'm going to Bethel Chapel, Mrs. Skeel.'

'No you are not. This isn't Sunday. What business do you have, tramping off to a chapel in the middle of the week?'

'The congregation meets on other days. Netty came with me once or twice. I want them to be told about her death. Her wicked murder.'

'Nonsense. It was no murder. She was a foolish girl, and made a mess of herself. That's all there is to it. No need for you to go wasting your prayers on that hussy, Jane Bowen.'

'I won't be praying for her, Mrs Skeel. She has no need of my prayers. I truly believe she is forgiven and safe with the Lord, who will be a better guardian to her than others have been.'

'I forbid you to step outside this house.'

'I am going to the chapel, Mrs. Skeel, whether you allow it or not. I shall pray for forgiveness, not for Netty Price but for myself. For my sin in failing an innocent child. What will you pray for, Mrs Skeel?'

7

He all but fell off his horse, slipping and staggering, foot nearly catching in the stirrup. Skeel rushed to the door, but Davy Thomas was already out of the stables, running across the cobbles to catch him under the armpits.

'Woah there, Cyril, lad. Don't you go falling flat on your face until there's someone soft for you to land on. Eh?'

They were both cackling like satyrs, by the time Skeel reached them.

'Ah. Skillers.' Cyril pulled himself up, unsteadily. 'You find me a little ineb – inebriated.'

Davy Thomas gave a filthy chuckle at Skeel's expression.

'Leave him to me,' she ordered, curtly. 'See to the horse.'

'I'll see you…' Cyril tried to talk over his shoulder as she led him away, but he didn't seem to know where he was supposed to be looking. Too many Davy Thomases for him to focus on, perhaps.

'Oh you will, Master Cyril, never fear.'

Skeel had him at last into the house, steering him to her parlour, pouring water for him to drink before he puked over her or her chenille tablecloth.

He swigged, grimaced and pushed the glass away. 'Is that the best you've got? Skillers? My silly billy skilly dilly…'

'Stop it!' She wiped his face like a naughty child and smoothed down his hair. 'What are you doing here, Cyril? Why this time? Have you been dismissed again?'

'Oh, the old men, the greybeards, with their wagging fingers and their—'

'What did you do, this time?'

He closed his eyes and let his head sink between his knees for a moment, then he sat up, waving his hand vaguely. 'Something about missing funds. A small amount. Barely nothing. How do they expect me to live, eh? Live like a gentleman, not some snivelling clerk. How? You tell me that, Skillers.'

'Does your uncle know you've been dismissed?'

'Uncle Teddy? Oh he knows all about it. Sent me home to join the ladies. Is this home, Skillers? Is this my home?'

'Yes! This is your home. With me. Don't I always look after you?'

'So you do, Skillers. So you do.' He slithered down in her chair as he spoke. The sentence ended with a snore.

She covered him up and went to fetch some strong coffee from the kitchen. No need to tell the mistress of his arrival just yet. Mrs. Merrick-Jones had other things on her mind.

By the time the ladies withdrew to their chambers to dress for dinner, Skeel had sobered Cyril up, drawn a bath for him, laid out fresh linen and shaved him herself, cursing him and blessing him with each firm sweep of the razor.

'You're good to me, Skillers.'

'Yes I am, and don't you forget it. There. You'll do.' She wiped a last streak of soap from his jaw line. 'Best come to the drawing room now. I'll let your aunt know you're here. For a brief visit. You've come home, like a dutiful cousin, for the express purpose of attending Miss Gertrude. You know they're off to a ball tomorrow, down at Stocklees? And great things are hoped to come of it. Mr. Thomas Tramworth, of Bryndeg Park is expected to be there.'

'Oho.' Cyril adjusted his tie and tugged his jacket sleeves into place. He was upright, examining himself in her mirror, turning this way, then that. Satisfied with what he saw. His voice was barely slurred. 'Snotty Tommy Tramkins. So they're plotting to shovel Gertie off their hands yet again.'

'Be good, Cyril.'

'Of course.'

'Don't breathe a word of the real reason why you've been sent home.'

'Could there any reason, except to escort my dainty little cousin to the ball?'

Skeel sniffed. She wanted to trust him, but experience told her want was not enough. Still, it was pointless wasting her time worrying. Cyril would be what he would be. She escorted him to the drawing room, where Mrs Merrick-Jones was already dressed and waiting.

'Your nephew, Master Cyril, ma'am, has just arrived from London.'

'Aunt Agnes!' Cyril bounded forward, hands outstretched. 'I couldn't...'

But his aunt interrupted, a letter in her hand. 'I was expecting you. Edward warned me. I know why you're here. Why do you do this, Cyril? Why do you always let us down?' She held up a hand to silence him. 'Thank you, Mrs. Skeel. You can go.'

The house was in a bustle. Skeel hated it. She liked to be surrounded by quiet regimented order, reflecting her command of the situation, but no one was in a mood for quiet order. The carriage was being readied, brass polished, leather cleaned. Gowns were being packed, servants were scurrying on the pointless missions that Miss Gertrude dreamed up every few minutes.

The ladies were being dressed. Easy enough for Mrs Merrick-Jones, who, despite her age, wore the latest fashions with a languid elegance, but no mean feat for her daughter. The absurdities of crinolines and bustles might be long gone, but the wasp waist was still de rigueur, and no amount of corseting and tight lacing could conceal the fact that Miss

62

Gertrude Merrick-Jones, at nineteen, had the waistline of a pregnant cow. In a few years, she would struggle to get through doors. Her little blue eyes would be swallowed up in the powdered balloons of her inflated cheeks. Dear Lord, let Thomas Tramworth take her, to have and to hold, before she expanded to bursting point.

The party was to stay overnight at Stocklees, a grand house south of Carmarthen. It had been decided that although Bertha Chantwell, lady's maid, would suffice to wait on to the mistress, the daughter would need at least two to attend to her, so housemaid Edie John was joining Mary Brownlow. And Charles, of course, would accompany them, so he could be assigned to act as Master Cyril's man, when they arrived.

Once they'd departed, the house would be silent again. Unnaturally silent. Cook's niece, former housemaid at Llys y Garn, was marrying a footman from Plas Abercwmdu, down the valley. The couple were going to run a grocery store in Fishguard. Attendance at the marriage ceremony was out of the question, with preparations for Miss Gertrude's ball dominating all, but Skeel had given the remaining servants permission to attend the evening celebrations, once the mistress had safely departed for Carmarthenshire. Permission on condition that they were all back to resume their duties by first light.

'Mrs Skeel, you did say... I hope it's not too great an imposition.' Mrs Phillips, who came in to do the laundry, had a child with her. Of course. Gwennie Phillips, her grand-daughter. Eight years old, pretty and shy. Skeel had agreed that the child, who would surely finish up in service at Llys y Garn sometime soon, could stay at the big house overnight, while the Phillips family, related to the bride in some way she couldn't be bothered to recall, headed off for the wedding party. She had forgotten the arrangement, but it was not a problem.

'Yes, yes, she can make herself useful here and keep me company, since the servants will all be gallivanting elsewhere. Well, girl, off you go to the kitchen. See if Cook can find you some bread and jam.'

The girl smiled bashfully, then ran off. She knew her way. She'd accompanied her grandmother before.

Skeel brushed off Mrs. Phillips' thanks, shooing the old woman away. She found Cyril standing in the doorway, watching.

'What are you doing here, wandering around the servant's quarters?'

'Looking for something to drink. Aunt Agnes has had the decanters locked up. So, you've hired a new kitchen maid, Skillers. A pretty little thing, ain't she? You should have told me.'

'I have not hired her. She's not a servant, Cyril. She's a child, staying here for one night. That's all. You should be getting ready.'

'Hand me a bottle and I will. You can't expect me to squeeze into a coach with Gertie, without some fire in my belly to sustain me.'

'Take it then. But for God's sake, just for once watch your behaviour. You'll have enough to answer for, when your uncle arrives.'

He took the bottle she offered. What harm could it do? It was already two thirds empty. But he must have found several more, despite his aunt's strictures, for when Skeel attended, on the terrace, as the mistress and Miss Gertrude were shoe-horned into the coach, Cyril wasn't there.

'Shall I send word to Mr. Lawson that you are waiting, ma'am?'

'No need, Mrs. Skeel. My nephew is not accompanying us.' Mrs. Merrick-Jones made it clear, with her pursed lips and distant gaze, that she had nothing more to say. Miss Gertrude merely scowled, wriggling to make herself more comfortable in such a confined space.

'Very well, ma'am.' The housekeeper stepped back and nodded to the coachman.

As soon as the carriage rolled away, Skeel hurried in search of Cyril and found him sprawled on a leather chesterfield in the library, hair ruffled, tie loose, collar unbuttoned, his eyes dim and half closed, his complexion dark with drink and resentment.

'Why, Cyril?'

'My aunt, in her wisdom, declared that I was no fit escort for my elephantine cousin. Would you believe it, Skillers? Am I not the complete courtly knight? Find me another bottle, for God's sake, there's a good Skillers.'

'You've had more than enough.'

'I'll be the judge of that. Send me a bottle.' He waved an imperious hand, then grinned. 'Send that little girl with it. She can cheer me up.'

Skeel was in no mood to be teased. 'Gwennie Phillips isn't here. I decide it was too much of a nuisance, having her here. I sent her home with her grandmother.'

'No you didn't. I saw Mrs Washerwoman waddle off with the other servants. She didn't have the child with her.'

'Cyril. Listen to me. You will leave her alone. You hear? She's eight years old.'

'Perfect. Sweet as honey. In London, you know—'

'I don't care what sort of depravity goes on in London. This is Llys y Garn and you will not—'

'I will not what, Mrs house…' He hiccoughed. 'Housekeeper? Eh. I'm the master here. Hic. In loco dom – hic – domin – hic.' He stopped, giggling. 'Need a – hic – bottle, so get me a – hic – damned bottle. And remember, you're just – hic – a damned servant.'

She stood looking at him for a moment, then silently withdrew. She summoned Jane, the only servant who had remained in the house. No one wanted tee-total, old maid Jane at rowdy, and probably drunken, wedding revelries 'Take this brandy to Master Cyril in the library.'

'Yes, Mrs. Skeel.'

Why did the woman presume to look at her, as if she had some right to judge her?

Jane returned. 'Mr. Lawson wishes to dine. He has requested claret and the port.'

Skeel took a deep breath. 'Very well. Do as he bids.'

'He's already intoxicated.'

'That's not for you to judge, Jane. You do as you're told.'

'I'll not help him engage in sin. What if he asks for Gwennie again?'

'Bowen, you're being insolent. Any more of such slanderous talk and you'll be out! Just do your duty and hold your tongue.' Let Cyril drink, she thought. Jane could look down her long pious nose all she liked, but at least he'd sleep quiet for it. Out of mischief.

Jane took him soup.

Skeel heard him roar. 'I don't want you serving me, you ugly old cow. Where's that pretty girl?'

Jane returned, thin-lipped, for the next course. Skeel, in silence, handed her a tray of cold cuts. She was right in her calculations. Thanks to the claret and the port, Cyril was sprawled on a sofa, snoring, before the fruit and stilton arrive.

Jane returned, muttering about dissolute corruption and the Devil.

'Wash the dishes,' said Skeel.

The child, Gwennie Phillips, was playing happily in the housekeeper's room, with a wooden doll that must once have had a face. She was crooning softly, but she stopped, put the doll down and stood up when Skeel came in. Skeel was the housekeeper. Skeel was one of those adult figures that required abject obedience, if not downright terror.

Skeel felt a small knot of disappointment. She'd had half-formulated ideas of mothering the child, while no one was around to see. Of curling her pretty hair, hearing her prayers, letting her sleep in the housekeeper's bed. But that was no longer a wise option. With luck, Cyril would sleep through the night, but if he didn't, if he came lumbering drunkenly to Skeel's chamber in search of yet more brandy, as he had been known to do, it wouldn't do to have him setting eyes on the girl

'Here you are, child. I've brought you a bowl of bread and milk. Eat up, and then I'll take you up to your bed.'

The servants' attic rooms were strangely quiet. Even in the middle of the day, there was usually someone here. Someone mending linen, changing aprons or washing off coal-dust. But Jane was still down in the scullery. There was the faintest rustle of a mouse, but nothing more.

'Here.' Skeel led the child to a room usually occupied by Polly, the under-housemaid. Polly had once shared it with Netty Price, but since Netty's death the second bed had stood empty. Skeel had aired sheets. She'd added a quilt – no need for the child to freeze.

Gwennie looked daunted by the prospect of a night alone, high in a strange, empty house. All her short life, she'd been crammed into bed with an older sister and a grandmother. There were some who'd relish the luxury of their own bed in their own room, but not Gwennie.

'You're not afraid, are you? This is where you'll sleep one day, if you work here.'

Gwennie turned big eyes on Skeel, sucking her thumb, an infant habit she'd almost grown out of.

'You're in luck. Polly's not here. She'd keep you awake with her snoring. You'll be a good girl now, won't you?'

Gwennie nodded, and obediently began to undress. Skeel stood over her till she'd wriggled under the sheet, shivering slightly. Skeel lay a reassuring hand on her shoulder, to pat the covers down, then left her, taking the candle. She caught a faint whimper as the door closed.

No! Get out!

Skeel didn't know if she'd heard the words, roaring through the fabric of the house, or if she'd dreamed them, but they jerked her awake. It must have been a dream, for all she could hear now was a scuffling and a sob and, from down the corridor, a clock striking the half-hour. She rose, pulled on her dressing-gown and opened her door. The corridor was pitch dark, but out of the darkness, near at hand, came the little sob again. And then, distantly, a bang. Again, 'No!'

Skeel still wasn't entirely sure if she had heard the word, or merely imagined it. She struck a match, stilling the tremble in her fingers, and lit her candle. Now she could see Gwennie, hunched, gown ripped, hair dishevelled, tears running down her bewildered face.

'Come in, child.' Skeel picked her up and placed her on her bed, unable to still her own trembling this time. 'Now tell me, what is the matter? What is going on?' As she spoke, fighting to keep her voice calm, to quell any incipient hysteria, she held the candle closer, examining the child. A tear in the arm of her nightgown, but no bruises. Her bare legs were thin, but not bloodied.

Gwennie opened her mouth to speak, but it was beyond her. The stifled sobs of confused anxiety in the dark gave way to an uncontrollable flood now that she had reached the comparative safety of the housekeeper's room.

68

'That's enough.' Skeel rocked her, but when that had no effect, she tried another tack. 'Calm down, Gwennie Phillips, at once! That's quite enough of this wailing. Stop it now, and tell me, what has happened?'

'He – he…'

'He? Who?' She asked, to force some precision from the girl, but it was a pointless question. As if there could be any doubt who He was.

'Mister,' gulped Gwennie.

'Mister Cyril?'

'And Jane.'

Oh of course! The busybody had to be involved. And yet, thank God she was. 'What about Jane?'

'Come to my room, m'm. Said she'd sleep in with me, because…' More sniffling. 'I was scared. I didn't like being on my own, and she said best not to, because – because…'

'All right. Never mind her reasoning. So Jane was in your room.'

'And he…' The sniffles turned back to howls.

'Mr Cyril was there? Calm down. Tell me. I'm sure, whatever it was, you misunderstood.'

'They were fighting. I was frightened. He was all strange and laughing and he called me Netty. I was scared! Jane, she said Run, Gwennie. Run away. So I did. He grabbed at me, but I ran. I want to go home!'

'All right! Hush, child. Don't make such a fuss. You're quite safe now. Now listen. Mister Cyril was just having a little joke. That Jane Bowen is a silly woman. She says and does silly things. Don't you go paying any more attention to her, you hear me? Now, lie down. You're quite safe. Nothing's going to hurt you here. Stay here in my bed. There. Go to sleep now. This was all just a nasty dream.'

The girl had a small child's eagerness to do as she was told, snuggle down and shut it all out. Skeel left a candle burning, safely out of reach, and lit another for her own use. Then she took a deep breath and stepped out into the dark corridor.

No imagined voice shouting 'No,' now. No voices at all. No movement. The hair was rising on the back of her neck but she resolutely kept going, her stomach knotting.

Cyril was sitting on the top tread of the back stairs, his head in his hands. How he'd managed to crawl up this far, in his drunken state, she couldn't imagine. He could have fallen and broken his neck. She hadn't thought of that, when she'd encouraged him to pass out. Hadn't thought that he'd actually go looking for a maid – a maid whose death he was too drunk to recall. Why hadn't she put Gwennie in another room? Any other room than Netty's?

She was almost on him before he registered her presence. Then he raised his head to face her, and every blotch and sag was highlighted by the ghostly flickering light. She could see, by that kaleidoscope of terror and denial in his blurred eyes, that he wasn't sure if he were awake, or trapped in some head-spinning nightmare.

'Skillers.' His voice croaked.

'What's happened?'

His face contorted. He buried it in her dressing gown, his shoulders heaving.

She wanted to keep him there, forever, but she had to ease him loose. She braced herself, swallowing bile, and paced down the dark passage to the bedroom door that stood open.

No curtains on the cracked window. Moonlight flooded the room with a ghastly pallid glow that intensified the shadows.

Jane Bowen was sprawled across the floor, her head up against the bed, hair splayed across the rumpled sheets. Skeel had never noticed Bowen's hair before. Was it really so fair, or was it the moonlight playing tricks? Her nightcap was wrenched back, the knotted strap biting into her neck. Her limbs were all akimbo, her gown rucked up, but more, Skeel prayed, from her slither down against the bed than from anything yet more sinister. Wasn't this sinister enough? The woman's face was dark, swollen, her eyes bulging and quite dead.

There was a stench of urine and faeces. One hand over her nose and mouth, Skeel flung the window open. A blast of chill air came in. An owl hooted.

Cyril had crawled along behind her, hauling himself to his feet against the door jamb. He looked in on the scene as if it were utterly incomprehensible to him.

'Is she...?'

'Hush.'

He stared at the dead face. 'I didn't mean to—'

'I said hush!' Skeel bent to feel for a pulse, just to gain some thinking time. She already knew there could be no serious hope of finding a sign of life. She straightened. 'She's dead.'

He shook his head. Perhaps he was trying to clear it. More likely, he was simply denying everything, to himself as much as to her. But there was no denying this.

'Don't! Don't stand snivelling. Oh, you fool, Cyril. Why? Why must you do this?'

'She attacked me. I don't know what happened. I can't remember.'

'Yes you can! You were drunk. You came looking for that child, didn't you? Didn't you?'

'Yes! Maybe. I don't know. Yes, all right. I was lonely. But she was there, waiting for me. Went at me like a wildcat.'

'Defending the child.'

'The child.' He looked around, almost eagerly. Dear God,

71

even now, with Jane lying there dead as his hand, he was hoping that Gwennie might be around, within reach, for him to play with.

Skeel despaired.

'What shall I do?' asked Cyril. He lurched forward, almost tripping on the corpse, and stared at it, the truth battering its way into his numb brain. 'I didn't mean...' He burst into tears, reaching for her. 'What shall I do, Skillers? Will they hang me? Not for a servant. She's just a servant. They won't hang me for a servant, will they?'

'No. No, they won't. I'll not let you hang.' Her mind was working... or trying to. It was as numb as his. She forced herself to be calm. Just think.

Through the open window came another owl hoot and, distantly, so distant it could be wafting from Elfland, a laugh. Another. A whisper on the wind. The servants were returning.

Her pulse speeded up again in panic. But no, she knew her subjects. They wouldn't be rushing. They'd be making the most of their brief liberty, stopping down at the Cemaes Arms for refuelling, hammering on doors until the bleary-eyed landlord let them in, to keep his windows intact. Their intemperance would give her a little time still, but she would have to act fast. Act somehow.

The solution came to her. A convincing story. Complications paraded before her. She answered them.

She took Cyril's face between her hands. 'Listen to me, child. Listen careful. You must do as I tell you. I will save you.'

Skeel crumpled her sodden apron into a ball and thrust it into the dark recess of the cupboard, She towelled her arms dry – she had got soaked and her arms ached from scrubbing the floor, stripping the sheets, changing the foul air in Polly's

72

garret, until there was no sign of anything untoward in the room. As silently as she could, she pulled on her nightgown again, listening with one ear for movement from the big bed where the child lay, curled up in disturbed dreams, and with the other for the distant sounds she knew to expect as soon as the draught stirred under her door – the muffled giggles, the snap of doors, the whispers, the creak of stairs...

It came, on cue. The first scream. And then another and another. Shouts and bellows and screams as if the servants were having a screaming competition. But not quite enough to wake the dead,

Skeel took a deep breath, laid a hand gently on the child who stirred in her sleep at the commotion, then pulled her dressing gown around her, lifted her candle, and headed resolutely for the back stairs.

'What is this commotion!' She kept her nerve, refusing to look into the gloom of the stairwell until the pleadings and pointings of Polly and Nancy and Mary and a very drunken Robert and Thomas forced her to look. To look at the dangling corpse, suspended from the upper bannister, the rope noose half-hidden by the cascade of tangled fair hair.

'Dear God in heaven!' said Skeel, a hand pressed to her bony breast. 'What has the wicked girl done?'

'Oh Sweet Jesus, oh Lord help us, it's Jane, oh she is dead, oh Lord...' The screams broke out anew and Mary John fainted. Polly Lloyd launched into full-scale hysterics. Cook was staggering back against the wall in preparation for a heart attack. Thomas Phillips the second footman, turned to lurch back down the stairs, shouting 'Murder!'

'Stop!' roared Mrs Skeel. 'Silence, all of you. Thomas! Stop where you are. There is no murder here. This is crime, but not murder. A suicide. The wicked girl has done this to herself.'

'But why?' wailed Nancy Davies, bursting into tears.

Skeel took a deep breath. 'I blame myself. After the foolish things this silly girl told me tonight... But no matter. The crime is Jane's, and so it must be—'

She stopped. Davy Thomas had sauntered in at the foot of the stairs and was staring up at the dangling corpse with prurient interest.

'You have no business here, Thomas.'

'Done herself in, has she? Saint Jane?'

'She'd never do that,' wept Nancy.

'Don't know how else she got there, then,' grinned Davy. His leering eyes met Skeel's, before flickering back to the body, assessing it, his red tongue licking his upper lip thoughtfully. His hand went up thoughtfully to his left shoulder, then his right.

Skeel froze, looked at the dangling corpse again, head twisted to the right. What had she done wrong? How could he suspect? Again, she felt his eyes on her. His hand squeezed his arm muscles meaningfully, then he mimed heaving a heavy weight up and over.

She struggled for breath, reliving her struggle with the dead weight of the housemaid, over the banister, while Cyril had stood by, whimpering and useless. Felt the burden slip from her grasp and the rope snap tight, biting into the already crushed throat. He couldn't know. Not for sure. She had to take charge, regain command. Defy the beast!

She turned her back on Davy Thomas, sweeping the maids before her. 'Robert, Thomas, cut the creature down. Lay her out decently in her room. I shall summon the police. This is a criminal offence. They must be told. Cook, make some tea. Polly, Nancy, take Mary to her room. Give her smelling salts.'

'Fetch Mister Cyril, shall I?' called the groom from below. She could hear the derision in his tone if no one else could.

She refused to turn. 'Of course Mr Cyril will be told, but he is no concern of yours, Davy Thomas. Leave him to me.'

'Oh you know I'll never do that, Nelly Skeel. Can't let you take it all on yourself.'

She span round. 'Get out! Out of this house. Go back to your sty, you filthy beast!'

He touched his forelock mockingly and turned on his heel, leaving her to wonder what the other servants had made of her outburst. Praying that they would be too involved in the drama that was Jane Bowen. She must get a grip. Now, more that ever in her life, she must get a grip.

8

'Mrs. Skeel.' Edward Merrick-Jones, master of Llys y Garn, stood with his back to her, staring out of the bay window of the morning room. He stopped.

She had been summoned, so presumably he wanted to say more than her name. She waited, hands clasped.

'You've been with this family a long time.'

'Yes sir. Forty-six years.'

'Indeed.' He turned to look at her, as if noticing her for the first time. 'That long?'

'Yes, sir. I first came to Llys y Garn when I was seven.'

'Ah. Of course. The years speed by.' For him perhaps. She'd probably been in service there a decade before he'd even noticed her existence. Maybe, then, his eye had casually skimmed over a cluster of housemaids, gathered for their Christmas boxes, or he'd irritably registered her presence if she'd been a little too late laying a fire in a room he chose to enter, but that was all. Once she'd been appointed housekeeper, he had taken note, in a lofty way, but he'd never considered it his role to concern himself with the lower orders. He wouldn't be concerning himself now, if necessity hadn't forced this on him. 'You've proved yourself very loyal.'

'I hope so, sir.'

'You take the honour of our family to heart.'

'Yes, sir.' Was that what she did? She had certainly never desired its ruin, that was for sure, because it would entail her own dismissal.

'We are grateful,' murmured Mrs. Merrick-Jones. She

76

looked ill, shocked to the core by traumatic events that she was not, in any way, equipped to deal with.

'Yes. Grateful,' repeated the master, turning back to the window. 'This – this business, with the housemaid, Jane Bowen. Shocking.'

'A very wicked thing, sir.'

'Yes. Quite. Upsetting for all of us. My daughter has been sent to stay with Mr. and Mrs. Tramworth, until this is all sorted and forgotten. You can imagine her shock, coming home from a ball, a pleasant party, to find our house occupied by screaming servants and policemen.'

He exaggerated. Order and a semblance of calm had been restored by the time Miss Gertrude and her mother returned from Stocklees. Only Polly was still hysterical. The rest of the household had subsided into silent shock.

'I'm sorry I was unable to remove the police officers before the ladies returned, sir.'

'Well, I have no doubt that could not be helped, Mrs. Skeel. You behaved very properly, I'm sure, and did whatever was necessary.'

She watched one of his fists punch into the palm of the other hand. Then he turned to face her again, feet apart, chest swelling. He was a big man, once powerfully built, now just portly, his whiskers grey, his bristling brows knitted.

'Now. I want you to tell me, to make clear – this girl, Bowen. She hanged herself.'

'Yes, sir. A wicked, criminal thing.'

'And it was because of some foolish notion she had, of being...' His frown deepened. He couldn't quite comprehend the idea of servants having feelings. 'Besotted with my nephew. With Mr Lawson. Is that right?'

'Yes sir. Truthfully, I had no idea till that night. If I had, I would never have sent her to serve him his dinner. She was always such a quiet girl, sir. Kept herself to herself. Perhaps too much to herself. Maybe it was because the other servants were out, sir. She must have felt she could speak at last.'

'And he rebuffed her.'

'Oh yes, sir. In a kindly way, I'm sure. There's no malice in Mr. Cyril. But I think she was unhinged, that's what it was. She started pouring out her heart to me. Such nonsense, sir. Such silly dreams. I'm afraid I was very sharp with her.'

'Of course you were, Mrs. Skeel. I'm sure you behaved impeccably.'

She caught the exchange of glances between husband and wife. They were all playing games here. So be it. She knew the rules of the game as well as them. Endless words must be spoken, but nothing must be said.

'I thought she'd gone quietly to bed, sir. It was only when the other servants came home that I discovered what the wicked girl had done.'

'Yes, yes. I just need to know – a few questions raised. I am told a doctor examined her body and found – it seems there were bruises, signs of a struggle.'

'Oh sir, I'm afraid that must have been me. When she spoke to me, when she broke down and came out with all this nonsense about love and so forth, she was in such a state, I had to slap her. I shook her. I was very firm. I thought I'd quietened her.'

'And Mr. Lawson?'

'He was in bed, sir. He knew nothing about any of it.'

The silence was a fraction too long for comfort.

'And the child. I understand there was a child at Llys y Garn.'

'Gwennie Phillips, sir. Yes, she was with me. She's very young, sir. Too young to understand what was going on. I explained how things were with Bowen, what a wicked thing she'd done. So that the girl wouldn't misunderstand anything she might have seen.'

78

'Yes. Good. Quite right. Her mother, I believe, is one of ours.'

'Her grandmother, sir. Mrs. Phillips. Helps with the laundry.'

'Yes. Perhaps, Mrs. Skeel, you'll see to it that she receives some form of compensation. For the distress. Whatever you deem appropriate. Let her understand we are distressed too, and we reward our loyal employees.'

'Yes, sir.'

He paused again. His wife heaved an audible breath. Now they were coming to it.

'You may be aware, Mrs Skeel, that there have been rumours. Certain foul rumours.'

'People will talk, sir. There's always gossip.'

'It seems Bowen attended Bethel Chapel. The minister there, Davies. Something of a firebrand, I understand. A trouble-maker. He's claiming that Bowen spoke of my nephew on more than one occasion. Not in terms of love. She suggested that he – I'm sorry to be so blunt in such a sordid matter, Mrs Skeel. Davies claims she'd referred to my nephew having vicious and unnatural tendencies, regarding little girls.'

'Her imagination, sir! Perhaps she said such vile things to disguise her own feelings towards Mr Lawson. I hadn't realised, until that night, that she'd been harbouring any queer ideas. I think, if she did say anything so wicked, it was prompted by jealousy, seeing Mr, Cyril so pleasant with everyone, but not paying any special attention to her.'

No! She heard Jane Bowen's voice, normally so flat and quiet, shouting defiance.

'This Davies is putting it about that Bowen was a devout girl who would never have contemplated the unforgiveable sin of suicide.'

'I would never have thought it myself, sir, until that night.

She was so cunning in hiding her feelings. The minister was deceived, as we all were.'

'I see. And you are satisfied, are you, Mrs. Skeel, that my nephew had no part in any of this unfortunate business.'

'Totally satisfied, sir! I am sure Mr. Cyril had nothing at all to do with the girl.'

'He never laid a hand on her?'

'No sir! Never!'

No! Get out!

'And you would swear to this in a court of law?'

'Yes, sir!'

Another sigh from the lady, as she sank back on the sofa.

'Thank you, Mrs. Skeel. I knew we could depend on you to protect the name and honour of this family. You'll not lose by it.'

'I'm only saying the truth, sir.'

'You've been very loyal. And for, what was it? Forty six years? We should consider a raise in your salary.'

'Oh, no need, sir. I ask only to continue in your service.'

'Of course.'

'To the end of my days.'

'What? Ah. Of course. No question. Of course. You will always be assured of a place here. Well, thank you, Mrs. Skeel.'

'Yes, thank you, Mrs Skeel.' Mrs Merrick-Jones stirred herself at last. 'We must try to resume a normal life, now this sad business is done with.' She re-tied a bow at her throat, as a signal that the other matter was now closed. 'I have something of a headache. Will you discuss the menus with Cook, please?'

'Yes, Ma'am.'

'And have one of the maids make the adjustments to Miss Gertrude's blue silk.'

'Certainly, Ma'am.'

'Oh, and can you also see that Mr. Lawson's wardrobe is packed up. Charles can take it to the station to be forwarded.'

'Mr Lawson is leaving, ma'am?'

'He's already left,' said Mr Merrick-Jones. 'I sent a man I can trust, Thomas, the groom, to accompany him on the night train to London.' He added under his breath, 'And make sure he stayed on it.'

'Yes, sir,' Her brain swam. Of course it was a relief that Cyril was safely out of the district, but with Davy Thomas as his companion! How could that be good? She would follow him, that was what she would do. Wrest that beast away from him, wherever it was he'd been sent. 'Shall I just pack his city clothes, sir, or will he require some country wear too?'

'Pack it all. Every scrap. Every sock, every collar. Mr Lawson will not be returning to this house. It has all been arranged by telegraph. He's taking up a position with an acquaintance of mine.'

For how long, she wondered. Had Cyril ever stuck with any position for more than a few months? He'd stay away long enough, she trusted, for this black affair to die down, but whatever the master said, she knew Cyril would be back in her parlour before long. Back where he belonged. There would be no more mishaps, no more disasters. She'd keep a hawk's eye on him in future.

'See that the lighter suits are packed in a separate trunk,' said Mrs Merrick-Jones. 'It will be sent out after him.'

'Ma'am?'

'To Ceylon,' said the master, snorting with acid satisfaction. 'He's going to be a tea-planter. He sails...' He consulted his fob watch. 'In two hours. Davy Thomas goes with him, to make sure he's safely on board in time. And that is the last I imagine we'll see of Cyril Lawson.'

No!

No! Let Jane Bowen's ghost scream the word for her. London, yes, or Scotland if punishment demanded it. Paris, even. But Ceylon. It was exile beyond all need. Far beyond reality and hope. How could he come creeping home from half-way round the world? They couldn't do this. They had no right to take her boy!

But they did, They had power, if not right, and he was gone. Gone beyond her reach and she had no chance to say goodbye. Sailing in two hours! It was too late for her to follow him.

She felt the blood drain from her and she couldn't say a word. Only bob a curtsey as her knees failed, and she staggered away.

9

'In a moment.' Agnes Merrick-Jones indicated the small oriental table in the window and Skeel set the tea-tray down. The mistress seated herself, still absorbed in the letter she was reading.

Skeel ached to sit down too, but that wasn't an option, even now, when she could hardly be termed housekeeper any more. Not since the household had dwindled to a single maid, a cook and a boy. Lady's companion. That was what she was, at sixty, but still she couldn't presume to sit in her mistress's presence without being invited.

So she waited for Mrs Merrick-Jones to finish the letter, fold it with a sigh, and gesture for the tea to be poured.

'Not bad news from Mrs. Tramworth, I hope, ma'am.' She could at least speak without waiting to be spoken to, these days.

'No. No word from my daughter. But she was well on the way to recovery, when we left. I'm sure there's nothing to worry about on that score.'

Gertrude Tramworth had had another miscarriage, the third, with hints from the doctor that she'd be unlikely to conceive again. The childless bride was naturally distraught, as was her mother. Distraught as people of their class were, giving weary sighs or petulant pouts. Mrs Skeel was not distraught. It wasn't that she wished stout Gertrude ill. She simply recognised a wider perspective.

Mr Edward Merrick-Jones had died, three years earlier, with little but the title to the estate to his name, and that had passed to Gertrude, his only surviving child. It was merely a matter of title. Her mother remained in residence and

Gertrude lived mostly in London. If there were to be no child of the Tramworth marriage – or if Gertrude herself were to pass away in a fourth attempt... Skeel didn't actually wish it. She merely perceived the possibility, opening the door to a happiness she shouldn't even dare to dream of – yet she did, constantly.

Seven years since she last spoke to her boy, urgent orders whispered on a dark stair, sending him to bed, to a pretence of deep sleep. Seven years since she last set eyes on him, looking shocked and grieved as he acted as temporary master of the house, leading a policeman into the library, to discuss the wicked suicide of a servant. If she had known then that their parting would be so abrupt or so prolonged, she'd have done anything to keep him. She'd have thrown up her position and followed him to distant shores.

But she hadn't been given warning. He was gone, his clothes packed up, his horse sold, every trace of him expunged, and for seven years his name had not been mentioned in the house. To the family of Merrick-Jones, Cyril Lawson might have ceased to exist. But there hadn't been a day, an hour, when Skeel hadn't thought of him, longed for him. Seven years she'd waited, for a letter or a word. Not one word. Nothing. But who knows, perhaps soon, at last...

If Gertrude died without heirs, and with her heart condition and other ailments, she could well die young, the child of Mr Edward's eldest sister would inherit. Cyril could come home. And then...

'What happened to the girl?'

The question came out of nowhere. Skeel had been thinking, as ever, of Cyril. Her first instinct was to ask 'Which one?' There had been so many. But surely Mrs Merrick-Jones was speaking of something completely different.

'You know the one,' said the mistress, sipping her tea, staring into its amber depths.

Had Cyril's dark-skinned natives picked the leaves that made his aunt's tea?

'Jane Bowen. The housemaid found hanging.'

Skeel gripped a chair back to steady herself. 'Bowen, ma'am?'

'I suppose she was denied a Christian burial, as a suicide.'

'I don't know, ma'am. They took her away.'

Took her away, God knows where. Yes, the hanged housemaid received no Christian burial, but there was a memorial to her in Bethel Chapel. Raised by subscription among her congregation.

Er cof am

Rhonwen Bowen

1871 – 1903

"Mae pobl ddrwg yn ffoi pan does neb are u holau,

Ond mae'r rhai sy'n gwneud beth sy'n iawn yn hyderus

fel llew ifanc."

Diarhebion 28:1

The wicked flee when no man pursueth: but the righteous are bold as a young lion.

Skeel was told of it by Charles. In an act akin to self-harm, she'd walked up the valley to look at it, one market day when the lanes were empty. Skeel was not welcome at Bethel.

She'd forgotten that Jane Bowen had another name. Rhonwen. Taken from her to be replaced by a servant's name, just as Skeel had been robbed of Eluned.

She's shuddered when she'd read the Welsh words. The words of her childhood. For forty years she'd been chiding the servants for speaking anything other than English, but it was still there, the old language of a world from which she had long been barred.

'She had a sister, did she not?' Mrs. Merrick-Jones wouldn't let it rest. 'A simpleton. What became of her?'

'The workhouse, ma'am, I believe. Or perhaps the asylum.'

'Left destitute, of course.'

'Yes, ma'am. I expect so.'

'It worries me, Mrs. Skeel. It has worried me all these years. On my conscience. I imagine you don't suppose I have one, but I do. I appreciate that you did what you had to do, of course, and we were grateful, but we all knew the truth. He killed her, didn't he? My nephew. Cyril?'

'No, ma'am! No!'

No! Still that ghostly shriek of denouncement.

'Loyal to the bitter end, Mrs Skeel. Well, no point dwelling on it now. He and his disgusting ways can't bring shame on us anymore.' The mistress looked thoughtfully at her folded letter. 'It seems he's dead. Mr. Norris claims that it was a bout of malaria. I hope that's what the death certificate will say. He's dead and buried out there, and we can wipe him from our thoughts.' She sighed. 'Be thankful you had no children, Skeel. You'll never know the grief they cause.' She tossed the letter in the grate. 'Tell Cook I'll dine early. Something light, I think.'

Skeel climbed the narrow stairs to the servant's quarters. Only a couple of the attic rooms in use now. The house echoed, empty, around her. He was there, on the top step, hopeless, helpless, waiting to bury his face in her dressing-gown.

They won't hang me, will they?

Her boy. Her own. What did she care what he'd done? She wanted him back. He was all she had – all she had ever had.

Her heart was breaking.

Her heart broke

'Ma'am. Please ma'am.'

'What is it, Gladys?'

'It's Mrs Skeel, ma'am. She collapsed.'

'Oh.' The mistress sighed. 'I suppose we must send for the doctor.' Another expense she could ill afford, in her embarrassingly straightened circumstances.

'I think, ma'am – I think she's dead.'

'Dead? Are you sure?' Agnes Merrick-Jones heaved a sigh of relief. It meant more upheaval and uncertainty in what was left of the household, but at least it would spare her the cost of a pension.

Eluned Skeel was buried at St. Brynach's church, in the parish of Rhydygroes. Her grave was marked by a simple stone bearing her initials, which was later moved to line the wall of the churchyard in order to make way for a bench, commemorating William Percival of Essex, died 1979, who frequently visited this valley.

Cyril Lawson is lost in an overgrown section of an Anglican cemetery in Sri Lanka. Beyond the malaria named on his death certificate, no details of his death were recorded. What became of Davy Thomas out east no one knows.

Two years after Skeel's death, the Titanic sank into the abyss. Two years later, Europe did the same, taking the two sons of Mr. Edward Merrick-Jones's younger sister, Alice Rowland, with it, but not before the elder managed to beget a daughter, Winifred, who eventually inherited Llys y Garn. After the death of two fiancés in the second world war, she lived out her life there as a recluse. On her death, in 2010, the house, in a considerable state of disrepair, was sold by

87

auction, and the proceeds distributed among distant relatives, living abroad.

Bethel Chapel stood empty for many years in the 1960s and 70s, before being converted to a holiday home. The memorial stone to Rhonwen Bowen still stands in the garden.

Interlude

The rooks would tell you, if they cared to do so, that the Victorian edifice, raised by Edward Merrick-Jones's father in the 1850s, replaced a more modest, though possibly more elegant house, built, in Queen Anne style, by John Myles, a merchant who had made a fortune in the West Indies and now sought to buy gentility in retirement. Alas, gentility absorbed all his fortune, so that his dreams were never quite fulfilled, and thus some of the older house, including the ancient hall, remained undemolished, housing kennels for a renowned pack of hounds that earned Llys y Garn its only mention in Fenton's *Historical Tour Through Pembrokeshire* 1811. The only known image of Myles's house is a badly faded and spotted watercolour, executed by Miss Frances Thomas, daughter of the house in the reign of George III.

Prior to the abortive rebuilding by the rapidly bankrupt Myles, the house must have been a Tudor residence of some dignity, raised by Dafydd ap Maredudd, or David Meredith, who fought beside Henry VII at Bosworth. According to the pedigree detailed in George Owen's manuscript history of the lordship of Kemes, c. 1603, his family had held the estate for some generations, but their fortune increased substantially in early Tudor times, only to plummet when their religious loyalties fatally undermined their social standing, and anti-Catholic persecution and fines finally reduced them to penury. The history of the house in the seventeenth century was mixed…

The Witch

1

1662

A cacophony of cawing and the sky above Llys y Garn was suddenly black with rooks. An omen? Devereux Powell frowned. He had no skill in interpreting omens, although his head was well equipped for other matters. Matters of money and business were his domain, not superstition and devilry.

Hinges creaked as the door of his chamber opened. His mother stood before him, in her Presbyterian black, tall, unbowed by age, her eyes as watchful as they had ever been, though time had withered her flesh and greyed the hair under her white cap. Superstition and devilry incarnate. If there were an omen in the flight of rooks, she would know it.

'Madam?' Filial duty obliged him to rise, though there was no filial affection in him. His mother's care had ever been the rod and fear of the Lord, not soft words and endearments. His father, in his time, had valued her stern righteousness, which had served him well in troubled times. But his father was dead, the times had changed and his mother's unrelenting piety had twisted with the years. It was fast becoming a curse upon her son's affairs.

Dame Cecily's black eyes shut for a moment and a shudder ran through her rigid frame. In recent years she had acquired a perverse dislike of this chamber, fancying that the Devil resided there. But then, Cecily Powell, in her growing madness, had a fixed and unwavering conviction that the Devil resided everywhere, lurking round every corner, and she was appointed to face Him down.

She stared around the chamber, in martyred defiance, before fixing on Devereux, her eyes piercing him in a quest for sin, even as she spoke of joy. 'My son, your wife is safely delivered, praise be to God.'

'So soon?' The last birth had taken far longer, hours of labour for a child that had only lived a week. 'And the child? Is it a boy or a girl?'

'It is a girl, born to bear Eve's curse. The child thrives.'

'Praise the Lord.' He frowned, more impatient than disappointed. 'A girl is regrettable, but there will be more sons, if God wills it. How does my lady wife?'

'Weary, but she sends her duty. Will you go to her?'

His mother followed him out in dutiful parade, across the courtyard, into the Great Hall, up the stone stairs to the stately bedchamber where his wife lay, recovering.

There was a bustle among the servants as soiled linen was thrust into the adjoining garderobe. A covered pail of noisome slops was hurriedly hidden from view. The air in the room was stifling, foetid with blood and sweat, as if it were a scene of death, but it was life, new and continuing, that had come out of it. His wife Beth rested on pillows piled high, exhausted as usual, but mercifully free of the flush of fever.

Since something was expected of him, Devereux gravely took his wife's hand.

'I am sorry, sir, that I can offer you only a daughter.'

'Well, well, madam. We have John and more sons will come in time.' Devereux glanced briefly at the swaddled infant that the midwife presented to him, its minute mouth puckering and tiny eyes already drinking up the world around it. He nodded, acknowledging that it was fit and well and his own. 'A wet nurse has been found?'

The midwife indicated a young woman, big breasted, clean skinned. She would do well enough.

'The child must be baptised,' said his mother.

Devereux glanced at the infant again. Healthy enough in its wailing and its colouring, its grip on life strong, for now at least. 'In good time. There's no need for haste with this one.'

'There is always haste against the Devil,' insisted his mother. 'Bind her into the covenant of grace with her God, and defy the Devil who hungers for her soul.'

'In good time, madam!' Devereux felt the touch of his wife's hand, admonishing him. He cooled his temper.

There was increasingly something more pagan than puritan in the old woman's all-consuming piety, obsessed more with the dark doings of the Devil than with the benevolence of God. Whatever it was that fed its fires, it was an ardour best kept confined here, within the walls of Llys y Garn, where there were few to hear or question. Perhaps this matter of the child's spiritual welfare could be used to further that end.

'Very well. You, my mother, shall have the command of the matter. The sole command, if you will, here at Llys y Garn. The works I have undertaken at Berevil Hall are near complete and as soon as my lady wife is fit to rise from her confinement, we shall return there.'

He caught the satisfaction in his wife's barely audible sigh. Berevil Hall, south by Pembroke, set amidst open fields and broad rivers, was her dowry and her home, comfortable and gracious as befitted a gentlewoman. The ambitious alterations he had decreed, in the latest style, would add to its dignity and in it she could play the role to which she had been born – lady wife of one of the rising men of the county. She had no liking for his patrimony, this ancient house, damp and draughty and creaking, buried in dark woods under lowering hills.

It pleased him, in a lordly way, that he would soon be

granting her greatest wish. Not that her wishes carried any weight.

'I mean to leave the children here in your care, madam,' said Devereux.

His mother was too well schooled to show her satisfaction. Her thin lips pressed together in acquiescence, she bowed her head, as if this were some burdensome duty she was compelled to shoulder, with humility and obedience. But he knew there could be no great pleasure for her than the prospect of beating Satan out of her grandchildren. She had striven diligently enough to beat Him from her son. Now the mad old witch could be fobbed off with a new generation.

His wife's eyes fluttered open a little wider, but she did not question his decision. It was not her place to do so. With such business in hand as her lord and master always had, she would understand that he had no wish for bawling children under his feet. He supposed she would feel some manner of distress, being a weak vessel and a mother, but as a gentlewoman, she would always expect others to have the care of her two chicks. Besides, she would be occupied soon enough with producing more. In good time, when this infant Elizabeth, mewling and wanting milk, was grown and wrestled into acceptable womanhood by the iron hand of her grandmother, there would be a place for her at Berevil. He would fulfil his paternal duty and see her safely married off, in some way profitable to his concerns. Until then, let her stay out of harm's way at Llys y Garn, in the house where she was born.

Outside, the rooks cawed. But Devereux has forgotten the notion of an omen.

2

Elizabeth, seven years old, was rejoicing in illicit liberty. Dame Cecily was on her knees in prayer or asleep, or both, for she could nod and pray and pray and nod, and it was not always easy to guess which was which, but it would keep her occupied for an hour or so. Joan, her attendant and spy, was busy mending linen, Thomas Rice, the steward, was out upon estate business, and elder brother John, who usually ruled imperiously over his brother and sister, was locked up with his tutor in punishment for the misdemeanours of the day before. So for a brief while, there was no one to command the younger children, to chide them into devout silence or to straight-lace them into solemn dignity.

Elizabeth skipped, paused and looked around, feigning bewilderment. She knew where Anthony was hiding. She'd know even if she couldn't see the top of his head above the water trough, because she had seen him glance that way before she closed her eyes.

Now he couldn't resist peeking out to see if she were near, so she looked away, pretending to hunt in the ivy, calling, 'Anthony, where are you?'

She caught a stifled giggle, but still she didn't turn his way. She peered behind the mounting block by the gatehouse in the west wing. 'Anthony!'

She skipped toward the Great Hall, and the steps to the door that gaped ajar. 'Anthony! Where are you?'

Even as she passed him, she pretended not to see and when he jumped out she gave a shriek of fright.

'You didn't find me!' declared Anthony gleefully, and she wouldn't spoil his triumph, for he was only five.

'Now I must find Huw,' she said.

'I know, he's in the hall,' said Anthony, treacherously. Now that he'd been found, he was impatient for the next game.

Elizabeth guessed where Huw ap Rhys would be. She had told him of the door to the tower, the last time he came to visit. But standing in the dim hall, silent and dusty, she pretended ignorance.

'Huw ap Rhys, where are you?'

Her words met no response except their own echo.

She could sense Anthony's apprehension, as he sidled up to her. The old creaking hall was no place to be alone, if you were only five and still in skirts.

Elizabeth led him into the store room at the end of the hall and gasped with fake surprise at the stirring of the moth-eaten hanging in the corner. 'Look!' she said, lifting the cloth aside to reveal the arch, the door standing ajar onto the winding stair. Anthony peered down into the gloom of the cellars with a little whimper of fright that he couldn't conceal, for all his efforts. If he would be a man he must not fear, but the dark undercroft was a fearful place to one so young and so small. She squeezed his fingers to reassure him and drew him after her, up the stairs into the tower. She was his dutiful, loving sister and would never let him come to harm.

If any of the servants observed them and reported what they saw, the children would be whipped, for certain. The tower was forbidden territory, an ancient thing falling into ruin, built, like the Great Hall, long before the noble gatehouse and the cluttered courts and ranges of Sir David Meredith, who fought with Henry Tudor at Bosworth. This ancient stonework wasn't safe, Thomas Rice said, in need of repair, and no repair was done because Sir Devereux Powell had no intention of squandering his gold on the upkeep of this old house. But for this moment, servants were busy elsewhere, Dame Cecily was drowsing over her Bible and Devereux Powell was far away in Berevil Hall, so there was no one to warn the children away with promise of a flogging.

There was a high chamber in the tower, whose beams still held, though the walls, thicker than a man's height, were stained, the floor boards bowing. Wind whistled in through the unglazed window. This was Elizabeth's retreat, the place where no one else ever thought to come, and she could hide from prying eyes. She'd told Huw of it, of how it was her secret place, so she was certain she would find him there.

But there it was – and there he was not. The chamber was empty. Where then? The tower door had stood open, so he must have climbed further, higher up the winding stair.

Elizabeth followed, up the last steps that had begun to crack and crumble. At the very top, out into the cold air, stones had slipped and fallen away entirely, and they would have to jump and hop and scramble up among the jackdaw roosts.

Anthony said nothing but she felt his terror and she was torn. 'Huw!' she called. 'I have found you. Confess it. I shall come no further. Anthony is afraid.'

'I am not!' roared Anthony, scrambling past her, onto the peeling lead roof that looked out over the house and the hall, over trees and fields and cottages and church and river and the whole valley, out to wide white sea.

There was Huw ap Rhys, their neighbour, eleven years old, in leather and homespun and not a scrap of lace to show his rank, laughing as he balanced on the crumbling parapet. The sun was behind him, turning his dark head copper.

'I didn't think you would dare to follow me here.'

'This is my house,' said Elizabeth. 'I dare go anywhere.'

Huw pulled a face and gave a mocking bow.

'And my house,' insisted Anthony.

But he meant it as their father would mean it; the house was a possession, with legal deeds on which he lay claim. For Elizabeth it was something more. It was hers because it was a part of her, the place where she, alone of the Powell children, had been born. How could she be afraid, in a house that was a part of her soul?

But she permitted Huw to hand her down from the whistling roof top. Anthony, determined that none should think him scared, was bounding on ahead, down the winding stair, but at the tower chamber he stopped.

'You must stay here and count now, Huw, and we shall hide.'

Elizabeth stifled a laugh. It was as plain as if written on the air that he meant to go down, to hide in the cellar among the ale barrels and the salt fish, to prove that his manly courage.

Huw looked at Elizabeth and winked. He'd guessed it too. 'I shall stay here and count then, but take care because I count fast.'

As he retreated into the chamber, Anthony was already flying down the stairs, giggling loudly.

Elizabeth tiptoed after him, as far as the hall, and stepped out from behind the old tapestry. There were a thousand places she might choose. She knew every inch of this tumble-down old house that no one loved but her. She knew one place where Huw ap Rhys would never find her – the cupboard behind the panelling of the deep doorway that led back into the hall. A cupboard built secretly into the wall by the old Meredith family, lords of Llys y Garn before they'd been crippled by fines and debts, and the usurping Powells had purchased their ownership. A place to hide their papist priests from the local magistrates and soldiers, who would root them out to have them hanged, drawn and quartered if they found them. That was what old Joan had told her.

Elizabeth cared nothing for priests and grisly executions. This secret place was hers, not theirs. Hers as much as the windy tower chamber, or the apple loft over the dry larder, or the little room behind the chapel, overlooking the beehives. With deft fingers, she felt for the concealed catch, clicked it open, and crept into the stifling space beyond, letting the oak panelling close back on her.

Darkness. Anthony would be afraid in here, but she was not. She was happy in the dark, feeling the fabric of the house, her house, around her. Joan said she was a strange girl, who must be in league with the fairies. Dame Cecily said she was a witch, who must be in league with Satan. But she was just Elizabeth, in league with this house.

Silence. She didn't mind that either. She liked space to listen to her own thoughts. But it was very silent now. She couldn't tell if Huw were near, searching for her. She hadn't told him of this place.

Out of the muffling darkness, she caught footsteps. Was it Huw, coming to look for her, now that he had found Anthony? There would have been no difficult in that, so why could she not hear the child's footsteps too? Anthony should be with him, his little feet trotting behind the older boy. But there was only one footfall that she could hear. Slow, heavy, full of doom, punctuated with the click, click of a stick.

Dame Cecily!

If she remained hidden, holding her breath, her grandmother would never find her. But then Anthony, down in the cellar, would be left to the old woman's wrath. The fear of the dark place, which he was striving so manfully to conquer, would be Dame Cecily's spiteful weapon against him, his punishment. She knew it.

Scrabbling for the latch, she burst from the cupboard – and there was her grandmother. Clad in sombre black, grey hair scraped back under her linen cap, beady eyes always watchful for sin, her thin lips that never smiled but moved only in silent prayer or harsh castigation. Like the raven that circled the hall and landed to pick at carrion, black wings flapping, its beak hard and remorseless.

'So, child, like your brother you scurry like vermin in the shadows, like the spawn of Satan, when you should be on your knees in prayer.'

All her short life, Elizabeth had been daunted by the old black crow, but now her care for Anthony gave her courage. The old woman knew where Anthony was. Doubtless, she had already locked him in. 'Please, madam, let me go to Anthony. He is afraid of the dark.' With her to keep him company, he would not be afraid, and the cellar held no terror for her.

She made to dart round the old woman, but Dame Cecily raised a finger, freezing her with black piercing eyes. 'Your brother does well to fear. Let him learn it hard and fast, until it possesses his soul. Fear of the darkness of hell, fear of Satan, fear of the Lord. But you.' The old woman had Elizabeth's arm now in a pinching vice. She leaned down and whispered in the girl's ear. 'You have no righteous fear. You are a daughter of the dark, are you not? A daughter of the evil one. You are a witch. Is that not so? It is Satan's power, moving in you, that gives you courage.'

'No, grandmother!' Elizabeth's fears for Anthony were swallowed up in terror for herself. 'Please, I am no witch.'

But the old woman's eyes bored through her as if she could read every sense in Elizabeth's body. 'Is that so? Why, then, are you not doing as any God-fearing child would be doing, wicked girl? Why are you not on your knees, as a dutiful daughter, beseeching God's mercy for your mother in her pain?'

Elizabeth felt a stab of guilt. Her mother, they'd told her, was in childbirth yet again, over at Berevil Hall. It was true, they had been commanded to pray for her. What if this baby died, too? Would Elizabeth be to blame by her careless indifference? The thought terrified her, yet she knew her prayers did no good. This was the seventh child that her mother had carried, and three had already died, for all the fervent family prayers.

'You have led your brother astray, teaching him to imitate your impiety and now he is punished for it. Down there he shall stay, in the cellar, alone, all alone in the dark, with the rats, until he learns his duty, to the Lord God and to his elders.' Keys jangled on the old woman's girdle.

'Oh no, don't leave Anthony down in the cellar!' cried Elizabeth, her voice loud and piercing. 'I beg you, please set him free!' There was nothing to be gained by begging mercy from Dame Cecily, for the old woman had none. But Elizabeth's words were intended for another's ears. For the eleven-year-old boy she could sense, lurking behind the doorway in the adjoining room, keeping himself well hidden from the unsuspecting old dame.

'No, he shall stay there until nightfall,' hissed the old woman. 'And taste the darkness of damnation, until it burns the sin of disobedience out of him and he learns submission to the will of the Lord. Let him spend the time on his knees, begging forgiveness. I will break the wickedness in him, as I will in you.' She shook the girl, thrusting her roughly back into the cupboard. 'Here you will stay, and may the darkness teach you to spurn the Devil when he gnaws at your black soul, witch!'

Elizabeth stumbled back into the gloom, cowering as the old woman's stick was raised. But it wasn't on Elizabeth, this time, that the blow fell. Dame Cecily's stick came down on the cupboard's inner latch, again and again, her righteous strength splintering wood, dislodging iron. Supernatural strength in that arm. The Devil's strength. 'No escape for

102

you now! Here you shall stay, until I see fit to set you free. Now, on your knees and pray, girl. Pray, you hear me? And next time Satan tempts you to wicked giddiness, when you should be at your prayers, He will keep you. Think on it, think yourself screaming for release and left to starve and choke and smother. Think of your parched throat, and your terror and think of Hell and know there is no escaping the wrath of God!' She stood tall, utterly insane, looking down on Elizabeth like the Satan she battled, then she slammed the door shut.

Darkness once more. Silence. Cold. After a moment, when the old woman's footsteps had receded, Elizabeth tentatively tried the door but it would not budge, its inner release catch shattered beyond repair. There would be no escape until Dame Cecily decreed it.

Or rather, no way out until Huw, certain that the way was clear from his hidden corner, crept up to spring the cupboard door open and set her free.

3

Dame Cecily was waiting upon her son. Devereux visited occasionally, and once they had been presented to him for inspection, curtseying and bowing in humble submission, his children could expect some licence, because their guardian dragon's attention would be elsewhere.

Liberated, they hid themselves in the draughty tower chamber that Elizabeth had furnished with a stool or two, cushions and a little chest to store her treasures.

Eight now, and tousle-headed, Anthony scuffed the worm-eaten boards and picked at the moss in the window with ink-stained fingers. 'It's very well for you, Elizabeth. You don't have to muddle your head with Latin verbs all day, as I do, while my pony is kicking his heels and calling for me to take him out.'

'No, I do not.' Elizabeth regarded her own hands, which were raw with pin pricks. 'Instead, I must sit and work by Dame Cecily's side all day. Will you change places with me? I would rather endure Master Rogers and his verbs active, passive, neuter and commune.'

'And deponent,' corrected Anthony, with a grimace. 'How do you come to know Latin?'

Elizabeth laughed. 'I hear you recite your lessons. I have looked in your grammar. And I've heard Huw labouring over much the same, have I not?'

'But no more!' Huw, sitting on the wide sill, swinging his legs, lifted his arms triumphantly. 'Enough of schooling for me.'

'Will you not go to Oxford, like John?' asked Elizabeth.

Huw and her elder brother were of an age, so it had seemed to her that as John did, so Huw must surely do, too.

'Not I.' Huw shrugged. 'My father would have it, if I showed a little more inclination, but I would rather stay on my own land and hunt the hills. Which is to say, I hunt, hunt thou, would God I hunt, and that is more than enough Latin for me.'

Anthony grinned. 'When I am a little older, I shall do the same as you. I shall kick Master Owen Rogers out of the house. I shall kick him all the way to the bridge and beyond.' He demonstrated by kicking the wall.

'A little older?' Elizabeth smiled. 'You will be an old man before then. You must endure Master Rogers and his learning for as long as our father decrees it. For years and years, perhaps. He will send you to Oxford to recite your Latin every day.'

'Oh no, not me,' said Anthony confidently. 'He'll not waste money sending me to Oxford, to rub shoulders with young gentlemen. He has John for that. I am no matter.' He was quite content that he had been left with Elizabeth and little Alice, when John, the first-born son and heir, had been summoned, two years since, to take his proper place in the noise and ceremony of Berevil Hall. Even with the iron hand and pitiless piety of their grandmother ruling over the nursery of Llys y Garn, Anthony had more liberty here in the old house, with the hills to beckon him whenever the old woman dozed off or drifted into mumbling over her Bible.

Elizabeth, was equally content with her exile in Llys y Garn, although she was forced to endure more of their grandmother's increasingly strange and muttering company than Anthony the reluctant scholar, or Alice, who was still with her nurse. This was her house, and her roots ran deep. One dreadful day, she knew, she too would be summoned to Berevil, to be presented to the world as her father's eldest daughter, and to play the lady among grand people and be sold to the highest bidder, but not yet, please God.

It was welcome news to her that Huw would not be going to Oxford, like John. Her elder brother had been dear to her. He had been rebellious against the rule of their grandmother, defiant in the face of punishment, ever ready with tricks and jests, and she had been happy to accept his imperious commands. But she scarcely knew him any more. He had become a stranger in the two years of his absence, a young man of the world. Now that he had returned to Llys y Garn, attending upon their father, he scarcely glanced his little sister's way, so full of himself and his golden prospects as Devereux's son and heir. But Huw, their neighbour from the old manor of Hendre Hywel, remained Elizabeth's everyday companion, as tied to this land as she felt herself to be, and she would miss him if he went, more than she could bear to think about.

'Huw Rhys, where are you!' John's strident voice echoed down in the Great Hall. 'Your father said you were here. Where are you hiding yourself?'

Huw glanced courteously at Elizabeth for permission to reply, then sauntered across to the chamber door. 'Here I am, up in the tower, John,' he called.

'What?' John's voice grew clearer as he pulled back the hanging and peered up the stairs. 'I am tired of old men jawing.' He came bounding up with a swagger and stopped at the threshold, with a laugh. 'What, Huw, still at play with the women and children? Or is it your father's game that you're playing?' He winked at Huw, who responded with a puzzled smile.

'Don't you know what the old men are talking of?' grinned John.

'Parish business?' suggested Huw.

'Family business, man. Didn't you know, you are to

106

marry my sister Elizabeth here?' John was amused, but Anthony looked bereft as if he had never before given thought to losing his sister. She was his closest, his only close companion.

Huw looked surprised, but not displeased. Elizabeth even caught a flicker of a smile. Her own feelings were more confused. She had always known that her future was fixed: she would be consigned to matrimony by the will of her father. But she hadn't expected to hear it spoken of so soon. She was only ten, not yet a woman, too young to think of such matters. And yet, if there must be a husband, was it not agreeable that it should be Huw? Her friend.

'A family alliance,' said John. 'Such honour!'

'Indeed, so it would be.' Huw smiled, matching John's mockery with his own. Devereux Powell of Berevil, Tageston and Llys y Garn might be a man of wealth, dignity and ever-growing influence, rubbing shoulders with the great and the titled, but he was merely the grandson of a leatherworker of Haverfordwest, a nobody who had purchased the estate of Llys y Garn from the family of recusants who had held the land for generations. Grandfather William Powell had married well enough, his son even better, and the family had trimmed its sails to every wind that had blown, till the Powells were among the most prosperous in the county. But still they were of peasant leather-worker's stock, while Rhys ap Griffith of Hendre Hywel, impoverished though he might be, was a gentleman of ancient blood and unimpeachable kin who could trace his lineage and hold on this land to the time of the Lord Rhys and beyond.

John would once have cared nothing for the difference in their blood or in their fortune, running, scheming, wrestling with his good friend Huw, but he was John Powell of Berevil now, and it suited his dignity to laugh at his friend, whose pedigree was so much longer than his purse. He laughed too at Elizabeth, the girl who was to be the passive pawn in this property exchange. 'So if the old men have their way, you will be wife to Huw ap Rhys ap Griffith ap Arthur ap Caesar ap Gog and Magog, and Llys y Garn will be your dowry. What do you say to that, little sister?'

'I will say nothing until my father speaks of it,' said Elizabeth, with seemly modesty, though the words hit her with the force of a hurricane and tore open a secret chamber within her that she had not realised existed. It was not the thought of marriage that stirred her, but the prospect of Llys y Garn as her dowry. It had never occurred to her. And yet, why should it not be so? It was her house, hers more than any other creature's. No one else wanted it, this insignificant appendage of the Powell fortunes. If she married Huw, Llys y Garn would be united with Hendre Hywel and it would be her home forever. Somewhere from deep in the very centre of her soul, a determination stirred into life. This was what she wanted. This and nothing else.

'Why must they marry?' pouted Anthony. He had seized Elizabeth's arm possessively, and was winding his own around it as if bind her to him for eternity.

John laughed even louder. 'Because Elizabeth must have a husband, instead of a little boy trailing at her feet. It is what women do, brother. Has Dame Cecily not taught you so? They are the weaker vessels and must have a lord to govern them or they will go to the Devil.'

'Elizabeth isn't a woman!' Anthony blurted out.

'Girls become women, silly boy. Or has our mad granddam been feeding you strange notions that she will turn Elizabeth into a toad before her womanhood comes upon her? I fancy she would if she could. But you shouldn't listen to such talk, little brother. Leave that to the women. It's time you came to Berevil, perhaps.'

108

'I don't want to go to Berevil. I hate Berevil!' Anthony was trembling in his petulance.

'You hate what you have never seen?' John patted him on the head. 'When you see it, you will love it well enough, and learn to desire better than this.' Lip twitching, John surveyed the dark damp chamber. 'To think this mouldering heap was all my father stood to inherit until our lady mother provided him with better.' He grinned at Huw, who listened silently, thoughtfully. 'You will have an ill bargain, my friend.'

'I don't think so,' said Huw quietly, with a sidelong smile at Elizabeth.

'The land is barely worth its keep. Although...' John reconsidered. 'Good hunting, as I recall.' He bounded up the winding stairs, to the open roof, avoiding the broken steps with one leap. They followed him, out into the sharp wind, to look out from the high parapet, over the courtyard and the gatehouse and the low sagging north wing, over the barns and byres, over the daub cottages and the pastures and the fields of struggling grain and the meadows, over the rushing river and the deep valley and the mounting forests, up to the high, lonely hills.

John drew a deep breath, his eyes sweeping around, taking in the realm of Llys y Garn that had been his only home not so many years before. Seeing it afresh, with new eyes and awakened memories. 'Yes, truth be told, I had forgotten. It may not be champion land like Berevil or Tageston perhaps, but still it is land and not to be relinquished lightly.'

He turned back to face them, lording it over them, knowing his power and young enough to relish it. He was the master. 'Your father must curb his ambitions, Huw. I shall speak with my father about this. I don't think this estate should be given up so easily. You must take Elizabeth with another dowry.'

109

Huw kept his counsel.

Elizabeth could not. 'I will have Llys y Garn!'

John looked at her wide-eyed, and laughed less in scorn than in amazement that she should dream of speaking up. 'It is no business of yours, little sister, to decide what will go with you to whatever husband our father chooses for you.'

'It is my dowry!' She said it as if it were something she had always known, though the knowledge had not found the light until today.

John looked down on her with detached indifference. 'That is not yet decided, and the old men may puff and parry and debate, but I say this land should remain a part of the Powell inheritance. All this. Seeing it now...' He waved his arm over the sun-bathed valley. 'I shall hold this one day, and I say I shall keep it. I shall pull down this old hovel, perhaps—'

'No!'

'But yes. Pull it down and build a proper house, fit for a gentleman, and it will do me very well. Yes, Huw, I think we shall find a purse of gold or some such, for Elizabeth's dowry. That will do well enough to patch your roof if your father still wants her for you.'

'No!' repeated Elizabeth.

John merely smirked at her with dismissive scorn, then turned his back on her. As if her wishes were of no account. As if this house were his, not hers. An anger that teetered on hatred boiled within her. She had never known such feelings before.

'It will be a good enough match for you, Huw, whatever my father offers with her,' announced John, bracing himself on the parapet to survey his future kingdom with lordly satisfaction.

Such rage rose up in her. This house was hers! Hers, and hers alone. Who would dare to snatch it from her? Not the arrogant, sneering lordling her brother had become. Never. She would not let him. Tears of fury, resentment and impotence blurred Elizabeth's eyes, and John was gone.

John and the parapet, gone.

John, gone.

There was a long moment of frozen time, when nothing moved, heartbeat stopped and even the wind was silent. Then Anthony's screams cut through to her consciousness. In a slow strange dance, he was bounding forward, and Huw had caught him, had caught Elizabeth, and was dragging them back from the open air where the crumbling parapet should have been, dragging them back into the darkness of the winding stair.

In a daze of disbelief, she followed Huw, her hand tightly clasped, as he half shooed, half carried the screaming Anthony down, into to the Great Hall and out.

Out, onto the cobbles of the courtyard, where servants were running, white-faced, shouting and wailing in terror, and dust was rising like the smoke of Hell.

'God have mercy on us,' whispered Huw as his father and hers, the tall, thin, grey Rhys ap Griffith and the heavy, fleshy Devereux Powell, emerged from the west wing to stand, frozen, with looks of horror and disbelief on their faces.

At last, with incomprehension as great as theirs, Elizabeth turned to look at the foot of the tower where the rubble of the parapet lay, and in its midst the broken body of her brother.

4

Elizabeth felt the wind cold and fresh on her face. It whistled round the weathered stones that thrust up from the short wiry turf, on the hill's high ridge. Did the stones whistle in reply? Some claimed they did. The Devil's Stones, they called them.

She listened. Something came, something as strong and clean as the wind. Something deep. She lay a hand upon them, drinking up the peace that flooded out of them. Stolen peace. By rights, she should be down by her grandmother's side, reciting her psalms, being berated for her ungodliness, but the old woman had nodded off, more often asleep than awake these days, berating hobgoblins, no doubt, in her twitching dreams.

Elizabeth was a woman now, a woman of birth and dignity; a woman who should not be wandering alone on the hills without a groom or waiting maid to attend on her. Her grandmother would flog her, with evil, pious pleasure, if she knew of Elizabeth's wilful folly, but Elizabeth didn't care.

She felt the thrum of approaching hoofs, then high upon the wind, the excited clamour of a hound. She didn't have to shade her eyes to see who approached. It would be Huw, riding out along the hills as he did every day. She stepped out to watch his approach and he reined in, smiling, leaping out of the saddle, the big dog loping busily around him.

'Elizabeth. Has the old lady released you for the day?'

Elizabeth smiled, not answering. 'I knew I would see you come this way.'

'Though I didn't think to see you step out from the Devil's Stones like a fairy.' He laughed.

Elizabeth laid her hand on the tallest stone. 'I don't think the Devil owns these stones, whatever the old wives say. You know the tale?'

Of course Huw knew the tale, having heard it from his nurse, just as she had heard it from old Joan. The Devil was quarrying stone for his own wicked purposes, when St. Brynach chased him away, claiming the stone for a church to be built in the valley to the glory of God. Determined to thwart him, the Devil crept back by night and flew away with seven of the stones, but St. Brynach's mighty prayers foiled him, doubling and trebling their weight until the Devil was forced to let them drop, where they stood still.

Huw eyed the grey, lichened rock with cautious scepticism. 'My father holds it to be a foolish myth of gullible old wives. He has studied the stones of the church and has found that they are quite unlike these. He believes that these must have been rolled along by the Great Flood, for nothing else could carry them here.'

Elizabeth laughed. 'And what do you think, Huw ap Rhys?'

'I think.' He grimaced. 'I think my father is a wise and scholarly man, so I will not contradict him – and nor will I tempt the Devil more than is good for me.' He grinned, but his hand instinctively rose in superstition to make the old papist sign. Many worlds met here.

Which of them was hers? Godly piety, old or new? The sane reason of enquiry? Or ancient magic captured in the deep rock beneath her? She knew what she should be: pious, unquestioning, obedient, wary of the Devil's wiles, holding herself deaf to strange tales and stranger feelings. But up here, she sensed another reality, a silver voice that whispered she was not a slave or a weaker vessel and she need obey none.

Wicked thoughts. Confusion brought her to her senses. 'I

must return. If my grandmother wakes and finds me gone, I'll have a whipping.'

'I shall escort you,' said Huw, gallantly. 'A humble groom for the daughter of the great Devereux Powell.'

She frowned at his mockery, but allowed him to accompany her down the hillside, the swiftest path through the thick woods that enfolded the house far below. She hesitated, for she hadn't meant to come this way, not down past the Devil's Quarry, which always filled her with dread. But now that she had chosen to remember her domestic duty, she dared not risk further delay.

'Elizabeth!' Anthony's voice, shrill with petulant panic, rose to greet them as they neared the woods. 'You should not have come out alone.' He was scrambling out from the trees.

She held out her hand to him. 'Has Dame Cecily woken?'

'She snores still, but...' Puffing with exertion, he tried to put on a dignity beyond his years. 'I don't care to see you unattended. There might be brigands.' He looked darkly at her companion.

'She is not unattended.' Huw ruffled the boy's hair. 'I am here to see that she comes to no harm.'

Elizabeth felt her brother's humiliation. He didn't yet know how to be what he should be, boy or man, friend or grandee. He had begun to treat her with disdain on occasion, as befitted a manly brother dealing with a mere girl, but at others he clung to her still, as if terrified of losing her. It disturbed her, at times, this deep flood of jealousy that raced in Anthony's veins, beyond the mere neediness of a child. He was tormented by any hint of attention that she paid another, even the little ones, Alice and Thomas. Ever since her marriage had first been mooted, his boyish admiration for their neighbour, Huw, had turned to a resentful aversion. Anthony was discourteous, blatantly so when he played the boy and slyly disdainful when he remembered he was a young gentleman.

'My sister should not be alone with you, sir. It is unseemly.'

Huw responded with a roar of laughter. 'Seemly enough, I think, since we are betrothed, and one day will be bedded.'

Red-faced at the words, Anthony was grappling to take her arm, to take possession. She permitted him, to soothe his self-esteem, but Huw had her other arm, his hound pacing easily behind, panting in their wake.

They came to the black pit, the dark dank walls of the Devil's Quarry, a sheer scoop cut out of the rocks under the crowding trees, oozing stagnant moss and black water. Legends abounded about this place, how the Devil lived here, how the souls of the damned whispered from the rocks, how the fairies drowned children here, how the bottomless mire could swallow horse and man. Perhaps it was those ghoulish tales speaking to her, but Elizabeth could swear she felt it breathing out an evil miasma of fear and choking desperation.

Beside her, Huw made the sign. She turned to him.

'Why do you do that?'

He laughed, self-conscious now of the gesture he had performed by instinct. 'It is the Devil's Quarry, is it not? A dark place, fit only for rapine and murder. There are such tales… Though my father says it was once considered a holy place, blessed by the saints.'

'Papist talk,' said Anthony.

'Devils and saints in one dark well,' said Elizabeth. 'I wonder if they fight it out still beneath the black waters.'

They all stared into the unfathomable pools.

Anthony took an instinctive step back, then corrected himself, turning the move into a show of bravado. 'Have you played this game, Huw? Scorn the Devil and cross the quarry. Can you do it? I can!'

115

He sprang lightly onto a stone, which jutted from the green slimy water, then a hop to a log, and to a flitch of wiry grass. There he stopped, teetered, turning in terror, the noisome pool already lapping round his toes.

'Come back!' Elizabeth seized Huw's arm. 'Fetch him back!'

Huw considered, took a stride to the stone, found his balance, stepped to the blackened glistening log, his hand out to Anthony.

But Anthony's terror had vanished, replaced by an impish grin. 'I can do it!' And he sprang onto another matted hummock, hopped to a ledge, sidled round under the dripping overhang of the cliff and leaped triumphantly back to firm land. 'See?'

Huw was left teetering, looking for whatever would bear his greater weight, as his hound ran up and down the edge of the mire in panic.

'Huw!' Elizabeth stooped for a fallen branch that she could reach out to him, but Huw had recovered his balance and stepped back easily to her side, laughing at his own folly.

'The mire will bear a boy but not a man, it seems.'

Anthony's mirth turned to sullen fury.

Elizabeth stepped between them. 'Forgive my little brother's pranks, Huw, and now you must leave us, before he leads us both into further mischief.'

Her eyes beseeched though her words strove to sound light.

Huw bowed acquiescence. 'Your word is my command, my lady.' He raised her hand to his lips, and smiled at Anthony, as a man would at a small child.

She watched him stride back up through the woods, without a care, then she turned to Anthony, who stood torn between satisfaction and peevishness.

116

'That was an evil thing to do!'

'What?' His pretence of surprise was pathetic. 'How do you mean? It was just a game.'

'You had murder in your thoughts, Anthony.'

'Not I!' Indignation came to his rescue. 'Don't presume to berate me, madam. I am not a child. I am the son and heir of Devereux Powell and you should address me with respect.'

'I am your loving sister, Elizabeth,' she retorted. 'And this is the Devil's Quarry and I swear, whatever saints may linger, He lives here still, for I hear Him laughing with glee at your malice.'

Anthony blanched, his lip trembling as he looked into his sister's dark eyes. 'I meant nothing!'

She corrected herself. 'Nor I.' Taking his hand, she forced a smile. 'Come now, my brave brother, take me out of this black place, and let us forget what happened.'

5

The low room in the north wing was thick with black shadows, like spiders' webs.

Why did Elizabeth think that? Was it because this room had been barred to her, when it had served as her father's private office, and fear of him left her with intimations of trespassing anxiety? Or were the webs woven by that spider, Dame Cecily, who had always hated this room, fixing her Devil-obsessed loathing on it for motives only her mad mind could fathom?

Whatever the reason, Elizabeth had learned to avoid the chamber, entering it, if she must, with a shudder. And now she must, for, of all the chambers in this rambling house, great and small, it was the one Dame Cecily had fixed upon, in her final warped perversity, to meet her end. The old woman's bed had been brought here, and here she intended to die, imprisoning Elizabeth with her in her slow decline.

'You go,' said Joan, the old nurse, busy with some nostrum on the fire. 'She sleeps, or scarcely knows when she's awake. I'll sit with her.'

'I should stay.' Elizabeth's demurral was half-hearted. Duty spoke loud, but the need to escape from this room spoke louder still. She stared at her grandmother, skeletal hands still and lifeless on the bed linen, the skull-like head sunk into its pillows, faint harsh breath coming from between the parted withered lips, veined parchment eyelids shuttered.

How was Elizabeth to regard the old woman? With respectful love, as the source of her own being? Love was a word that Dame Cecily herself would scorn. Love was simpering folly, or ungodly lust, a distraction from thoughts of the soul's welfare. Had there been a time, when a young Cecily Lloyd had laughed and played and dreamed of love and worldly things? Perhaps she had been a solemn pious girl from birth, snared into insanity by the terrors of Hell. Or perhaps she had always been an evil spiteful witch.

Hate. No, Elizabeth must not hate her grandmother. It was not permitted. Dutiful attendance was permitted. Commanded. So Elizabeth dutifully attended. Knowing that the end must be near, she had sent word to her father. When he arrived at his mother's side, it would be for him to attend, but until then, the duty was hers.

Airless, noisome, suffocating duty. Surely there would be no sin in a brief escape, out into the clean air, to taste the breeze, fresh off the hills, just for a moment or two, to steal herself for her return to this shadowed, suffocating temple of death.

Joan had stoked the embers, ready to make herself comfortable in Elizabeth's place. Elizabeth rose from her stool, succumbing to the temptation, and leaned briefly to confirm that the old woman still slept.

Saw the black glint of eyes between the barely parted lashes.

'So, you would abandon me,' croaked Dame Cecily.

'The child must rest,' said Joan, coming forward with an audacity she would never have dared when the old woman had been haler.

'She is no child,' snapped Cecily, life surging back into her. 'A woman. And more. More and worse, this one. Is that not so?' Her eyes were open now, fixed on Elizabeth, one claw-like hand clamped around her wrist. Then her glance flickered to Joan, and her fingers groped for the stick that had lain, ever ready, by her free hand. Too feeble to thrash,

119

she could still jab.

'Get out, woman. Go. Go on, get out. Leave me with my granddaughter. She and I must speak before the Lord takes me.'

Joan looked to Elizabeth. In the past, no servant would have looked to another for confirmation of Dame Cecily's commands, but the old era was passing.

Elizabeth nodded, watching Joan bustle out and longing to follow her. Her grandmother's nails were biting into her arm.

'A woman, cursed by the sin of Eve.' Cecily gurgled. For a moment Elizabeth thought she was choking, then understood it was laughter. 'And a witch,' said Cecily. 'That's what you are. The mark has been upon you from your birth. Church water couldn't wash it out. I have witnessed the wickedness work within you. You think you escape me? I watch you, always, wherever you think to hide. I have seen you up there on the hills, at Satan's altar, at the stones, worshipping Him. Confess it!'

'No, madam! I worship none but God, and seek only to obey his ordinance. I have walked on the hills, it is true, but nothing more.'

'Nothing more? You do the Devil's work, whoring with that Huw ap Rhys.'

'That is a false lie!' For a moment, Elizabeth imagined that the old woman had some evil magical power to observe from afar, even though she had been confined to the house for years, never venturing beyond the courtyards. Then, in a flash, she understood. Cecily had no supernatural vision, but she had a grandson. A grandson more than happy to follow and spy on his sister, and report her doings, if it would bring her to heel, chained to his side. A grandson happy to embroider his tales with malicious untruths about Huw ap Rhys. Hurt though she was by Anthony's treachery,

Elizabeth maintained her dignity. 'I am a maid still, grandmother. I shall swear it on the Holy Book, if that will content you.'

'Swear, would you? And tempt the Lord to strike you dead? He will, be sure, for He knows what you are. A whore and a murderess. Oh yes, a murderess. Who threw your brother from the tower, witch?'

Elizabeth struggled for breath, horrified by the accusation. 'It isn't true! John fell. The parapet gave way. I did not touch him!'

'Who made him fall but the Devil, at your command? You wished it and you willed it, is that not so? A true daughter of Satan. Heed the words of Holy Scripture. Thou shalt not suffer a witch to live!'

Struggling with her own shock and anger, Elizabeth looked down on Dame Cecily. 'Why did they suffer you to live then, grandmother?' The words hovered on her lips, but she didn't voice them. 'I fear the Lord and seek His grace,' she insisted doggedly, fighting tears. 'I am no witch.'

The gurgle again. 'You recite the words of the godly, but your heart is black heathen. If it were not, it would have you on your knees, day and night, living as I have lived, shutting my ears to the whispers of Satan, closing my eyes to His bewitchment. That is why they have suffered me to live, girl: because I have renounced the Evil One and His treacherous gifts.' She spoke as if she heard Elizabeth's thoughts louder than her spoken words. Her nails sank in deeper and Elizabeth flinched.

'You feel Him now, do you not? In this chamber? You feel the cold breath of His malice on your face, reaching for your soul. Even so He reaches for my soul, but I deny Him. I deny Him! Why do you think I chose this chamber at my very end, if not to show that I deny Him, that I will not heed His lies? Kneel, girl! Bow your head and pray. Beseech the

121

Lord to cleanse you of the filth that suffocates your soul.'

Drilled by years of obedience, Elizabeth was already on her knees beside the bed, but a scream within her would not allow her head to bow. It would not permit her to accept this assault as meekly as she should. She must speak.

'I beg God's mercy on my sins, but I am no witch, grandmother! I shall pray for you, that your soul may find peace from the cruel and evil thoughts that beset you, but I am no witch.'

'Devil's spawn!' shrieked the old woman, and Elizabeth felt the shadows of this hateful chamber close around her. 'They will hang you, and leave you on a gibbet for the crows, for you refuse to relinquish Him.'

'I do relinquish the Devil!'

'What is it that He tempts you with? Huw ap Rhys, the hot beast and his honey-tongued lust? You would grunt and sweat and play the harlot with him, would you not? Or is it more? Is it this house He offers you? I know your dark desires. I know you crave this house more than your own salvation. You pant after it, as a hart after water. You slew your brother for it. Do not lie to me, girl, for I feel it in you. You want this house, Satan's gift to you, as payment for your black soul.'

Elizabeth, her hand free, knelt back. While the old woman had raved about Huw and harlotry, Elizabeth could scorn her accusations. But the house – there the old woman spoke with corroding cunning. This was Elizabeth's house. Not the Devil's, nor God's, nor any man's, but hers, and her grandmother's malice sullied it. The fight rose within her. 'My father thinks to offer this house as my dowry. Is he the Devil, madam? Do you call your own son Satan?'

'He is the Devil's instrument, maybe, and knows it not. Yes, that is the way of it. But I will defeat Satan. Even now, on my deathbed, I will spit in His face and undo His work. I will bid your father remove you from this place—'

'No!'

'Yes!' Dame Cecily had her victory at last, seeing the panic that Elizabeth could not disguise. 'That is the way to suck the Devil out of you. Take this house from your wicked grasp and give it to another. I shall speak to your father. He comes, does he not? You have summoned him to see me die. So be it. I shall speak, and no God-fearing son would dare refuse his dying mother's last command, to take you hence.'

'No.' All dutiful obedience gone now. Elizabeth's piety was stripped from her by a cold fury. A fury that urged her to strike, to tug the pillow from under the old woman's head and press it on her face, so that she need no more see the woman's malice, or hear her spite...

Yes, there was the Devil, summoned by His true disciple in this house. Elizabeth would not heed Him, but neither would she let His malevolent disciple rob her of her heart's desire. 'You will not speak to him, you hear me?' She rose to her feet, looking down on the shrivelled remains of her life-long torment. 'You shall not speak!'

Dame Cecily's black eyes opened wide at this rebellion. Her head rose from the pillows, the blood flooding her paper-white features, as her fingers grappled again for her stick, to beat the girl as she had beaten her so many times before. But her fingers would not grasp. They would not obey. Words poured from her open mouth, but they were merely gurgles and splutters, as her face twisted, distorting itself. She fell back, struggling to regain the last vestige of a control utterly beyond her now.

Elizabeth stared at her for a moment, then rushed to the door, flung it open, calling to Joan, who came hurrying.

'She has had a seizure. Where is the physician? What should I do?'

'Your father, madam. He is approaching, even now. He

will say what must be done.'

Elizabeth, freed from her preoccupation, caught now the jingle of harnesses, the thud of hooves. Her father was come at last. She returned to the dark chamber, and her grandmother's bed. She touched the clenched hand and looked into the dribbling, lopsided face.

'Your son is coming, madam. He is here. You wish to speak with him, do you not? Speak then, if you will.' She shivered at the vengeful triumph possessing her.

The house was in formal mourning, and yet there was more life and noise and bustle than there had been for many months. All spoke low, with dutiful solemnity, and moved about the place with the slow-paced dignity of the grave, but there were so many of them now. Devereux's retinue was an army, occupying the quiet, forgotten halls and passages of Llys y Garn. Elizabeth found their presence distracting.

She should be praying for the old woman, who now lay cold and stark beneath the slabs of St. Brynach's church, down in the valley, but she could not. Dame Cecily's mad soul had escaped at last, to God or to a darker master, and prayers would not avail her. Nothing of her remained, except her words.

Witch.

On her knees before the open Bible, Elizabeth caught her reflection in the streaked glass of the casement. What is it in me that the old woman recognised? A reflection of herself? Am I a witch? Are my prayers to Heaven unheard because I am predestined to be barred from grace? Does God know me for a true child of Satan?

She dug her nails into her clasped hands as punishment for her impiety. 'I beseech Thee, Oh Lord…' But still the thoughts would not go away.

She rose smartly to her feet, facing her reflection. 'I am

not a witch.' The words fell flat. 'If I were a witch, Satan would answer my prayers.'

'He did,' whispered her grandmother's voice.

The memories came back, of her anger with her brother and how he fell, her anger with her grandmother and how she was silenced. But Elizabeth had not prayed for her brother to die, or for Dame Cecily's tongue to be tied. Had she?

'Pray to Him,' whispered the voice. 'Put Him to the test. See if He answers.'

A prayer leapt to Elizabeth's lips. No. Not that. Not yet. If she would test the Devil, let it be with a foolish prayer of no consequence.

And not here. She stared at the words of the Bible. How could she pray to the Devil with its sacred pages open before her? Where then? Up there. Up at the Devil's Quarry, where, surely, He resided in the rocks and foetid mire.

Slipping secretly from the house, before an attendant could bustle up to escort her, she climbed up through the woods, almost running in her haste one moment, frozen in doubt the next. She felt the darkness around her as she reached her goal. The dankness and the horror of the place. Stiffening her resolve, she stared into the dark oily water, chin raised defiantly.

'If I am thy child, Satan, then serve me. Do my will. Make...' She hesitated. 'Make Huw ap Rhys appear to me.'

A branch snapped and she shrieked with terror, her arrogance dissolving. What wickedness and impiety was this? She could not take the words back, though she longed to. Where was the lightning bolt? God would surely strike her down.

Silence. Nothing stirred. No lightning. No Huw descending on her through the trees. Such sweet relief!

Mingled with such aching disappointment.

She couldn't stay in this place. Better to walk on and pretend such foolishness had never occurred. Up, out of the quarry, out of the woods, up onto the hills, where she could see clearly and not let the venomous words of an insane old woman tempt her into further wickedness.

She climbed to the stones, and stood there in aching solitude. There was none to stand by her. No rider came thundering along the hills, no great hound bounding through the heather. Huw rode out every day, without fail, but this day there was no sign of him.

What was she doing? Tempting God and the Devil yet again? Coming to this place where she had been so certain she would meet Huw, in order to fulfil the Devil's bargain for Him? See how her wickedness was thwarted. For once, there was no Huw. It was God speaking, God shielding her from her own sinfulness. She should give thanks.

But as she rambled back down through the woods, it was not thankfulness she felt. No sense of grace and salvation, only of abandonment. For if the Devil failed to answer her prayers, who else would? Not God. He demanded sacrifice and self-denial. He would never give her her heart's desire. He bestowed only pain and suffering to cleanse her of her wicked, worldly desires and teach her the fear of the Lord.

Repentence and forgiveness were what she needed now. She must pray, to the one true God and no other - pray for patience and endurance of all that life would demand of her.

By the time she reached the house, she has almost taught herself renewed godliness. She was no witch, but a chastened, pious girl, who would live henceforth in devout resignation to God's will.

In the courtyard by the water trough stood two horses, their harnesses jingling as they stamped. Horses that she knew. She turned cold as the door opened and Huw stepped out, smiling to see her.

'Elizabeth! My father thought to pay his respects to yours, so you see, here I am.' He bowed, with the old mockery of high-born humility. 'I am here, as ever, to serve your wishes. Command me, mistress.'

6

'Elizabeth.' Anthony's lip was trembling, his face miserable.

She told herself that, whatever the cause of his present grief, she could never forgive him for spying on her and sneaking to their grandmother. But she couldn't sustain her anger. He was just a foolish, innocent boy, terrified of what the world held for him, terrified of losing her.

Elizabeth reached out a sympathetic hand, to stroke her brother's hair. 'What is it, Anthony?'

'It isn't fair!' For one moment more, his eagerness for her comforting embrace governed him, but before she could put her arms around him, he had remembered himself and all that he must be. He pulled back, attempting a smirk of haughty satisfaction.

'No, no, all is well, Elizabeth. I have good news. And you too perhaps. You will go with me, I hope.'

'What—?' Elizabeth had no time to question him, for Thomas Rice was ushering her into the chamber where her father waited, and he would brook no delay. Anthony relinquished her with a brave smile, and she entered, dropping a deep respectful curtsey.

Devereux Powell turned reluctantly from the window and his consideration of political manoeuvres down south. He never wasted attention on his children until they became useful assets in his mighty schemes, but perhaps the time had come to consider this girl and her potential value. Others were certainly fixing their thoughts on her, manoeuvring to negotiate.

He looked her over, surprised to find he had such a daughter. In all those years that she had been out of his thoughts, she had become a woman, and a comely one at that.

'So. My lady mother is dead.' He was in sombre mourning for Dame Cecily, and it suited his fleshy bulk better than the ostentatious finery with which he usually advertised his ever-increasing wealth and status. Honour thy father and thy mother, that thy days may be long upon the land which the Lord thy God giveth thee. A gentleman was obliged to mourn the passing of his dam, but within his calculating heart there was only relief that the old witch had gone at last, to leave him in peace and cause no more embarrassment. Her wild, unorthodox religiosity had grown worse with the years. Promises of hell fire for all papists were well enough, but her screeching rants against the King and the iniquities of his court were another matter. If she had been anything other than his mother, he would have had her locked up in a madhouse and left her to detect Satan in the eyes of her gaolers and fellow lunatics, but confinement at Llys y Garn had served nearly as well, with few but rooks and sheep to be troubled by her insanity or hear her treasonous denunciations.

But the grave was a safer prison still. Now that the lead was sealed and the stone was closed over her, his burden lightened. It was time to attend to other family matters. Such as his children.

'She desired to speak of you, child.' In the three days that Cecily had lingered after Devereux's arrival, the old woman had tried repeatedly to master her disobedient tongue, but to no end. 'You and this house.' He had gleaned that much.

The girl's head rose fractionally. What was it he saw there? Fear? Guilt?

Devereux debated, juggling shillings in his fleshy hands,

behind his back. He suspected that his mother had wished to pledge him to offer this house as Elizabeth's dowry, but for all her struggles, she had been unable to voice her command. Just as well, for the property was his to dispose of, not hers, and as his mother had failed to utter any comprehensible word, he could now do as he chose without risking accusations of filial impropriety. What did he choose though? The idea of a dowry was not without some merit. There was logic in it.

'You will understand, child, that there must be changes in this household. Your brother Anthony, my son and heir, is returning with me to Berevil. He cannot be permitted to linger on, in obscurity, now that he grows to be a man. It is time he took his rightful place in the world. To that end, he is for Oxford. I have informed him of my decision.'

The girl bowed her head in dutiful acquiescence. Of course. Acquiescence was her only option. She was his to command, just as Anthony was. The boy had been sullen – an evil trait that a few good beatings would correct, but he would soon embrace his new life when he discovered the pleasures it had to offer. Pleasures he could barely have dreamed of, exiled in this rambling old house in the woods, confined with a mad grandmother.

There were other children to consider, too. He'd lost count of the children miscarried or dead in days, but there were two others who had survived.

'The babes, Alice and Thomas.' Devereux dragged up their names with a hint of query. 'They are young. Thomas, they tell me, is ailing. They are best left here, to make or mar, as God wills. But you, I am not so certain about.'

Still her head was bowed. She was still, so still she seemed frozen to the spot. Then he noticed her fists were clenched. Fear of him, perhaps. That was not untoward. As a man should fear God, so a child should fear her father.

'You are, what, fourteen, fifteen years of age?'

'Fifteen, sir.'

'Yes, yes.' The finer details of her existence were of no real importance. 'And I don't doubt you have been properly schooled in simpler matters, but it is time, perhaps, that you should take your place at your mother's side at Berevil, to learn the ways of the world and become a lady as befits my daughter.'

The fists clenched tighter. Her head came up, white-faced. 'Sir, I had thought to remain here and care for the little ones. To teach them…' Her words dried up.

Devereux's sharp little black eyes watched her intently. Did she speak with an insolent presumption that must be crushed? More probable, perhaps, that she spoke as a child, nervous of stepping into a wider arena. Her intent was really of no importance, but her trembling suggestion was not entirely objectionable. It fitted well enough with another idea.

He nodded. 'A proper womanly desire. Fit for one destined to be a virtuous wife and mother in good time. Our neighbour, Rhys ap Griffith, has called upon me. He deigns to remind me that there had been some talk of a match between my daughter and his son, Huw. What do you say to that?'

He asked because he was curious to gauge how genuine her apparent humility and obedience was. There was something about the girl that hinted of a wilfulness, carefully restrained.

Her eyes were lowered again, but he fancied he caught the flicker of desire in them. 'If my father wishes it, I am happy with the arrangement, sir.'

'Are you, indeed?' Devereux snorted amusement. So that was how the wind blew. 'Huw Rhys is a man for the maidens, so I hear. Well, well. It is a match worthy of some consideration, certainly.' He inhaled deeply, making his decision. 'I think it is fitting that a Powell should reside here, least my name begin to be overlooked in these parts. Very well, you will have the younger children in your care. That is good. I shall send for your aunt Ann. She shall have a care of the household and act as your guardian. In a year or so, perhaps… ah, you are pleased with my decision.' Yes, there was no doubting that flash of joy. 'Well, so be it. But understand, you will behave as the daughter of Devereux Powell, not as a wild thing of the woods. Keep to your prayers and your duties, obey your aunt and learn to live according to your station, madam.'

He studied her, the child he had barely noticed for fifteen years. She was dark and slender, less voluptuous than the court beauties he had seen in London, but a match for them in other ways. None of the heavy features of the Powells, nor of the fair delicacy of her mother's line, like Anthony, but vibrant with some inner fire. She was his flesh, but he could see nothing of himself in her. It worried him, this sense of her otherness, something not quite within his control. For a moment he fancied that he had been twisted and wound like a thread on a spindle, by this girl who feigned obedience, who bowed her head in humility but whose thoughts, in a fierce kingdom of their own, were closed to him.

He frowned, determined to command. 'As for Huw ap Rhys, you will treat him with proper courtesy, as a neighbour and gentleman, but no more. There may indeed be a betrothal, when I have given proper thought on it, but I'll have no wantonness, you hear me, or you'll feel a rod across your back.'

She was wise, it seemed. She said nothing, bowing her head again.

'Very well.' Devereux was satisfied. Matters had worked out well enough. A son and heir must be on view to the world, but once the boy was despatched to Oxford, he'd not be in the way. And the girl was content to stay at Llys y Garn. Sooner or later she must be brought into the light, decked out and attended to, but for now she could be put aside again, while he took time to consider. Hugh ap Rhys. There would be no financial capital to made of it, but a ready match with Rhys ap Griffith's son was not without its political benefits, and it might save him tedious efforts in that quarter.

He grunted dismissal, and Elizabeth curtseyed again, retreating from the chamber, her face a model of calm acquiescence until the heavy oak door shut behind her.

Elizabeth threw her head back and laughed in glee. She had her home still and, with renewed talk of the betrothal to Huw, there was hope that it might be her home forever. It was the answer to her most fervent prayer that she…

The image of the Devil's Quarry rose up before her. Her challenge, her prayer, not to God but to the dark one. A shiver ran down her back.

Who was it, God or the Devil, who had answered her prayers?

7

Beth, wife of Devereux Powell, looked down from the oriel window of her confinement chamber and hated what she saw. Hated it because she hated everything about this God-forsaken house. It had killed her first born, her promising son, John, and though the tower that had hurled him down and crushed his bones had been hurled down in its turn, its stonework scattered, on her husband's orders, still she fancied the house was waiting to devour more. By ague and rheumatism, if by nothing else. It was draughty, damp and inelegant, its former grandeur long decayed.

She endured with a good grace the jolting journeys that took her periodically to her husband's other lands or to London, relishing the high company and elegant fashion that awaited her, but she detested the upheaval of coming here. Devereux came once or twice a year to Llys y Garn to inspect the property and receive his rents, but she seldom accompanied him, content to remain in elegant Berevil Hall, with her small dogs and her important neighbours.

But this year, she had no choice in the matter. Infectious fever was abroad in the south of the county, and with yet another confinement so near, her husband had dictated that she must travel north for the sake of the unborn child.

She obeyed. Of course she obeyed. That was what a wife did. That and dutifully bring forth child after child. There must have been a time, long ago, when she anticipated her confinements with eagerness as well as dread, praying for the wail of a healthy offering to present to her lord. But there had been so many still births now, so many miscarriages and ailing infants that survived barely long enough to be baptised, that she could no longer bring herself to anticipate anything but the usual futile ending.

Was that the child, stirring within her? She felt a flutter, but it was one with her aches and swellings and inevitable nausea. Perhaps this one would live, after all. Another son, please God, for though Anthony was said to be thriving at Oxford, so too had John, and all his promise had come to nothing. Little Thomas, sinking day by day by all reports, would not last long. She was reconciled to his loss even while he lived. And the girls. What use was there in two healthy girls? Young Alice was a bonny child, full of life and vigour, but still a girl. And Elizabeth…

Elizabeth was down below, in the garden under the mulberry tree, with Huw ap Rhys. Her mother watched, lips pursed. The girl had sent her maid away on some excuse and permitted the man too much freedom. Far too much. She had been left to run wild for long enough. Doubtless Devereux's sister Ann, the nominal head of this household, fretted in small anxious ways over her wards' dignity and dancing lessons, but she didn't notice what a sharp-eyed mother did. A mother who had seen and spoken with her daughter barely a dozen times in sixteen years. She could see with fresh and critical eyes.

Beth shuffled her aching bulk away from the window and sank with relief into the velvet chair that stood ready by the fire. She gestured to the maid. 'My daughter is down in the garden. Bid her come up to me.'

Her eyes closed, in search of ease while she waited. The birth was very near, she could tell. Let it be over with, let her have a few brief days of respite before it all began again.

She opened her eyes at the sound of the door, and looked upon her daughter, sinking in a respectful curtsey. All semblance of propriety, but what lurked within? Something

135

not so curbed and dutiful. It must be rooted out.

'I have been watching you, child.'

She saw Elizabeth's glance flit to the oriel window, a blush at the realisation that for once there had been watching eyes. This chamber had stood cold and empty for so long, she had forgotten the vantage it offered.

'Madam?' A tone of innocence. She acted well. No harm in that. A woman should master such a skill, just as long as the part she acted was the proper part.

'You have been with Huw Rhys.'

'Indeed, madam. He is our neighbour and visits often. My father bade me treat him with respect, as I trust I do.'

Beth raised her hand for silence. Too ready with her words. Naturally the girl had learned to play poor Ann, like the fool the old maid was, but she would not play her mother in the same way. 'You are pert, child. I saw. He had his hand upon your breast.'

'There were wasps, madam.'

'And doubtless he was brushing them away from you.' A twinge within her. She gestured to her maid who brought a cup of spiced wine, but it cloyed, curdling in her stomach. 'You will inform him he will forego such courtesy henceforth. The son of Rhys ap Griffith is no fit companion for the daughter of Devereux Powell. Sir Devereux as he will be, by Christmas, God willing.'

There was utter falseness in the girl's meek demeanour. She dared to answer back. 'My father wishes us to be betrothed, madam. I didn't think there could be harm—'

'Betrothed? You father does not wish for any such betrothal, whatever idle thought he may have had once.' Beth was an actress too. She too could lie with conviction. '*Sir* Devereux Powell need not seek to ally himself with an impoverished house of insignificant squires. There is no betrothal.'

The truth was that Devereux had not yet made any decision on the subject, and had not deigned to discuss it with her. But here, confined among women, she could pretend that she was autocratic mistress in the matter, and she did not want this match. She had always nursed a secret hurt that as the niece of a baronet and distant cousin of an earl, she had been married beneath her. Devereux might have wealth and inexhaustible energy in sowing political and social connections, yet by birth he was barely a gentleman, of the second generation at most. But years and experience had taught her it was the social order of the present, not the blood lines of the past that mattered. Her husband, God and the King willing, would soon be a baronet, and Huw ap Rhys, with nothing but a moth-eaten pedigree to his name, was nothing. He would add no dignity to hers.

But Elizabeth, it seemed, would not be told. Perhaps she recognised wishful thinking in her mother's words and understood Beth's true powerlessness. 'My father spoke of a betrothal and I have prayed for it, since it was his will. I cannot think—'

'You do not think, child. You obey your father and mother, as the scriptures command, and we shall decide whom you will or will not marry. You have been confined in this house for too long. No more. It is time you took up your proper station. A daughter's place is with her mother, until a suitable husband is found. A match suited to the status of a baronet's daughter. You will return to Berevil with me, and let us hear no more of this foolish betrothal to a penniless nobody. You understand me?'

The girl understood, that was clear. There was such fury in her glance, though she cast her eyes down for fear they would burn. Her hands were clasped in modest supplication, but there was no modesty in her words. 'I am betrothed to Huw ap Rhys and I will marry him!'

Such outright defiance was like a slap across Beth's face. Unheard-of impudence in a child. 'You will do as you are bid, and if you do not swear obedience now, I shall have you whipped and locked up in your chamber until...' A sharp stab of pain. She gripped the arm of her chair.

'Madam?' Her maid had come forward, anxious.

Beth held her breath until the pain passed. 'It is time. Summon the women. Where is the midwife? Now.'

Her women gathered round, helping her up, mopping her brow, guiding her to the birthing chair. This was something Beth had endured more times than she could recall. This ordeal would be Elizabeth's one day, but for now the girl was superfluous. The maids bustled her from the chamber.

Elizabeth stared down at the grass around the mulberry tree. Stained by the juice of fallen fruit. Blood. Spilt by her. Blood to stain a murderess's hands.

'Sweetheart, the pain will pass.' Huw placed his hands upon her shoulders. No one now to disapprove. 'It's only natural you grieve for a mother's loss.'

Her eyes met his, wondering. He could not understand this thing, yet to him alone she could speak of it. Why? She was not so simply to imagine some romantic fancy. She wanted Huw as her husband, but that was not love, not the love of passionate tales, of Tristram and Isolde, of Dido and Aeneas, of David and Bathsheba. Did Hugh love her? As much, perhaps, as he loved any other lass in the parish. But they were bound by something stronger than mere love: their mutual yearning for a match that would secure Llys y Garn as his property and her perpetual home. That was the devilish lust that drove them both.

'I killed her.'

'No, sweetheart.'

But yes. It was a sin, her greatest yet, to have killed her

own mother and its weight tormented beyond endurance. Her mother. A hallowed tie, even though Beth had never been more to her than a distant figure of obligatory respect. Any maternal affection that Elizabeth had ever received had come from her wet nurse and spiky old Joan. And yet Beth had borne her and there was a sanctity in that, which she had desecrated.

'My hatred killed her. My wickedness.'

'Hush, sweetheart, it was no such thing.'

'It was! I hated her for denying me this match, and my anger killed her. My anger kills anyone I hate. It's an evil spirit at work in me.'

'No! You did nothing.'

'I hated my mother; she died. I hated Dame Cecily; she died. I hated my brother John; he died. How can it be other than witchcraft? The work of the Devil?'

Huw tried to comfort with good hard reason, though she could see the superstitious alarm in his eyes. 'Dame Cecily was an old woman, far beyond her time. What had you to do with it? She was many years in dying. And a loose stone gave under John. It was an accident. How could you be to blame? Where you stood, you could not have pushed him. Your mother, God keep her soul, died in childbirth. As my mother did. It is a cruel thing, but women do die so. It was not your doing. Stop this rash talk or you will have the parson ducking you for a witch.'

'And if I am a witch, Huw ap Rhys?'

For a moment he seemed unsure whether to laugh or shiver. But there were higher demands driving him. He smiled. 'Then I shall wed a witch, my love.'

She could only shudder, remembering her sins and wickedness, and the Bible's injunction.

Thou shalt not suffer a witch to live.

139

8

Smoke from the open hearth rose to the blackened rafters of Hendre Hywel . This ancient house was like its owner, a dilapidated ruin of forgotten rank and dignity.

'The child's death was hard on you, girl.' In his high oak chair, Rhys ap Griffith's spine was no less rigidly upright than the carved wooden panels it barely touched. He was a man who did not know how to bend, yet he sought, in his lofty, ascetic way, to offer a crumb of human comfort. He had a concern for this girl; she was valuable and must be nurtured. 'Remember, she is with God, free from the trammels of this world and past all pain now.'

'Yes indeed, sir.' Elizabeth mouthed pious compliance, but knew it was meaningless. There may have been release for little Thomas, when he died four months since, for what had his sickly life ever been but pain and misery? He had ailed from birth and wailed and snivelled his discomfort to the last. But Alice had been a happy child, overflowing with life and health and hopes, until the smallpox had swept her away like refuse in the gutter. Where was the mercy in her pointless death? She had not wanted to be with God in Heaven, she had wanted to be here, in this world, alive and loving.

Like Elizabeth. Whatever the scriptures promised, she had no hunger for bliss in another life. She no more desired a city of pearl and translucent gold and cold, heartless, precious stones, than a lake of fiery brimstone. She wanted only this, her life, her place, her breath.

But she could not admit this. It was forbidden. She must

pretend devout resignation at the loss of her little sister. What could Rhys ap Griffiths understand of her inner fury? His concern was all for the long dead and the intricacies of his ancient pedigree.

Lit by the red glow from the hearth, his son smiled in sympathy on her and reached out his hand to squeeze hers. She smiled back painfully, conscious of Rhys's black eyes on them both.

'Your father is doubtless grieving his loss,' said Rhys. Did he speak with irony? When had her father ever grieved, even for the loss of his first wife after nigh on twenty years of marriage? Even for his eldest son John? He was the child of Dame Cecily, beaten by her into heartlessness. If he had ever known true grief, he had never let it interfere with the business of his life.

'He is an unlucky man,' said Rhys complacently. One son was all he had, from a wife long dead, but Huw was strong and healthy and would thrive. Sir Devereux's endless tilling of his fertile soil had come to this; a dozen children dead and now just two remained, a boy and girl. This girl. Though the boy would take the greater part, the lands in the south and in England, the girl must have a dowry. Llys y Garn. A certainty now, unless fate decided to smile upon Sir Devereux's bed at last, and add complications to the brew. 'How does his new wife fare? The Lady Margaret? Is she with child yet?'

Elizabeth fought back a blush. The Lady Margaret, not ten years her senior, did not share confidences with a step-daughter who lived on the other side of the county. 'I had not heard so, sir.'

'And he leaves you barren too.' Rhys's old thin lips stretched into a smile. 'He should be attending to the marriages of the children that God has already seen fit to grant him. It is time that you and Huw wed.'

141

Huw laughed. 'I would have it so, sir.'

'And I, sir.' Here, at least, Elizabeth could be certain there would be no opposition to the plan.

A dragonish papery rustle escaped from Rhys. His laugh. 'I see that well enough. So it should be. You should have been wed and nursing a child at your breast long before this. When does your father next come to Llys y Garn? Michaelmas, I suppose.'

'I believe so, sir. It is his usual custom.'

'Very well, so be it. At Michaelmas I'll call on him and we shall have you settled. Now off with you.'

Elizabeth was glad to be dismissed. Her rambles led her to Hendre Hywel often enough, but not for the pleasure of Rhys's company. His son proffered his arm as they picked their way across the muddy cobbles of the yard.

'Michaelmas. Less than two months away. Will they close on it at last, do you think?'

'If your father has his way, they will.'

'Your father is not so eager. I trust he hasn't hatched other plans for you?'

'None that he has told me of. Rest easy, Huw. I think nothing delays my father but reluctance to give my marriage any thought at all. His great business affairs are his only concern.' Except for this delay, she was happy to be out of her father's thoughts, for what might become of her, if she occupied them more?

'My father will bring you to Sir Devereux's mind,' Huw assured her. 'He is set on this, and growing impatient. As am I, sweetheart.'

'And I.' She admitted his kiss. What harm was there in it? There was none to witness their closeness, as they walked back towards Llys y Garn.

'We shall be man and wife by Christmas, God willing.'

'I pray so. Indeed I do.'

142

He was full of easy loving nonsense, was Huw. She knew it and did not care if it were false, for he would be her husband, and she would honour him as such, and there would be tenderness and companionship and children – and they would both have Llys y Garn. For that she would pay any price.

The wall surrounding Llys y Garn reared up before them. Aunt Ann, no longer having younger children to occupy and worry her, would be fretting on hearing that Elizabeth had walked out alone again.

'I must go to my aunt,' said Elizabeth, pulling her hand from Huw's. 'She will be in tears, if I am absent any longer.'

'Elizabeth?' From the trees, a young man was approaching them, leading his horse. 'There you are!'

For a fleeting moment she didn't recognise him, the height, the swagger, the arrogant tone. Then she knew him again. 'Anthony!' She rushed forward to greet him. 'What brings you here? We did not expect you.'

'My father was so full of mighty business with the tedious greybeards, down in Berevil, I thought to clear my head and come to visit my sister. And truthfully, I could not abide another hour of the Lady Margaret's pretty prim prattle.'

'Hush. Don't say such things of your step-mother. Have you seen our aunt?'

'I have, and I had to flee her too, before her hen-twittering drove me mad. So I rode out to find what had become of you. You should not ramble in the woods, sister. Here. You, sir. Take my horse.' Anthony casually flung the reins to Huw, who caught them instinctively.

'Anthony!' reproved Elizabeth.

'What?' He strove to look bewildered, then looked a second time on Huw. 'Ah. It is Huw Rhys. Forgive me, sir. I mistook you for a groom.'

Huw smiled away the laboured insult. 'How are you, lad? You grow fast. Almost a man, I see.'

'Not a man, sir! A gentleman!'

Huw bowed. 'I honour your noble descent.'

'Come,' said Elizabeth hurriedly. 'Anthony, come in with me. Huw.' She dropped a curtsey. 'I thank you for escorting me safely home, sir. I shall see you soon, I trust.'

'Not soon enough for me, sweetheart,' said Huw, raising her fingers as if to kiss them, then, leaning forward, he kissed her lips instead, before turning to saunter away, whistling.

Anthony stared after him, smouldering. 'How do you permit such uncouth incivility, Elizabeth?'

'There was no incivility.' She took his arm to turn him away, beckoning to the groom who'd hurried up from the stables.

'I say there is,' insisted Anthony. 'It is time you learned to consider your position and mine. You are the daughter of Sir Devereux Powell, and my sister, and you should behave in a way that does not besmirch our honour.'

'Anthony.' She spoke sharply, still the mistress in this relationship. 'I am betrothed to Huw and you will not speak to me in such a way.'

'Betrothed to Huw Rhys? Ha! A nobody. You are bewitched by his pretty looks and words? Then that means you are no better than a dozen doxies in the village that he has bedded. There are a score of brats, they say, that have his looks. That is the man you simper over and think to wed?'

Elizabeth breathed deeply to calm herself. 'I am the woman he will marry. What do I care what others he has bedded? I shall be his wife.'

'You shall not, if I have any say in it!'

She fought down her exasperation. 'Who would you have me marry then? What decrepit old gentleman of our father's

144

acquaintance have you picked out for me?' She mocked lightly to appease him, holding his hand.

'Why should you be so eager to wed at all? Marriage is a dangerous thing for a woman. You would do better to leave it alone.'

It was true. Yet the dangers of matrimony were those of being alive and she would brave them, and more, to have what she sought. 'You would rather have me die an old maid, like Aunt Anne?'

Once she would have been certain how he would have replied, with a sullen pout, wanting to keep her to himself. But he had changed. Grown up and away from her. He scowled. 'If you must wed, I would have you wed someone who will bring honour to our name.'

'Ancient blood, perhaps? Huw has that. More ancient and honourable than ours.'

'I shall be a baronet. Since I have but one sister left, I would have her marry a lord. Now that Alice is gone...' He shrugged.

'You have come here to grieve for her with me,' she said sadly, hoping to restore the brother she once knew.

'Yes, poor Alice,' he said indifferently. 'But think, now you are the only daughter of the house. No sister to lay rival claim to our father's attention. Are you not secretly glad that little Alice is out of the way?'

'Glad?' Elizabeth dropped his hand, shocked. 'How is this, Anthony? How can you speak so callously of the sweet child? I loved her and I believed you did so too. Did you not? Have Oxford and Berevil Hall bred such coldness in your soul, as to dissolve all affection in you?'

He jerked his head up and away, as if in contempt, but she caught the blush on his cheek. The glint in his eye, even. 'Alice was well enough. A sweet little maid who had no vice in her. But it was God's will, was it not, and now she's gone.

145

They all go. There is nothing to be done about it, so let us forget her.'

'I loved her,' Elizabeth repeated, recognising the conflict in him, desperate to win him back. 'Just as I love you, Anthony.'

But he had recovered, stepping back from his hesitant redemption, too well schooled now to surrender. He laughed complacently. 'So I should hope. For I shall be head of the family. Don't fear, Elizabeth, I shall serve your interests well, if you remember your place and respect mine.'

He swaggered on and she followed him into the house with a chill sense of desolation and loss.

9

Michaelmas, and mist hung on the trees. Llys y Garn was bustling, for Sir Devereux was in residence and the usual lax and somnolent life of the house was swept away by an invasion of officious lackeys, grooms and secretaries.

Aunt Ann was forever distressing herself, fluttering and flustering from chamber to chamber, worrying the servants in the kitchens for fear of presenting anything less than the best. Anthony was lording it in the stables, making needless demands about the housing of his fine new horse. The parson and his curate were being dined on game pie in the parlour. Tenants were waiting their turn to pay their respects and their rents.

And Devereux was closeted with his neighbour, Rhys ap Griffith.

Elizabeth sat quietly in the courtyard, watching the doves circle round their cote. She had known that Rhys would call. She would be patient. She would be still. No Huw to distract her for this desperate moment, but he would appear soon enough, when all was settled, she was sure of that.

If it were settled. She could pray. To whom? To a God whose goodness she no longer trusted or to another? No! She would put aside these evil thoughts of devilry and witchcraft and listen no more to the dark voices within her. Mouthing the vow, she swore she would marry Huw ap Rhys, be a good wife and mistress of Llys y Garn, and that was all. It was a vow she made to the house, to the hills and forests and the stones. Let God or the Devil listen if they would.

Rhys ap Griffith emerged, and her heart quickened. He saw her, no hint of a smile or frown to tell her what to

147

expect. She rose, her knees buckling beneath her, into a curtsey more accidental than intentional. Rhys said nothing. He merely nodded his grey head solemnly in acknowledgement. As he mounted his sturdy horse, Thomas Rice bustled out from the north wing, seeking her.

'Madam, Sir Devereux wishes to speak with you.'

Devereux paced, impatiently. He still had need to speak to the parson about the church repairs, John Davies about the mill, Morris ap Thomas about the harvest, and a thousand other matters. This little domestic matter was an importunate annoyance.

But it was a matter that must be addressed sooner or later, and better perhaps to have it out of the way now. He looked at the young woman before him. She was ready for marriage, without doubt. That was what women, after all, were for; marriage and children, though God's arrangements in these matters were beyond his comprehension. His first wife was scarcely ever without a child in her belly, though little good it had done, and his second had still not conceived, after more than a year. He wanted more children, more pawns to move around the board, but for now he must deal with the pawns he had. There was a Philipps daughter that he had in mind for Anthony. And for Elizabeth? A dozen potential suitors lurked in the wings, if he were to study the matter in depth; men who would welcome alliance with the Powells, each with something to offer in return.

But here was Rhys ap Griffith pressing his son's suit, refusing to let it go, nagging like an old woman, and there was profit of sorts in it. Rhys had nothing except his antique pedigree, but that pedigree had a considerable value to a man who had none of his own. It would tie him in and win him influence with all the gentry of the northern county, where, apart from this estate, he had little connection.

It could be of value. And to have a daughter married and off his hands so easily was a benefit indeed.

'Well child, you doubtless know what our neighbour Rhys ap Griffith wanted with me.'

'I believe so, sir.' She was meek and biddable, just as a woman should be. That was good.

'Your betrothal to his son. He wishes me to settle. What say you to that?'

She raised her eyes. A flash of fierce spirit in them. How would young Huw like that? He would doubtless know how to curb it, once he had the mastery of her.

'I am content to wed Huw, sir.'

'But should I be content to arrange it?' A rhetorical question. It was not for her to answer. And she did not, wisely, though he caught her quick glance gauging his reactions. Perversely, he must argue. 'I don't know what benefit I shall reap from such an alliance. A threadbare squire with nothing but his name. And he presumes to ask for Llys y Garn as your dowry. He asks of me!' He was aware of her stillness. 'A man with nothing in his purse should, I'd have thought, be content with a bag of guineas and have done.'

He turned to face her full on, and found her black eyes boring into him. Eyes that, were he of a superstitious frame of mind, would give him pause for thought. Eyes that called to mind his mother's, as she spiralled into venomous madness. Did it pass in the blood? Best, perhaps, to hand her quickly on to others, before it revealed itself. 'But I should consider the welfare of my own blood, should I not? My daughter must have proper habitation, and the marriage will bring the lands of Llys y Garn and Hendre Hywel together, which would be a fitting inheritance for my grandchildren.'

'Father, I do thank you with all my heart.'

Her warmth took him by surprise. When had he last

evoked such enthusiasm from a child of his? If ever? A small additional satisfaction for a troublesome matter so easily settled.

'Well well, that will do. You may go. There is much, I am sure, for you to do as you prepare for the journey to Berevil Hall.'

'Berevil?' She was shocked.

He was impatient to be done now. 'Yes, indeed. You must journey to Berevil with your aunt, tomorrow, to prepare for your marriage. When you return, it will be as wife of Hugh Rhys and mistress of this house. Let that content you. Now go.'

Elizabeth withdrew, relief overwhelming her disappointment. A brief stay at Berevil was a small price to pay for the attainment of her true goal. The marriage was set. Soon, there would be no going back, for her father had already sent for his lawyers. Papers would be drawn up. Nothing could come between her and this marriage now.

'Elizabeth.' Anthony caught her on the stairs. 'You look brimful of happiness. I wonder what brings that about?'

She smiled on him. 'I am returning with you to Berevil, little brother.'

His supercilious smile broadened. 'That is good news indeed! Far better than I'd feared. I hate to see you abandoned here in such neglect. My sister should live as a lady. No more of this dreary old house.'

'I go to Berevil to prepare for my marriage to Huw ap Rhys.'

'No!'

'Our father and Rhys have come to an agreement. The attorneys have been summoned. Soon I shall be wed.' She felt his shock, saw his clenched fists and his rigid jaw, but it could not undermine her overwhelming joy. She would have the whole world rejoicing. 'Be happy for me, little brother.'

'Happy? Do you jest, madam? How can I be happy that a sister of mine be given to a tuppenny, pig-swilling, bare-arsed—'

'To our neighbour, Anthony. A man of ancient honour and lineage, and if I am content, why must you object?'

'I will not permit this marriage.'

She laughed. 'It isn't yours to permit, Anthony. Our father has set his mind on it. Would you presume to gainsay him?'

'Yes! Oh, I see. Locked up in this place and knowing nothing of the world, you imagine I am just a silly boy still, and our father will brush me aside like a buzzing fly, if I presume to question him. You are wrong. I am his son and heir, sister; I am a man and he speaks to me of his affairs. He will listen to me. Believe me, I know how matters work with him. Today, he was beset with business, and he thinks to be rid of you with the least trouble to himself, but he hasn't yet considered the ills of such a match. When I speak of them, the folly, the futility, the degradation, he will listen with both ears. There are a hundred better men for you to wed. Men of wealth and rank, who will add to the honour of our name, not drag it down.'

'Let there be a thousand dukes and earls and moneybags, there are none that I wish to marry!'

'Your wishes are no matter. This is Powell business. There are no papers signed yet, and never doubt, sister, when we are away from the witchery of this place, when we are back in Berevil and he can see clearly how his affairs should best prosper, he will understand that this marriage was ill-conceived and cannot be countenanced.'

He had become so confident. Seventeen and knowing so much of the world. She could no longer be sure if he spoke as a jealous boy, bragging in order to assert his own importance, or as a man of sense and true cunning. Fear

151

ripped through her happiness. Perhaps he spoke the truth. Perhaps he was now regarded with respect and interest by Devereux, and his words could indeed sway their father, while she, adrift in Berevil, the mere daughter of the house, waiting on her indifferent stepmother, would have no influence at all. She could sense her dream, on the very brink of fulfilment, slipping away, dispersing in mist.

No. She would not relinquish it. She would have Huw, and Llys y Garn with him. The two were one. What other suitor would demand this house as her dowry and be content for her to live here? Only with Huw could she be certain of that, and she would not weep, but fight for it. She had no sword or pistols, but still she would fight, with whatever weapons she had.

'Anthony, you will do nothing, say nothing. I command it.' She had the weapon of her authority as his sister to whom he had always deferred.

For a fleeting moment he was once more under her spell, cowed by her fierceness. Then he recovered. 'You do not command me, sister. It is I who command now, and I say this marriage shall not be.'

She would speak no more to him. She would not look at him, for fear of what her anger would do. She brushed past, head high, her thoughts whirling, seeking a solution.

Down in the courtyard, Huw was dismounting, sent by his father to press his own suit. He smiled at her, contented, and she strove to smile back with equal warmth, as she hurried to greet him. 'Come in, Huw, and take some wine to seal our betrothal.'

'I'll take a kiss for that,' he said, following her into the house, into the sunny chamber where she usually sat to her work. 'No harm in that now, I think?'

'Be patient, sir. I am told I must go to Berevil tomorrow.'
'Why so?'

152

'To prepare for our wedding.'

'Prepare? How?'

She gave a hollow laugh. 'Doubtless I shall be told, in full measure.'

'Then I shall claim two kisses now. It is my right as your lord, is it not?'

Like the kisses he had claimed from every girl in the valley, it was said. She would not begrudge him, but—

She caught the creak, the faint shuffle, behind the heavy oak door that stood a hair's breadth ajar into the adjoining chamber. He was there, Anthony, she knew it. Behind that door, listening, spying on her as he had when their grandmother was alive, a spoilt and jealous child still, despite his assumed assurance. Was he kneeling through there, with his eye to the keyhole? So be it. Let him see. In fury, she pulled Huw to her and kissed him on the lips, with twice the passion he had ever presumed to shower on her.

He laughed.

Was it the wind, whistling through a loose casement, or did she catch a muffled squeak of rage? So. For all his boasting, Anthony did not dare step forward to challenge this liberty. He merely lurked in the shadows, a sullen little boy, impotent in his spying, who could only watch and bloody himself with what he saw. That was how it would be, then. The battle was drawn, and she knew now how to win it.

She steadied herself, easing herself away from Huw's embrace. 'Here, sir. Drink your wine. I must go prepare for tomorrow's journey. But I cannot bear the thought that I shall not see you again until our wedding day.'

Huw ap Rhys was willing to make sacrifices for such a prize. 'Fear not, sweetheart. I shall ride to Berevil, to sing at your window, and beg another kiss or two.'

Her finger was on his lip. 'Ride no further than this house,' she breathed. There was such fierceness within her, its heat would surely set the chamber ablaze. 'Tomorrow. Two hours before dawn, before the servants stir.' She spoke clearly. 'Come to me, Huw, as my betrothed, as mine in the eyes of God. In the Great Hall, where no one will disturb us.'

He looked at her thoughtfully. Then he smiled and bowed. 'I'll be there, sweetheart, never fear.'

'I do not fear!' she whispered, to herself; 'I will not fear.'

The crescent of the old moon was edging up into the night sky, out of the black mass of the forest. Elizabeth had lain, tossing, sleepless, waiting for it, the curtains of her bed drawn back. Too much depended on this moment. Let it slip away and she would be imprisoned in Berevil, while Anthony's persuasive poison did its work, souring and overthrowing the distant arguments of Rhys ap Griffith. There was no lawyer yet on hand to seal the matter irrevocably now, so she must seal it herself, with all that she had.

She rose softly, careful not to wake the maid who slept at the foot of her bed, wrapping a cloak around her against the dawn chill as she slipped out into the courtyard.

Night shadows spilled across the cobbles, and a flitting shadow with them. She was sure of it. A flitting shadow, determined not to be seen. Anthony. She could not see him, but she saw the shadow flit, and what servant would bother to conceal himself so furtively? It was Anthony, watching for her at this early hour just as she had intended him to do. She had spelled out her intention for his benefit.

She climbed the steps to the side door of the Great Hall and, wary of the creaking hinges, opened it. The arches of the passage within opened onto cavernous darkness, a devouring chill and the stale smell of damp. The hall was seldom used. It had been a year and more since Devereux entertained the local gentry here, and when it was not required for banqueting, it stood in silent neglect. No hangings on the stone walls or gilded portraits on the panelling. A few worm-eaten benches gathered dust, the ancient table tilted against the wall, its trestles stacked.

She'd left the door behind her ajar. No need for Anthony to risk its creaks and groans when he followed her, as he was surely doing. She crossed the passage to the low door on the far side, which gave access to the gardens.

Huw was there, pacing, the faintest glimmer of moonlight catching on his dark hair.

'Sweetheart.' He came to her, arms outstretched. Huw her husband, her beloved. Huw the philanderer, curious to know what pleasures might come of this early morning tryst.

'Come in.' She spoke low, drawing him on into the huge emptiness of the dark hall, and heard a hasty scuffle away to her left. It might merely be a rat, scurrying in the shadows – but she knew it was not.

'You are my husband,' she said.

'Soon, sweetheart,' agreed Huw. He sounded content, complacent, yet she knew, she could feel the same urgency in him to have the deal done. No need to fear his reluctance.

'We are betrothed,' she said. 'And a betrothal is a marriage for all but the parson. I must go to Berevil, and I shall pine for you.'

'And I you, sweetheart, but the delay will not be long.'

'I don't want delay.' She stared at him and took his hand, leading him to the stone stairs. A complicated dance, this. One whose steps she must get perfect, if she were to succeed.

One half-second Huw resisted, then followed her eagerly, up the steps to the creaking gallery that gave access to the upper chamber.

She had no intention of going in, but up they must go until the shifting shadows below told her that all was as she had intended. Anthony was down there, lurking, ready to follow them up on tiptoe once they had slipped inside the bed chamber. But at its door she stopped.

She had intended to stop there, pretending to be seized by sudden second thoughts, but it was a genuine chill that froze her. It was a cold room of death. The great bedstead stood black, its carvings writhing in the dark, the ropes loose, the hangings packed away.

'No!' She paused, her shudder real enough, hand to her throat as if surprised by her own thoughts. 'Not here. Not in the chamber where my mother died.'

She turned sharply, back down the stairs, moving so quickly that the scurrying shadow below almost revealed itself in its urgent need for concealment. Huw was noisy on the steps behind her, willing to play her game, though puzzling over her intent.

A creak, a shuffle, an echo. She heard it clearly and knew her brother had taken the bait she had set. Late last night, she had left the door of the secret papist closet agape in readiness. Anthony, panicking in his haste to conceal himself as they came down the stairs, would have found no better hiding place. He was in there, she was sure. The ornate panelling in the deep recess of the doorway under the gallery appeared almost seamless in the dark, but, pulling Huw in her wake, she could feel the false panel ajar by the merest fraction of an inch. Turning to face her future husband, she threw herself back against the secret door, hearing its catch click shut.

'Here,' she said urgently. 'I am your wife. Take me.'

Would such a man as Huw ap Rhys need more encouragement? He had kept circumspect till now, respecting her rank and her own discretion, but now that her discretion was dissolved, why hang back? He took her in his arms, would lay her down, on the cold slabs, on her cloak, but she'd have none of that.

'No, here.' She stood, fierce, a panting tigress, so he took her there, her back pressed to the panelling, her fingers clawing him as she responded with a passion scarcely human. The daughter of Sir Devereux Powell. Witch woman.

Afterwards, as they recovered their breath, she pushed him away, straightening her skirts, and spoke sanely again.

'I must go, Huw, before I am missed. My maid will be up to rouse me.'

'Take care, sweetheart.'

'I shall. We shall meet next to wed properly, before the parson.'

'I wait only for that day.' His mock gallantry came so easily.

She slipped out, down the steps to the cobbles again, hurrying back across the courtyard. His now, by deed. By witnessed deed.

Huw watched her go in the grey welling light of the coming dawn, leaving him to stand and think, in the empty echoing hall. Now he could freely acknowledge the amazement he felt at her ardour. An ardour greater than all the girls, willing or cajoled, that he'd bedded over the years. Such dark passion and such determined calculation.

Calculation to match his own. His way lay back through the passage, through the gardens and the woods, but first he paused, at the site of their passion, in the little low doorway under the gallery. He looked thoughtfully on its dark panels, still stained with their sweaty handprints. He knew the panels and their significance. It was he who had opened them once before to set Elizabeth free. But he did not open them now. He turned and sauntered out, smiling darkly.

Aunt Ann was fretting. It was her mission in life. Her only mission, now that her charges were either dead or grown. Her brother Devereux would never leave her to starve in utter obscurity, since it would reflect too ill on him, but nothing remained for her except bitter charity. She must fret over that, and over the agonising discomfort of a journey that she dreaded, and over Elizabeth, who was fey and wilful this morning, and who neither ate nor spoke.

Ann fussed, which was foolish for it only annoyed Sir Devereux further. Now that he had eaten largely, he was impatient to be on his way. He frowned at the stool where his son should be seated and summoned the steward.

'Tell my son, if he cannot rise on time, he must forgo his breakfast. Bid him ready himself. We leave within the hour.'

Elizabeth waited in silence, her fingers knitting together in her lap. Soon she would be released, and in her turn she would release Anthony, face down his mortification and his rage, and settle once and for all with him. Soon. For now, let him sit in the dark of that locked hiding place and consider what he had been obliged, humiliatingly, to overhear. He knew now that she no longer had a prized maidenhead to bestow on any other suitor. If it was the honour of their name that concerned him so much, he would not dare oppose the match.

Thomas Rice came bustling back. 'Sir, your son is gone.'

'Gone!' fumed Devereux. 'Gone where?'

'Sir, his chamber is empty, and when I questioned the servants, I found a stable boy who saw him ride out an hour since.'

'He presumes to ride on ahead of us?' Devereux swelled and grumbled over this slight to his precedence. His son should follow, not lead.

Silent in her place, Elizabeth was frozen. How could this be? She was so certain that Anthony had concealed himself within the secret cupboard. He couldn't have escaped without aid. Could he? There was no possibility of escape from within, since her grandmother's superhuman malice had splintered and destroyed the inner catch.

And yet he was free. An hour ago, servants had seen him riding off. Was it possible that he had never been there at all? Perhaps the shifting shadows had been no more than her imagination, and Anthony had slept on in ignorance.

No, no, no. She had felt him. Felt his spite and rage. He had been there. But somehow he had prised his way out, and now he had ridden off in sullen dudgeon, risking even his father's displeasure.

Her father was impatient, and Elizabeth was bustled to her preparations with the rest. She barely had time to catch the arm of the stable boy who attended to their coach. 'You saw my brother riding away?'

'Yes madam, he took the bay.'

'Did he speak? You heard him?'

'He called, my lady. "Tell my father I will not wait." He was in a great temper, my lady, cursing as he rode, and spurring the beast on most cruelly.'

Yes, she could imagine his resentment and shame urging him to a rash disregard even for their father's displeasure. It was what he would do, her petulant, mortified brother.

'Oh Elizabeth, we must leave.' Aunt Ann was almost in tears in anticipation of their departure.

'Come Aunt.' Elizabeth helped the silly woman into the coach, and paused just a moment longer to look upon her home. Then she too stepped up. 'Let us be gone.'

10

Waiting. Forever waiting. Elizabeth stared out of the window. Between ever shifting clouds, the spring sunshine poured down on the formal garden of Berevil Hall, yew and holly clipped to fantastic contorted shapes, the very turf figured out of its natural state. All forced, all constrained, all tortured, like her.

Spring turning into summer. How long ago was it that she had journeyed south, thinking foolishly to be wed by Christmas? Months had become an eternity as hopeless grief and guilt turned to stone.

Guilt had set its claws in her when they arrived at Berevil to find no Anthony awaiting them. No Anthony, that day or the next. Enquiries had been made, the father furious with the errant son, while Elizabeth, heart in mouth, told herself that she must speak. The stable lad's story must have been a lie. Surely Anthony was imprisoned still, in the secret cupboard in the hall of Llys y Garn. She must speak.

But then came word; the fine bay gelding had been found wandering on the hills, girth snapped, Anthony's glove snagged in the reins. So there was no purpose in her speaking out, for the truth was plain. Anthony had ridden out and been thrown. He lay injured perhaps, cause enough for her distress, but he was not her prisoner. Day after day, the search had continued, with nothing discovered, except Anthony's hat, shredded and floating in a tumbling stream.

Little by little, the search parties had relinquished their questioning and prodding and delving. No body was found.

And then Elizabeth knew.

She wondered if she had always known. Had she ever

truly believed the servant's story, or had she chosen to accept the convenient lie? She no longer knew what had governed her silence. Was it confusion, a lingering fury with her brother or a fear of betraying Huw? For Huw it must have been, riding out from the stables on Anthony's horse, wearing Anthony's hat and cloak, swearing Anthony's oaths.

How much had Huw guessed of her intent in meeting him in the Great Hall? Not to slake lust but to taunt and trouble the spiteful boy who would wreck their hopes. It had been Huw, conspiring with her, and Satan in him. Her master. It was the Devil that had stopped her mouth, kept her still and silent while her brother endured the parched, suffocating terror of imprisonment and the snuffing out of the last frantic struggle to breathe.

In her mind, she endured it with him, sharing his frantic, screaming pain and fear. It was too late to speak. Too late to do anything but accept the guilt and let it burn it into her heart, carbonising and hardening until she had no feeling left, no thought for anything but her one obsessive goal.

For months she had nothing to do but brood on it in silence. Her father had thoughts only for his missing son, his heir, his grasp upon the future. What interest did he have in the trivial fate of a girl? Anthony was all.

But all hope had gone now. Devereux knew it, acknowledging the truth with bitter anger against fate. His son was gone for good and all that remained was Elizabeth. At last his attention turned to his daughter.

A servant ushered her into his chamber, and she looked upon a man whose flesh had begun to fall in sallow folds. He was ill, and ill-tempered with it.

'Sir.' She curtseyed, speaking softly, no longer daring to pray, for good or ill, just willing.

Sir Devereux pushed his chair away and stood facing the fire, the beringed fingers of his big hands working behind his

161

back. 'I wish to speak to you of your marriage.'

She stared at his broad shoulders. At last. Her prize. Though it was befouled with grief and guilt, she would finally have her house. The house that entombed her murdered brother. What did it matter if she gained a husband and Llys y Garn at the expense of a lifetime of penitence? There was nothing else.

She could picture, clearer than this chamber in Berevil Hall, the dark carved panelling at Llys y Garn. She could picture herself opening the secret cupboard, candle aloft, her throat as dry as his must have been, her heart thudding in a terror equal to his. Nothing would cleanse this sin but at least she could ensure Anthony's remains were laid decently to rest. Would that suffice to pay off the Devil?

'Sir Philip Tyrce,' grunted Sir Devereux. 'You have not seen him here. He has lands in Gloucestershire and Bedfordshire, and he has the favour of the King. He will be an eminently suitable match for you.'

The words washed over her like ice. 'Sir? I don't understand. I was to marry Huw ap Rhys. We are betrothed.'

'Betrothed!' He turned at last to face her, eying her with distaste. 'There was no betrothal. You will forget such talk.'

Desperation drove her. Who was this Sir Philip Tyrce? What would a man of Gloucestershire and Bedfordshire care of her or of her world, her dreams, her house? 'But it was agreed.'

'Silence!' Devereux drew a deep breath of rage. 'Who are you to argue with me? Somewhere, madam, my son lies dead. Do you understand that?'

Her heart thudded. She understood. No one understood better. 'Yes sir.'

'My son is dead, and my lady wife will not give me others.' The Lady Margaret, for all her noble connections, was as barren as his hopes. He stared at his daughter. 'You

162

are all I have. Heiress to my estates, my land, my wealth, all my concerns, here and in London and abroad. My only surviving child.'

He waited to see if the knowledge had sunk in. Until now it had not.

'Do you imagine that the sole heiress to Sir Devereux Powell would be parcelled off to the son of such as Rhys ap Griffith?'

The Devil laughed. From the walls, the floor, the ornate ceiling, from the sooty darkness of the fireplace, He laughed. His face gloated from the plasterwork, from the flashing glass of the window panes. His malicious victory encircled her, but she would not submit. She cried, helpless in her defiance, 'I would marry Huw ap Rhys!'

'You would marry? You will marry as I decide. Do you imagine I have done all I have done in this world, to profit the beggarly son of a worn-out line? You will marry Sir Philip Tyrce.'

'I have lain with him!' The threat of shame and disgrace that she had once thought to use to silence Anthony was now her only weapon. 'I have lain with Huw ap Rhys.'

Her father's face flooded dark red. There was spittle on his lips. His flaccid hand stung her face, a ring catching her cheek. 'Whore!'

'Huw's wife!'

'No, harlot, nothing but a whore! I'll have you whipped!' He paused, looked down at her stomach for any tell-tale swelling. 'Did he get you with child?'

She longed to say yes. Just as she had longed, in the dark, night after night, for it to be true. But the truth betrayed her.

'No, I see not. Then I need not beat it out of you.' He stepped back, the deep crimson of choler fading, his small black eyes busy again with calculation. 'You will speak of this to no one. You hear me, whore? Defy me in this and I

163

shall have you locked up where you'll never see the light of day again. You will not disgrace the name of Powell. I do not permit it. Sir Philip Tyrce is a man of the court and they are all whore-mongers there. He will not be over-nice on such matters, for a match such as this, and once you are wed, let him deal with you as he wishes, and as you deserve.

'Now, take yourself out of my sight, where I need not be reminded that you are all I have. Get out, you poisonous whore! Get out!'

The wind hissed around the Devil's stones, and the hounds paced, eager to be on. But Huw ap Rhys sat still in the saddle, gazing down over the trees to the rook-haunted roofs of Llys y Garn. No smoke rose. The house stood empty and decaying, a wasted asset in some foreigner's purse.

His loss, his impoverishment, his own doing.

Such a little thing. A sin of omission to have walked away, knowing, as certainly as Elizabeth had known, that Anthony was trapped within the forgotten priest hole. And the worse sin of commission, slipping into the stables in the dawn confusion of departure, sowing the lie that Anthony had departed in one of his infantile sulks.

Elizabeth could have betrayed him, but he knew she would not. She had never meant the boy to die, he was sure, but he was less tender, as determined on the match that would bring him this estate as she, and bruised by years of contemptuous insults from Anthony Powell, scion of the upstart leatherworker of Haverfordwest. He would not stand by and have the arrogant boy threaten his longed-for achievement.

So he'd acted, and in acting, he had destroyed the very thing he sought. After the chaos and clamour of the search, when the dull weight of grief had rolled in, Huw's father had ridden to Berevil to press his suit. He had argued, threatened, nigh on begged, but to no avail. A son of Rhys ap Griffith was no longer fitting match for the heiress to the Powell estate. Huw lost the house, the land, the honour and prestige, and lost Elizabeth too. She had been shipped off, willing or no, to wed some lord in London.

He would never see her again, that was certain. Her new master had no place in his busy life for this estate. He'd sold it to fund his latest venture, a grant of land from the king, in the Carolinas. So dark, passionate, witch-girl Elizabeth lay far beyond Huw's reach now, to live out her grief and die in an alien world, as much a slave as those who laboured on her husband's lands. She was lost beyond an ocean of salt sea and salt tears.

The present absentee landlord of Llys y Garn had plans, he'd heard, to pull down the rambling old house and build something new, more worthy of a gentleman in this new, prosperous age. Perhaps, in time, he'd offer it as a daughter's dowry, but it would not be to the likes of Huw ap Rhys and his sons. The dream and the hope were gone, God's justice on the Devil's schemes.

Nothing gained by sitting there in the cold wind, staring down on what he had lost. Huw turned, and rode back along the hills, to the snivelling, discontented bride his father had found for him, and his sturdy threadbare brats, screaming under the sagging tiles of the smoky barn of his home.

Sir Devereux's second wife, Lady Margaret, did not give him more children. His own fortunes decreased sharply, due to political miscalculations in the reign of James II and he died in straightened circumstances.

The descendants of Huw ap Rhys remained at Hendre Hywel, their fortunes diminishing, until the manor was rated at no more than a farm and they were no longer listed as gentlemen.

Elizabeth Tyrce died in 1693, aged 31, it is said of a fever, at her husband's mansion near Charleston, although dark rumours persisted that she had long been insane, a condition inherited from her grandmother, and, during one of her husband's many absences, had locked herself in her room and starved herself to death.

Interlude

The Tudor era saw one of the many ambitious remodellings of Llys y Garn.

Dafydd ap Maredudd, companion in arms to Henry VII, whose rising status encouraged him to add wings and court in the latest style to Llys y Garn, had inherited a modest manor, with a stone hall, a scattering of timber buildings, and a small show of fortification, with a stone tower and gatehouse dating from the fourteenth century, raised not in fear of foreign invasion or civil war, but largely due to internecine quarrelling among neighbours in the locality. The estate changed hands many times, being in the gift of the lords of Cemaes.

Gerald of Wales, in his *Journey Through Wales* 1188, mentions a Hywel ap Ednyfed, known as Hywel Croch (Howell the Vociferous) whose land contained the holy well of St Bride, with a miraculous statue reputed to foretell the future. "A certain man, cursed with a nagging wife, thought to consult the statue, which swore that he and his wife would find great peace, and so it was, for the man, coming down from the hill, fell in the river and drowned."

The Holy Well of St Bride has been putatively identified with a deep spring on the hillside above Llys y Garn, though no trace of a statue has been found. Apart from local court records recounting a string of disputes over the property, little is known of the history of Llys y Garn before the Black Death. Perhaps the rooks could say more...

The Dragon Slayer

1

1308

'Accipe, soror, viaticum corporis Domini nostri...' Father Emrys's soft hypnotic drone was lost in the rising scream of agony.

And lost still further in the roar of Owain ap Elidyr. 'Stupid fool! The wood is damp. Would you have us all choke to death?' Angharad could hear the thwack of her father's stick across the servant's back, feel its echo in her own flesh. She peered out, but could see little through the blue haze that struggled to find its way out through the blackened thatch. She caught sight of the servant, Guto, scurrying out, bent double, but it didn't stop her father shouting, as he aimed a kick at Guto's rear. Nothing ever stopped her father shouting. He was the great grandson of Hywel Groch, whose roar could shake rafters. Owain's roars were so loud, they drowned out the screams of his wife.

Then for a moment, his roaring ceased. But the screams did not. They cut through the plank panelling, through the smoke, through Marged's hands, clamped over Angharad's ears as she clung to her sister. They echoed in Angharad's belly and heart and head, till she thought they would scream within her, forever. Screams carried on a wave of muttering women and the lulling voice of the priest.

'Per istam sanctam unctionem...'

The piercing shrieks rose again.

A spider was crawling up the rough-hewn pillar of oak, tiny body, long legs groping its way upwards, upwards. Angharad fixed on it. *Look at the spider, keep looking,*

170

nothing else, just look at the spider. She willed it on. *Up! Up! Escape!*

'Paradisi portas aperiat…'

For a blissful moment the screams subsided into a long animal moan, a deceptive promise of peace. The young priest emerged from the dark suffocating chamber, where Angharad must not look.

'Enough!' She could see her father's arm rise to cross himself, out of habit, even as he swelled up like a bullfrog, to bawl out the priest. He'd kicked the damp wood from the fire but smoke was still swirling like tentacles of rage. 'Have you done the thing? Given her her absolution? Then go. Back to your books, Master Priest, and let the women get on with it.'

'But if the baby should—'

'Out! Away!' He was shooing Father Emrys out as he shouted, thrusting him between the shoulder blades, and with the priest went the moment of respite.

The screaming began again.

'Shut her up!' roared her father. 'Enough! Three days of this! A man cannot sleep.' He was thumping on the panels of the dark chamber. 'If she must die, let her do it quickly. What keeps you, woman?'

Old Ina, the midwife, emerged from the smoky gloom.

'The child won't come. I cannot do it.'

'I command you to get it done!'

The outer door was flung open wide, white light pouring in, churning the smoke into ghosts that rose to writhe in panic among the timbers. A bird flew in, beheld the scene and flew out again.

Gwilym ap Gruffudd ap Hywel Groch, their kinsman and neighbour, came in, pulling with him a little man in cap and gown, clutching a leather bag.

A couple of the stitches on the bag had frayed. Angharad

171

noticed. She looked hard at the bag. It was only a bag, but she would look hard at anything that took her thoughts away from all this. Fraying stitches. Soon the seams would part. Rip apart. *Make it go away.*

'Who is this man?' snarled Owain. 'He is, what, another priest?'

'Of sorts, cousin. He is a physician. He can remove the child.'

'Let him to it then.'

'Your wife still lives, cousin.'

'Not for long. She's received the sacrament. Why wait? Do it!'

Angharad didn't understand the words, but she understood her sister's arm tightening around her, crushing her face into the felted wool of her gown, prayers coming in bursts of panic. Baby Ieuan, beside them, was blessedly too young to understand more than the flood of fury. It left him whimpering, but uncomprehending, as he clung to them.

Angharad buried herself, trying to hide in sister Marged's eleven-year-old body. She could no longer see the bag and count the stitches, but she could still hear her mother's straining gasps and piercing screams.

And her father's roar. 'Do it!'

Do it. Do it. Do it. The roaring had wormed its way into Angharad's blood, a thunder, a flood that filled her head. Roar, roar, roar. Marged was clutching her too tight. She couldn't breathe.

Ina's pleading voice rose into a high-pitched squawk. 'You cannot! She's not gone yet!'

'Out of the way, woman.'

And then more screams. Such screams. Screams that would never leave her. Marged's screams too, releasing her tight hold in her own convulsed distress. Freed from the smoke-scented wool, Angharad breathed in the sickening

172

stench of the shambles. Women were screeching and sobbing, and someone retched. There came the feeble wail of an infant, but the screaming had stopped. At last the screaming had stopped.

Angharad could see nothing. Her eyes couldn't focus. She was drowning in the smell of hot blood and bowels.

'A girl?' roared her father. 'All this for a girl?'

Marged was up on her feet, stooping to lift baby Ieuan, grabbing Angharad's hand, pulling her away, out of the smoke and the reek and the darkness, into the chill white wind of coming winter. She tugged them away from the hall, across the churned mud, to the shelter of the brew house walls. She set the baby down, released Angharad's hand, then braced herself against the wall and vomited. After that, she sank down on the wet grass and buried her head in her arms, shaking.

Angharad tentatively touched her sister, trying to embrace her. She couldn't understand, in words or in images that made any sense, what had happened, but she knew, instinctive as a leveret or a trembling fawn, that Marged was now all she had.

Marged lifted a tear-stained face, and forced a smile that brought more tears gushing from her blue eyes. 'Here, little ones.' She drew them both against her and rocked them to and fro.

Out from the house came her father, big and bullish, kicking the little man he'd called physician into the mud. Gwilym ap Gruffudd followed, throwing down a couple of coins. The little man groped for them, then struggled to his feet and loped away, shoulders hunched.

'A girl,' said Owain, raging because he could not live without something to rage about. 'Isn't it enough that I must impoverish myself to buy husbands for two of them, without a third to drain my purse?'

173

His cousin soothed him, gravely. 'It is too soon yet to say that the child will survive.'

'True. That's true!' Her father stopped in his stomping tracks. 'Very true, cousin. They die.'

'Many die. It is God's will who lives or no. Although this one looks well enough.'

'No! You are wrong, Gwilym. This one fades. Look again and you will see it. I think she'll die.'

'And yet…'

'She'll die.'

'Owain, think on your soul.'

'Think on my purse, rather.'

They carried Crystin, wife of Owain ap Elidyr ap Rhys ap Hywel Groch, to a barn. She couldn't be left in the house, but the women would attend her through the night, amidst the hay and sacks of oats. They'd washed her and wrapped her in clean linen, before they brought her out, but Angharad saw the linen staining, seeping, red and brown and sour yellow, even as they hauled the sagging corpse across the cobbles.

Tomorrow she would be taken away, down the valley, for Father Emrys to say Mass over her, and she would be buried under the walls of St. Brynach's church, at Rhyd y Groes, safely shriven, though only the saints knew if she'd heard the priest's words through her own screams, or if, in her agony, she'd found room for any thoughts of a future heaven and hell.

For four years, Angharad had clung to her mother, seeing her face when she opened her eyes in the morning, hearing her soft, lilting voice as she closed them at night. But all she would ever remember of her now were the screams, the smell of blood and the slowly spreading stain on white linen in the twilight.

174

The child, so crudely hacked from her mother's dying body, did not live. It was strange, some said, that she should pass so swiftly, when she had seemed as sound as any baby at her birth, even though she had been wrenched out so unnaturally, in a shower of blood and guts. When the attendants had swaddled her, they had remarked that all her limbs were clean and straight, and she had wailed with good lungs, drinking in God's air. She had suckled the wet nurse, eagerly, and taken nourishment. And yet, as was God's will with so many infants, in the night, briefly unattended while the wet nurse hurried to fetch ale on Owain ap Elidyr's command, the baby had ceased to breathe.

At least there was cause to be thankful that her mother was gone before her, for Crystin's mourning would have been sharp and bitter. No paradise for the little mite. Her small soul would waste for all eternity in Limbo, because she had not been baptised.

She was a girl.

2

Angharad kilted her skirts up and held out a hand to Ieuan, helping him to scramble up among the scrubby oaks and holly, to a spot where they could sit, out of the way, and watch the exotic, bustling scene.

'I didn't know the world had so many people,' said Ieuan, his five-year-old eyes stretched wide in amazement and alarm.

'More than a hundred,' said Angharad, guessing wildly at a number beyond her reckoning. The notion excited her, like a door opening somewhere inside her, but she knew it frightened Ieuan. He was a soft child, solemn and thoughtful, preferring predictability to novelty. He would have preferred to stay safe at the llys, chiding and soothing the puppies, but his elder sister was set on attending Curig's fair this year, and she would not leave him unattended at home. Who could say what would become of a small boy, alone and defenceless, if their father chanced upon him, in one of his rages? And Owain ap Elidyr was always in a rage, over one thing or another. Ieuan had pleaded, promising to stay concealed and quiet in the hay, where their father would never see him, but Marged would have none of it. She had bundled them both out of their blankets an hour before the June dawn. Angharad had leapt up willingly enough, eager for the promise of new sights and adventure, but Ieuan had dragged, whimpering all the way on the long forest trek to the borough, terrified of this plunge into the wide world.

Angharad, secretly, felt a tremor of fear too, as their close wooded world was left behind, but that was drowned out by exhilaration, at the sight of new faces, the sound of strange tongues, the unexpected greeting her round every turn.

She thrilled as the estuary opened before them, such a mighty river, with its acres of mudflats and salt marshes, rolling out to vast, dark sands and the wondrous, glittering sapphire of the sea. She'd glimpsed the sea from the hills, but here it was so close, she could smell the salt, see the foam dancing on the curl of the waves as they seethed across the beach. To think that it stretched from here to the ends of the world.

From the viscous black of a mud bank, a great flock of raucous water fowl rose up in sudden panic. Another herd of black cattle was being waded across the river, lowing their resentment, the drovers hopping from stone to stone, hollering, their hounds barking. Surely, the whole world was coming to the Borough. Along the meadows, buyers and sellers, beggars and peddlers, merchants, drovers, peasant women, squires, were shouting, arguing, bargaining. Laden carts creaked and rumbled, rolling precariously in the ruts. Hurdles were dragged by sturdy men. Pack horses clipped and clopped and swayed under their bulging loads. There was a constant roar of voices, but few of them roared in anger, like Owain ap Elidyr. Children laughed, without fear. Music of every description drifted this way and that – drunken voices raised in song one moment, the blare of shawms and the thrum of tabors the next.

'It is too noisy,' complained Ieuan, creeping closer to press his pained ears under her arm.

'It is the world,' said Angharad, drinking it in and loving it all, but she slipped her arm round his shoulder, to comfort him. 'Look. Here comes Marged.' She leaped up to wave.

Their sister came striding along the track, her servant, the great, hulking, fair-haired Watcyn, pushing recalcitrant traders out of her way, as if she were some grand dame. He was fond of Marged was Watcyn, and dutifully protective, but she could take care of herself, well enough. She had a round face, with freckles, and one tooth missing when her father threw her against a stone, so her grin made her look like a cheeky boy. She was always busy, mistress of the household these last three years, caring for the little ones, pacifying their father, organising the servants, spinning, mending, praying... anything but standing still and letting dark thoughts creep in.

She looked around, in a moment of anxiety, then spied the children.

'Come down! I've bought us a barrel of salt herrings, and Watcyn has saved me from a snatch-purse.' She grasped their hands as they slithered down from the trees, swinging them out of the way, as the wet, muddy cattle came lumbering past. Their own cattle had been driven down the previous day – barely a dozen and nothing else to sell. Their father might choose to fancy himself a lord, with a pedigree to match the King of England, but it was hard enough for his household to feed itself from the oats his land produced.

Marged licked her lips. 'Let's find a place to sit and eat. I'm famished.'

They settled on a vacant meadow patch, with a salt breeze in from the sea to cool the summer heat. Angharad loved the smell of it, the scent of salt and storm and faraway places that would be forever beyond her reach. She breathed it in, deeply, as their servant laid out their oatbread and sour cheese, ale and a jug of buttermilk.

'That will do us,' said Marged. 'Go and gather that samphire, Watcyn. I see no reason to pay that knave good money for it, when it's there for the picking.'

'You'll be safe here, girl?'

'Of course we will.' Marged poured a bowl of buttermilk for Ieuan, who drank it, thirstily.

Angharad lay back in the grass. The sun stroked her face, and painted crimson through her closed eyelids. Then a shadow crossed, and when she opened her eyes, there was a girl standing over them.

A smiling girl, as old as Marged, or older, plump and fair, well-nourished, her clothes of the finest woollen cloth – finer even than their father's best tunic. Her linen was bleached white, like snow.

'Good day to you.' She began in English, saw their struggling expressions and slipped easily into comfortable Welsh. 'Will you give me a sip? I've not sat down all day.'

'Sit and welcome.' Marged handed her a bowl. 'You've come with the traders?'

The girl subsided with a satisfied sigh. 'I have. I am Johan. My father is Nicholas Hamblyn. He trades out of Bristol, which is our home.'

'That is a very distant place,' said Marged.

Angharad didn't know where Bristol was, but she supposed, from Marged's look of awe, that it was at the end of the world.

Johan laughed. 'Not so far. We sailed along the Severn channel and around the coast. After this, it will be to Ireland. Some voyages take us much further, to the low countries and France and Spain and the Middle Sea.'

'You travel with your father?'

'Always.'

Now Angharad was truly awestruck, not by the thought of such voyages, but by the notion of being confined with a father for so long, and yet being able to smile.

Johan wriggled her rump into a more comfortable position and corrected herself. 'Except once when I was ill and stayed in Bristol with my grandmother. Which was well enough, for I love her dearly, though she is a scold. But I would sooner travel with my father, as I must if I am to learn the trade. We deal in wool and woollen cloth. So many fairs and markets, I sometimes forget where I am.'

'Why must you learn the trade?' asked Angharad.

Why?' Johan laughed. 'So that I can carry it on, little one. I have no brother, so my father teaches me.'

Marged passed bread. 'How will you go travelling, when you are married?'

'Married? Time enough for that. I'm fifteen. I don't think I'll take a husband until I am twenty, and then, if trade goes well, I'll look for one that takes my fancy.' She caught, as Angharad did, that fleeting look of wistful longing on Marged's face. 'You mean to marry sooner?'

'I am to be married next month,' said Marged. 'It is arranged.'

'You are young for that.'

'Fourteen.'

'And arranged for you. So your father, I suppose, is a lord?' Johan's quick glance appraised their threadbare homespun, patched and moss-stained.

Marged laughed. She escaped into laughter. 'My father would have you believe it. He is Owain ap Elidyr ap Rhys ap Hywel Groch, and Hywel Groch ap Ednyfed was a very great man. Dewi Mynyw wrote an englyn in praise of his hospitality.'

'Is that a good thing?'

'My father will tell you it is a very good thing. A great thing. He boasts of it. Hywel Groch was a great man – with many sons. And those many sons had many sons, and what share my father has of the great man's lands would scarcely feed a goose. But my uncle, my father's brother Maelgwn, has died, unwed, and my father thought to have his land at Cwrt Isaf, which lies beyond Rhyd y Groes. He considers that since our kin has held it from time out of mind, he should have it by right. But the truth of the matter is that

180

they all hold what they have now from the Lord Fitz Martin, who cares so little for our pedigrees that he has granted Maelgwn's land to Maredudd ap Hywel instead. Now Maredudd is also of our kin, though very distant, being the grandson of—'

'Hold!' Johan clapped her hands to her head. 'I have a father and a granddam, and that's enough of kith and kin for me. You Welsh love your family shackles. So this Maredudd holds the land your father lusted after. I understand that.'

'Yes. And so I am to wed Maredudd,' said Marged. 'My father thinks a grandson on the land will do well enough.' She smiled, but Angharad saw her fingers clutch and twist at the grass beside her.

So this was what it was all about, the talk of marriage. Angharad had heard it spoken of, or roared about, at home, but Marged always brushed it aside, as if it were a matter of no consequence, a very small matter, to celebrate and smile about, and then forget. Girls must marry, so now Marged would marry, and that was all there was to it. But now Angharad understood, there was far more to it. Blood and land and ancient rights. It was her father's business, this match, and nothing of Marged's choosing. It was to gain control of Cwrt Isaf, and it was to be next month. Next month! Angharad had not realised. That was so soon.

Johan blew out her cheeks and leaned back on her elbows, skirt up above her knees, bare legs wide, toes wriggling the fine leather of her shoes. 'Ah well, if your father thinks himself a lord, I suppose there is nothing for you but marriage or a house of nuns.'

Again, that determined laugh from Marged. 'Oh, our Welshmen don't care to have their virgins running off to nunneries. They want them on their backs, with their skirts up. We have no house of nuns here.'

Johan thought about it. 'No, you are wrong, I think. I do

181

recall one, hereabout. Well, many miles north of here, but in these wild Welsh parts. We took the drover's road past it once. But I would never recommend such a place, unless you truly have the saints whispering in your ears. Who would seek to be confined behind cloistered walls, when there is all the world to explore?'

'I would love to see the world,' said Marged. 'But I have explored as far as this borough, and that is all I'm likely to see.'

'Go on pilgrimage. Go to Canterbury. Rome. Santiago. Jerusalem!'

'To the shrine of St. David perhaps. One day.' For a moment, the dream got the better of Marged. 'Oh, but I would like to go! Jerusalem!'

They all crossed themselves. Even Ieuan's eyes shone at the thought of Jerusalem.

They could all go, sail to the Holy Lands, like the crusader knights, walk where the Lord had walked, touch the stones of the sacred city, see the very centre of the world...

But they never would.

Through the rest of the long June day, the children wandered through the fair, gazing open-mouthed at the business and the sleight of hand, the entertainments and the diverse nature of the world, while Marged bargained, admired, poured scorn and bought needles.

Angharad kept hold of Ieuan's hand to keep him safe, and they stopped to listen to the increasingly drunken musicians. Angharad itched to join the dancing, or the raucous play of other children, but Ieuan was too nervous, so they hung back, out the reach of trampling feet, and watched.

They saw Johan, with her father, a jolly man but shrewd with it, hugging his daughter, clapping a man on the back, clipping an over-nifty boy round the ear before some small purchase disappeared from the back of his wagon.

It must be strange, a delightful thing, to have such a father, though he wasn't a lord but a mere merchant, with no blood or kin to boast of.

Johan spied them in the throng and beckoned them over. 'The little one looks tired. Let him sleep here.' She lifted Ieuan and tossed him up into the wagon. He looked startled, but when Marged laughed and nodded, he snuggled down without more prompting on a heap of thick felted cloths.

'You've purchased us some waifs, daughter?' Nicholas Hamblyn bent down to examine them closely. 'Are you sure of their quality? I think they breed finer ones in Pembroke.'

'No, no, father. These are the very best. I bit them to be sure.'

Angharad was confused. She fancied they were joking, but she had to look to see if Marged was laughing, to be certain. Marged smiled, her freckles dancing, so it must be a jest. Unless…

'Have you bought us?' she asked.

Nicholas stroked his beard. 'Hm. Is it a bargain though? What did you pay, daughter?'

'Two marks apiece. I haggled.'

Marged laughed. Her eyes shone with tears.

'Marged is already sold,' said Angharad.

'Hush!' said her sister.

'Marged is to be wed,' explained Johan.

'Ah. Is that so?' Nicholas smiled. A kindly, understanding smile as he gazed on the young bride-to-be. He held up a finger, then rummaged in a chest in the wagon. He couldn't find what he wanted, so he leapt up and delved further.

It was Angharad's turn to laugh – he looked like a ratting dog, digging for quarry.

His head came up at last and he held aloft a small brooch.

183

He reached for Marged's hand and planted it in her palm. 'A gift for a Marged. St. Margaret. I picked it up in Sicily. It seems we cannot buy you, after all, so I must restore the purchase price.'

Angharad marvelled at the wondrous thing. It was enamelled with a tiny image, skilfully done but fearful: a woman being swallowed by a dragon. Or was she fighting her way out of the fell beast?

Marged was staring at the brooch too. 'You could buy me, if you wish – take me with you.'

Nicholas smiled into her eyes, in sympathy, then gently closed her fingers over the brooch. 'Alas, no. Stay and be a happy wife and mother. But what are you doing, Johan? Leaving our guests to starve? Let us eat. Sup on dry land, before we haul this wagon to the ship and our victuals and stomachs are tossed on the waves.'

They ate well. Better than they had ever eaten in their lives. Such exotic food as never graced their father's tables, even when he chose to feast. Fine wheaten bread, fresh mackerel, a rabbit pasty, spiced ham and sweet, dark raisins. They ate, they drank. Marged and Johan huddled together, gossiping and giggling. Nicholas told tales to Angharad and Ieuan, that set even the solemn boy rolling with laughter.

Then Angharad sang, as she sang at home when her father was not there to hear. He'd cuff her ears if he heard her, like as not, although, once or twice, when entertaining visitors he thought grand enough, he'd have her brought out to sing to them.

'She is a song-thrush and a nightingale, this one,' said Nicholas, patting her on the head. A little Welsh song-bird. I wish we could take her with us, to sing us to sleep on the waves.'

'And Marged, too, to be my sister,' said Johan, embracing her, as if their friendship were of many years

184

standing, not of a few brief hours.

'Alas, my child, if I could, I would purchase you a dozen sisters. But we must be content. All of us must be content.'

So the dishes and jugs were cleared away, and the table and stools piled onto the wagon, with the canvas roped tight around it. Angharad watched as the heavy cart trundled away, along the estuary to the jetties, where Nicholas's ship was waiting.

Marged wept, her shoulders heaving.

Angharad gripped her hand. 'Would you truly go with them and leave us?'

'No! Not for the world.' Marged sniffed and brushed away her own tears, though her hand tightened within Angharad's fingers. 'But you know, I must leave you soon for a husband.'

'I wish you wouldn't go.'

'I wish I wouldn't, too. But look!' Marged's back stiffened. She forced a wide smile. 'There is Watcyn. Not too drunk to stand, I hope. And Guto. It's time we headed for home.'

3

'See to the horses!' Owain ap Elidyr was roaring again. 'Come! What's keeping you, you filthy lickspittles. Do you not know who I am?'

Roar, roar. Was he ever not roaring? Sometimes, it seemed to Angharad, that his roar had begun to swell, louder and louder, as his fortune decreased, smaller and smaller, until one day there would nothing left of him but a roar, Or perhaps, if all went well and the saints bestowed on him the grace to prosper again, he would begin to speak softly once more. Softer than she had ever heard him speak. If God granted him all the wealth of his desires, all the lands of Hywel Groch, all the lost honour, all the esteem, would he start to coo like a dove?

Angharad found herself, despite her anxiety, smiling at the thought of her father gently warbling. She could not even imagine what he would look like, with his face at peace, not red and scowling, beetle-browed. No, a smooth brow and a smiling mouth were contrary to nature, with Owain ap Elidyr.

But it might be that his fortunes were about to improve at last. His purse might begin to fatten again, if he, as guardian to a grandson born in wedlock, were allowed to hold this land of Cwrt Isaf on the far side of Rhyd y Groes. Maredudd ap Hywel had no sons by his first wife, but two acknowledged bastards who could lay claim under the old ways, and Owain had always been the loudest champion of the old ways, but now he embraced the law that recognised only legitimate sons. Let the bastards come sniffing for their

186

share – Owain had arrived here first, to roar in this courtyard, determined to take possession when the moment came.

To support his claim, he'd brought his sons with him and that was an uneasy matter. Young Ieuan was no harm, still as quiet and meek as ever, and would doubtless be attending on Father Emrys, who was waiting in the hall. But Siencyn and Hywel, the elder sons, were another matter. They were swaggering young men, newly returned to their father's hearth from the halls of kinsmen where they'd been raised, as if Owain really were a great lord and not a growling, penurious bear in a miserable den, holding shreds of ancestral land by English sufferance. It seemed to Angharad that all her brothers had learned from their fostering was a respect for their father's claims to greatness and a readiness with their fists. Now they were home, they were learning to roar like their father. They were prowling now, outside, ordering servants, swearing oaths, calling for ale as if they already ruled this place.

But at least they did not enter the solar. That was one place forbidden to men for a while longer. It was a place for women's business.

Angharad, at twelve, was considered old enough to attend her sister, along with her kinswoman Elain, and Meleri, daughter of Ina the midwife, who had inherited her mother's skills.

Though he did not presume to enter the birthing chamber, Owain's presence was felt, like a hurricane rattling the timbers of the house, making all the women tense, when they should be calm and soft. His hunger for possession was battering at them.

It wasn't the house he craved. This homestead at Cwrt Isaf was no different, no more grand than his own at Llys y Garn. Here were the same heavy blackened timbers, the same soot-soaked sagging thatch, the same cobbles and mud without and the same stale dampness within. It was the land, the meadows and woodlands that he ached to have added to his own. He was like a wild boar, scenting a straying child, itching to charge and trample and feast.

Among the women, here in the dark, there was no room for thoughts of land or wealth or patrimonies. This was an older, deeper concern.

Marged gripped her sister's hand, pulling her down to kiss her, and Angharad felt the racing pulse, though Marged smiled bravely. And briefly. The pains gripped again, and she muffled a squeal, biting her lip.

'There, now, hold her,' said Meleri, and Elain, behind the chair, gripped Marged under her arms, supporting her. The baby was coming.

'St.Margaret!' cried Marged, in a fleeting moment of panic, her fingers groping.

Angharad cast about in the straw and found the brooch her sister had dropped. She pressed it back into her sister's hand and Marged clenched her fingers around it, her panting breath easing.

'It won't be long,' promised Angharad, as if she understood the matter perfectly. Cows and cats and dogs she knew about, but women... She shuddered, trying to thrust out of her mind the memory of her mother's long, bloody, screaming death. 'Not long.'

'I – ah – I hope not. I pray not, or our father will wear a furrow in the yard.' Marged managed a laugh, before convulsing again. Too late for talking now. The pain came on like a charging army, and the sweat of terror drenched Marged's face.

'Come now,' coaxed Meleri, on her knees between Marged's legs. 'Come, come.'

Marged's squeal turned to a scream that she couldn't

188

stifle. This gateway of pain was the only escape for her now. Three times, since her marriage to Maredudd ap Hywel, a man nearly as old as her father, she had conceived. Twice, she had lost the child, in the early months, and had had to bear the scowls and rages of husband and father. Though she had offered up dutiful prayers that each child would be brought to full term, though she had schooled herself to weep and wail at each miscarriage, Angharad knew the relief she'd felt when the bleeding told her she would not be brought to this.

But now this had come at last. This thing, men were quick to tell her, that she was created for. The pains were her just torment, as bearer of Eve's sin.

Angharad wiped her sister's brow, and the sweat from her lip. It was all she could do. Twelve was a terrifying age, teetering on the brink, old enough now to be considered a woman, a property to be disposed of by men, but too young to know much of what she should be doing here. She could only content herself with prayer and let Meleri and Elain handle the rest.

'Benedicta tu in mulieribus, benedicta tu in mulieribus, benedicta…' Angharad kept whispering, feeling a fire burn within her, as the memory of screams and blood rose up, refusing to be quenched. She must quench it. Block it out, block it out.

'Ah…' Marged sagged down into cousin Elain's arms.

Meleri sat back, breathing deeply, in the soiled straw. 'It is a boy.' She was rubbing the infant, slapping it. At last there came a feeble, mewling cry. She reached up, handing the baby to Angharad.

Angharad looked on her nephew. A small shrivelled thing, blue and miserable. Like a new-born rat. Was this how the Saviour had looked, when laid in the manger? It was a thing both wondrous and disturbing.

189

Marged's waiting woman was standing by with water and fresh swaddling linen. Someone must have rushed out to tell Owain, because Angharad could hear his roars of triumphant delight, every bit as loud as his roars of anger. He had what he wanted – a grandson to give him governance of these acres.

Marged, the first swooning relief of expulsion over, was pressing the brooch of St. Margaret to her lips in fervent thanks. Then she looked for her child.

Angharad brought him out of the gloom so that she could see.

And Marged, with greater age and experience, saw more than Angharad had seen. In an instant she was in a panic, struggling with her helpers. 'A priest! Fetch the priest. Don't let them take the child. He must be baptised. Now!'

'Hush!' soothed Angharad. 'Don't fret. Be still, Marged. If you wish it, we shall call Father Emrys in.'

'Yes, you had better,' said Meleri. Elain peered at the child and nodded, sagely. The child was small, puny, barely able to draw breath. 'Put him to the nipple. Let him feed.'

'Yes. No!' Marged still couldn't settle. 'Baptise him first.'

They fetched the priest from the hall and Ieuan came too. He was fast becoming the priest's shadow, forever hovering at Father Emrys's side, among his musty books and candles and incense burner. It was safer, quieter, than hovering in Father Owain's company.

Father Emrys blessed Marged, took one look at the infant, and proceeded, without wasting another moment, to baptise Rhys ap Maredudd into the body of the church and into hope of salvation. Ieuan and Angharad stood godparents. The men of the family watched from the door in glowering consternation.

Only when it was done could Marged relax, taking the

190

feeble wisp of a child to her breast.

'Away with you all,' commanded Elain. 'She's not finished yet.'

No, Marged's labours must continue. Meleri knelt, massaging her, while Marged concentrated on her son.

'He will not feed.'

'Easy, girl. It will come.'

But it did not come. Nothing came, not the child's feeding, nor the afterbirth. The time wore on. Marged strove. Meleri strove. Elain bit her lip and muttered prayers. Angharad knelt motionless, the child in her arms, cold dread in her stomach. There was no escape. Eve's sin, eternal retribution. She froze in dread and desperation. For an hour. Another hour. And another. The sky outside darkened.

It was over. Somehow. The sobbing and grunting and panting subsided at last, and Meleri was busy sweeping away a bundle of bloodied tissue and straw. Marged, washed clean, was being helped to her bed, her face white from loss of blood, expressionless.

Angharad cradled the infant, her nephew, who didn't cry and didn't move.

'Is he dead?' asked Marged

Angharad nodded, drawing the linen across the tiny blue face.

Where there should be grief, there was only a sad resignation. Marged heaved a sigh. 'He was baptised.'

A moment of silence and stillness. Then the roars began. Someone, with no thought for Marged, had officiously carried the news to Owain ap Elidyr. No holding him now. His daughter's confinement was ended and he stormed to the bedside.

'Well, you have ruined our hopes, girl. What now, eh? Instead of bringing me land, you lie there, useless, and I must buy you another husband.'

191

Marged said not a word. What purpose was there in saying anything? She was a thing to be disposed of, of no greater account than when she had first been disposed of at fourteen.

Her husband Maredudd had died five months ago, falling from his horse, while hunting, and striking his head on a stone, leaving an unborn child and a widow of nineteen. Marged had sat through her mourning dry-eyed. She had been an obedient and submissive wife, holding her tongue and minding her house, as the church and her menfolk demanded, because what else could she be? There was no ship to carry her away to a different life or kinder loving. This child had been her one hope of a sort of freedom. Owain would have had his land, and she would have earned a little peace.

So she had not wept for the man who had covered her repeatedly, with all the love and tenderness of a bull on a heifer. No more had Owain, at the loss of a son in law. Far from it. He had thumped the table and called for ale, for his daughter was bearing the son and heir, and he would claim wardship, whatever the bastard sons of Maredudd ap Hywel might have to say on the matter.

But the child, after a few faltering breaths, was dead, and Owain's fury was set on wings. Carrion wings. He stormed. He thundered. He struck servants and threatened floggings. The whole cymwd could hear his anger at his loss, echoing round the hills. Deer took flight in the woods, rats crouched low in the granaries, while Owain raged against his loss. But he did not go home. While he remained at Cwrt Isaf, who was there who would dare command him to leave, for lack of a claim to the land? It was a moot point he was prepared to argue with boot, fist and sword, and his sons were prepared to fight with him.

Siencyn and Hywel, seventeen and fifteen, and strangers

to each other for so long, had found a liking for each other, instead of the vicious brotherly rivalry that fostering so often bred. Or at least Hywel had found a great admiration for his towering, bullish elder brother, and followed him, eagerly aping his words and actions. Neither of them had anything other than scorn and indifference for their younger siblings. They attended their father now like a bodyguard, armed and bristling, ready to challenge anyone who argued. As the days passed, many came, with arguments prepared. Supporters of the bastard sons and other kinsmen of Maredudd ap Hywel with claims of their own. Acidly polite messengers from Fitz Martin's steward. A cleric from the abbey, questioning some supposed grant of land. Wise old men clustered at the gate, recounting genealogies, ready to lend their authority to this or that claimant.

While the men argued, Angharad sat, stood, knelt, by Marged's bed, as her pallor gave way to the flush of fever, and aching pains began to rack her limbs, leaving her moaning, barely remembering where she lay or who Angharad was.

'You are not to leave me,' whispered Angharad. 'Fight, sister. Don't surrender. This life is not so bitter. Come back to me.'

'Come back?' Marged's eyes flitted from Angharad, to something only she could see, too weak to lift her head from the pillows. 'I shall sail away.'

'There is no ship to take you,' said Angharad. 'You cannot sail away.'

'Take ship with Johan and her father. Sail to Constantinople. Is Curig's fair soon? Will she be there?'

'She will be there.' Angharad kissed her sister's hand. It was November. Curig's Fair was not for seven months.

'Good. That is good.' Marged's clenched fingers twitched on the blanket. 'Is that Johan? I see her.'

'No, Marged. It's Ieuan. Your brother. He has brought Father Emrys.'

Marged looked at her sister, recognising her through the blur of her fever and almost smiling. She withdrew her hand, leaving on Angharad's palm the enamelled brooch. 'No more,' she whispered. No more fight. The dragon had devoured her.

'Daughter.' Father Emrys was standing over her, weighed down with solemn holiness.

'Is it time?'

'It is time to pray, to show contrition and to be at peace with God.'

'You baptised my son.'

'I did. And now I shall anoint you, as you go hence. Give your soul nourishment for your journey, daughter.'

Marged wasn't listening. 'You baptised my son. Not my sister. My little sister. The baby.'

'Alas, yes, the baby was not baptised. Your father was unwilling.'

'I baptised her.'

'Daughter—'

'I knew he meant to kill her. I could not let her go into the dark. I baptised her.' The words came out, some strong, some mere whispers, as she rambled. 'With water. In nomine Patris et Filii et Spiritus Sancti. I named her Gwenllian. My father, when he's in his cups, when he is angry with the world, he shouts "Remember Gwenllian,' so I baptised her Gwenllian. So that he would be forever shouting her name, though he did not know it. I baptised her with water. In nomine Patris. Then he killed her. Later. In the night. But I baptised her.'

'Daughter.' Father Emrys frowned. 'Beware. He killed her, you say? You speak of a terrible sin laid upon your father.'

194

'He sent the wet nurse away and smothered her.'

'If that – if it was indeed so, a mortal sin before God, then another must answer for it. But now it is time to think on your own sins, child, for it is you who stand before God.'

'I baptised her. That was enough, wasn't it? She's not in Limbo. What I did…'

'Daughter, it is not permitted for women to administer the sacraments. No doubt you meant well, but only the holy church and its ordained priests can deliver salvation from the stain of sin to which we are all born.'

Marged sank back on her pillows, the last fight draining out of her with his denial. The priest, armed with his merciless dogma, laid out linen cloth. Ieuan knelt beside him as his assistant.

On the other side of the bed, Angharad held a candle, both hands wrapped around it. A fine wax candle. The church's candle, fit for the sacrament.

It had been enough, she thought, whatever the priest said. He was wrong. What Marged did for the infant Gwenllian had been enough. St. Margaret, bursting from her dragon, shimmered in the candle light, promised her it was enough. St. Margaret and all the saints, Anne and Veronica and the Holy Virgin, held the soul of Gwenllian safe, as they would soon hold the soul of Marged, no matter what the cold, hard fathers of the holy church said. She fixed her eyes on the candle flame, following its flicker, its bending curtseys, the white gold glow streaming up, up, up, into the darkness, sailing away.

A man of Fitz Martin was with her father and brothers, offering gracious words armed with barbs and scythe blades in exchange for Owain's growling rants. The men saw Angharad approach and turned to her.

'Well, girl?'

'My sister is dead, father.'

The Fitz Martin man piously crossed himself, bowed and withdrew.

Owain waved her away, irritably. 'No matter, no matter. It was the child that made or marred.'

Siencyn, as tall as his father and wearing a scar on his face like a prized jewel, looked her over. 'The other one is of an age to wed, is she not, father? Maredudd's kin...'

Owain turned his attention back to her. 'Yes. Of course. If the argument goes their damned way and one of his sneak-thief kin in granted the land, we could arrange a match. You are right, my son. All need not be lost.'

Siencyn's hand, beneath her chin, jerked her head up. 'You won't lack for takers with this one's looks. She's no speckled whelp like Marged. Marry her off, Father, before she's tempted to play the harlot, and you'll be robbed of the fee for her maidenhead, with nothing to show for it.'

'I have no mind to play the harlot,' said Angharad. 'Nor any wish to wed.'

They stared at her. 'Who asked you, girl?'

Hywel laughed. His voice was still high when he laughed. 'Whatever husband you choose, Father, he'll need a bridle for this one.'

'A whip, too, and welcome. Go on, get out, girl. Go and bury your sister. Do what women do. We have more important matters to see to.'

So Angharad turned away, to bury her sister Marged and the child that had killed her.

4

'Angharad! Here she is, our little song bird.' Laughing with delight, Johan came bustling up to hug her, pushing through the crowd as soon as she caught sight of her.

Angharad returned the embrace, tears of relief in her smile. 'You are pleased to see me, then?'

'My little Welsh sister. But not so little now. What has a year done? You are grown to be a woman. Of course I have longed to see you again, and here you are. Let me look at you. And feast my eyes, too. You are a rare beauty, Angharad ferch Owain.'

'That is silly talk, Johan ferch Nicholas.'

'No, it is the truth. I shall show you your own dark eyes in a mirror. There are women who would murder for such.'

'You think I have never seen my own eyes in the water?' Angharad shrugged off the flattery. 'I feared you would think less of me, coming here alone. Last year, when I told you of Marged's death…'

Angharad crossed herself, and Johan instantly followed suit.

'Oh Marged, Yes, last year I was dull and uncharitable. Forgive me. The news took me ill. I did so grieve for her, I wept all night. She was a good and loving friend and sister. So I must be your sister now, and love you as she did.'

Angharad hugged her again, letting the tears flow.

'I bought a mass for Marged's soul,' said Johan.

'You did?' Angharad seized Johan's hands and kissed them. 'I begged my father to do so, but he would not. Still, I pray for her, nightly.'

'And I have no doubt little Ieuan does too. Prays for her and all of us sad sinners. Too fond of his prayers, that one. More than his victuals. Has he come with you, this year, the little brother? Hanging on your skirts, as ever?'

'He too is not so little now.' Angharad laughed, rejoicing in the freedom to do so. There had been little laughter for the last two years. 'Heron legs! Very odd he'd look, hanging on to any woman's skirts. But he's still as quiet as an owl. He never cared for the noise of the Fair and came only because he must. But he has another refuge now. He sits at home with Father Emrys, learning his letters and his Latin.'

'I knew it. He'll be for the cowl, for sure. But surely you didn't come alone?' Johan peered around for the lumbering servant who had always dogged Marged's steps.

Angharad pulled a face. 'That would never be permitted. My brothers Siencyn and Hywel accompanied me. Or I accompanied them.' Angharad glanced about her, to make sure they were not within sight or earshot. 'They are tucked up in one of the ale houses, and I have escaped their thoughts for a moment. They have sent Watcyn on an errand, and I was able to slip away in search of you.'

'Well, I am thankful to them that they both brought you and forgot you.'

'They will remember me soon enough. They brought me unwillingly enough, bade me stay home and mind the fire and the spinning. So I went to my father. He was dead drunk, and did not know I was there, but I took his snores to be a blessing, and I told them he had given me permission to come, to buy good cloth for my wedding.'

Johan's sunny smile faltered just a little. 'Are you to wed, little one, and not yet fifteen?'

'So they tell me. I am to do as they command. But not yet. They plot and connive, but all their fine schemes go awry. First they would have had me married off to a kinsman of Maredudd ap Hywel, my sister's husband, if my father was denied the land of Cwrt Isaf. But the Lord Fitz Martin, whoever, or wherever he is, saw fit to give it to an Englishman of his, a William Lange, who rides off somewhere, against the Welsh, or the Irish, or the Scottish, but doesn't come here. So all the Welsh are fuming, Maredudd's kin, my father and brothers and all.

'Now my father has in mind to marry me to Rhodri ap Gruffudd, who holds a good estate along the river. Rhodri's wife is barren and ailing, so we wait for her to die, and she is proving most obstinate.' Angharad shook her head, with a twisted smile, and crossed herself. 'My father beat me raw when I said I would not marry Rhodri, so now I say nothing, and pray that his wife will live.'

'I shall pray for her too, the poor lady. May she find health again and outlive them all.'

'Amen! But what of you, Johan? Were you not to marry when you were twenty?'

Johan chuckled comfortably, linking arms with Angharad as they strolled and hustled their way through the milling crowds of the fair. 'Well, there are a couple of fine lads with fine purses that I have my eye on. When I am good and ready, I shall make my choice. But for now, I am content. My father's eyesight begins to fail, and he can no longer travel easily without me. We no longer go so often as far as we once did, but we keep to our yearly pattern around these isles.'

'I'm glad that Curig's Fair lies in your way. How far have you travelled, Johan, in earlier years?'

'Oh, almost to the moon and back, I swear. To Constantinople. Only once, and then back by the skin of our teeth – we had a quarrel with a Venetian ship. We have been to the Hetland isles in the far north, but only because our ship was blown off course in a storm and nearly wrecked.

We've traded with the Moors in Spain, and fought off pirates once.'

Angharad looked at her companion, marvelling that there could be so much in the world beyond the green woods and bleak hills of her homeland. So much strangeness and adventure that Johan must surely be half-beast, half-warrior princess through all her travels, yet here she was, happily linking arms with her little Welsh sister, kicking horse muck out of her way, and rubbing her round belly.

'I'm hungry. Let's eat, before I go and harry that Ranulf Attewood, who is seeking to oust my father with the local wool traders.'

They fought their way through to Johan's wagon, and sat under an awning, as a servant brought soft bread, fowls and pies, and wine from Gascony. Johan's father Nicholas, stopping to eat with them, was affable still, though he had to look twice to recognise Angharad. She could tell that he began to see the world in a haze. But his other senses were sharp enough still. He stroked her face, on greeting her, as if his finger's touch could supply the certainty his eyes lacked.

'Fair Angharad it is. And doubly welcome, if you'll sing to me.'

'So I shall, If you will first tell me tales.'

So they ate, and father and daughter regaled her with tales of the low countries and the cities of the cold Baltic sea, of Brittany and Aquitaine, of the hot olive groves around the Middle Sea, the decaying grandeur of a Rome bereft of its Pope, and the gilded venial glories of Venice.

Angharad drank it in, wide eyed, as if harvesting images to feed her dreams, and within, her heart shrivelled at the thought of her return to her dark, smoky home and the rocky, grinding horizons that hemmed her in.

'You're a knave and I'll set the dogs to snap off your cods,' said Johan, hands on hips, while Angharad stood by, laughing.

Ranulf, the rival wool merchant, loped away, disgruntled, snarling over his shoulder, 'You have no dogs.'

'Then I'll bite them off myself!'

'She will, too,' said Harri ap Robert, fingering the coins Johan had paid him. 'And some of us would not say no.'

'Hold your tongue, you, or I'll have my silver back.'

'Lady.' Watcyn, the hulking servant, touched Angharad's shoulder and she span around. 'Your brothers are waiting. They bade me fetch you.'

So they had remembered her at last. She wondered if Watcyn had been secretly dogging her steps all day. He was as careful of her as he had been of Marged, but for Marged he had had felt true devotion, while her little sister, usurping her place was simply his master's valued asset he must guard, least harm should come to her. Least she escape.

She sighed. 'I must come then. It would never do to keep my brothers waiting.'

Watcyn gazed expressionlessly at a clod of mud on his shoe.

Johan saw how it was and brushed the wool farmers aside to embrace Angharad. 'So, it must be farewell for another year, little sister. Fear not. I shall pray for the ailing wife with all my might. May the saints perform a miracle and restore her to health. Now, are you set? Do you have your package?'

'I have.' Angharad hugged her tighter, loathe to let go. But she must. With a sigh, she pulled free. She lifted the bundle that had lain, half concealed by her skirts and thrust it at the servant. 'My fine wedding wear, Watcyn. You can carry it.'

He grunted, shouldering it, and led her through the crowds, heaving men, horses, cattle and pigs out of her way.

201

Outside an alehouse, Siencyn stood, watching her approach with dark irritation.

Hywel took his cue from his elder brother and put on a fine show of impatience. 'You're keeping us, girl.'

'I'm sorry, I didn't know your business would be finished so soon.' Business with the ale casks and the dice, she guessed, spending what they didn't have to spend, with their cattle ailing and little else to sell.

'You came here to fill your dowry chest,' said Siencyn. 'Where are your purchases?'

'Watcyn has them.' She took her bundle from Watcyn. Johan, hearing her mission at the fair, had prepared it for her. Enough but not too much. She untied it sufficiently for them to glimpse fine wool, dyed a soft grey green. 'This and linen for shifts and coifs.'

Siencyn eyed the quality suspiciously. 'How much did this cost you?'

'I spent only what our father gave me.' Which was true enough. He had given her nothing, being drunk and snoring.

'You've drained his purse enough, girl. No more on such gewgaws. This match may yet come to nothing.'

'Yes, brother. It is in the hands of the saints.' And if sweet St Margaret, St Agatha and the Holy Mother of God had any mercy, Rhodri ap Gruffudd's wife would recover and thrive, to laugh in the face of Owain ap Elidyr and his sons.

'You're looking to marry off this girl?' A man, leading his horse, had stopped to listen. Now he stepped forward.

Angharad recognised him – William Lange's steward at Cwrt Isaf, a swaggering young man whose very presence in their valley, let alone by their side at the Borough fair, set her brothers' teeth on edge, their faces darkening, their fists clenching on the pommels of their knives.

'What's it to you, Robert ap Tomos?'

202

'She's a prize worth winning. Another Nest, is she not? With such a face, surely she cannot be a maid still.' The admiration that Robert ap Tomos professed, as he studied her, was as full of insolence as his words. He looked her over as he would look over cattle, or horses, or whores.

Angharad turned away, cheeks burning with anger, but her brothers had wrath enough for all.

'Take your filthy eyes off her, cur. She's not for you to ogle.'

'But perhaps I will offer for her.' It was a suggestion designed only to provoke. For the last year, the provocation had steadily flowed both ways. More than once their servants had come to blows over slights and boundaries and grazing rights, while their masters circled each other, groping for causes to bring a suit to the Lord's court.

'You,' roared Siencyn. 'You would offer for my sister? Robert ap Tomos? Robert of nowhere and no kin? Robert from the midden?'

Robert laughed, leaping into the saddle, looking down on them with contempt, his clothes, his horse and his manners far finer than theirs, though in their eyes he was nothing. Whatever parentage his Welsh mother claimed for him, he was said to be the bastard of some English knight. 'Perhaps I'll wed her, and see if one sad sprig of Hywel Groch's line can be curbed and cudgelled into decent obedience.'

He thought his lofty mounted height made him untouchable, but it was a mistake he would not make again. Before he could set spur to his beast, the brothers had leaped on him and brought him down in one mass of flailing limbs, hurling him into the dust as his horse staggered in its attempts to avoid trampling him. In a moment, a crowd had gathered, eager to egg on one side or another, or both. Stranded on his back like a beetle, Robert's knees came up and his boots caught Siencyn a midriff, sending him flying

203

back into the crowd. But Hywel was there to kick the steward back down before he could rise, spitting invectives, stamping on limbs and guts. Then Siencyn was catapulted back into the affray by helpful hands, and seized Robert by collar and belt, to heave him into the steaming, squelching cattle muck that had accumulated by one of the emptying pens. The crowd roared approval, indifferent to causes, but happy, by this stage of the day, to witness any mayhem.

'Back in the midden where you belong, snuffling swine,' snarled Siencyn. 'And keep your filthy eyes off any daughter of Owain ap Elidyr ap Rhys ap Hywel Groch? You think we'd sully our blood with yours?'

Little of Robert ap Tomos's finery was left, or his scorn. Only red-faced fury as he wiped muck from his eyes and mouth, spitting and gagging. Then his men reached the scene, and the brothers' servants stepped up in turn, fists flying. Knives were drawn.

'Come, lady, I must get you away from here,' said Watcyn, torn between duty to her and a desire to join the fracas.

'Yes, take me away.' Angharad turned her back on the scene, hurrying through the crowd, seeking only distance between herself and Robert ap Tomos's foul insults. Hopeless to seek distance from the glowering resentment her brothers would doubtless take out on her, when they finally broke free from the mêlée and came rolling drunkenly home.

She wished she were free of them all.

5

A cuckoo called across the valley. Soon, in a month or two, it would go. Vanish. Puff.

Angharad leaned back against the trunk of an oak, plaiting long blades of grass and listening to the strange, illusive bird. Where did it go? Or the swallows, who gathered in loud, twittering congregations around the house one day, and the next were gone, not to be seen again until the spring. Did they burrow deep into rock to sleep away the winter gales? Or did they secretly take ship, like Johan? How was it that a mere bird could escape, and Angharad could not? Such wise fools, the birds. Wise to leave, fools to return.

Perhaps the wiser birds of the woods knew better, the blackbirds and thrushes, the robins and wrens. They knew there was no escape, so why waste their strength in fleeing, when the winds of the world would carry them straight back? Perhaps it was that knowledge that quietened their song, after the urgent clamour of their springtime ardour. Their mates had been found, their young had been fledged, and the truth of their captivity had returned to stifle their souls. Only a drowsy intermittent song haunted the woods now.

There was a stillness under the trees, a hush. She listened to it, drinking it in. No, it wasn't the empty hush of despair. It was the quiet stillness of expectant life, not death. The oaks, imprisoned in the rocky soil, flexed their gnarled branches, rejoicing in their burst of fresh green. That freshness would grow heavy and weary in the summer heat, the sad green would fade to russet, the leaves would fall, and the trees would be left in the biting winter winds as barren skeletons, rattling their bones. But every time they died, they lived again, meeting another spring, year after year after year. Death and then life again. Resurrection. Always the return of life, unconquered.

Angharad turned to press her ear against the rough bark of the oak, listening for the sap rising. The pulse of the world.

Was it true of all things, this conquest of death? Would her mother live again? And Marged? It was the doctrine that the Holy Church taught, so she must believe it, or die apostate and damned. She wished it to be true. There had to be a promise of life renewed, for them all. Even for the baby Gwenllian, who was surely baptised, though all the priests in Christendom denied it. She prayed that their time in Purgatory would be short and their sufferings mild. What great sins had they committed, to require a painful purging? Rather, it was the sins done to them that should be purged, with fire and ice and biting winds.

For herself, she acknowledged frankly she was not without sin. She was disobedient and wilful when she should be submissive. She was a wicked daughter, for though God and men gave her father authority over her, she would never honour him, as the scriptures commanded. She would have a hearty pricking and whipping in Purgatory before she could hope to taste the eternal bliss of Paradise and see her mother and Marged again. Oh, but though she longed for them, that was not the escape she wanted. Not the joys of another world, but the promises of this. This life. Freedom. She wanted the rising sap in the green woods, the breeze from the distant sea, the birds singing, and her own song, the pulse of life in her own veins. She wanted to live.

She watched a warbler alight on the branch above her.

206

She was so still it didn't notice her existence, until she raised a hand – and then it flew away, bobbing, dipping through the greenery. Escaping.

Her basket dug into her hip as she swivelled to follow the bird's flight, its jabbing reminding her of her mission. She had no business to linger, day-dreaming of swallows and sap and seasons. She had been ordered to carry Ieuan his supper, and though, at a safe distance, she cared nothing for her father's command, she cared a great deal for Ieuan and he must be hungry.

She tucked up her skirt, singing her lingering defiance as she climbed on, up through the trees. Her round-about route, as she had rambled, this way and that through the forests, had brought her close to the holy well, under its dripping crags. She veered aside, to its brink.

St. Bride's well. It was said there had once been an image of St.Bride here, a statue that could work miracles, healing wounds of mind and body, but it had vanished. Perhaps the saint had reclaimed it, not wishing to dwell so close to the roaring blasphemies of the house of Hywel Groch. Or perhaps it had sunk into the green waters. Siencyn lost a hound here, a year since – one of his favourites. It bounded over the crag above, and fell, and the mire had swallowed it before anyone could reach it. Perhaps the hound hunted with the lady now.

Angharad knelt and thought of her. The lady of this dark pool. St. Bride. St. Margaret. She touched her breast, pressing the linen of her shift against her skin, so that she could feel the little brooch she always wore there, where her flesh could touch it. Holy Virgin, Mother of God. The lady who owned this well could be any of them. Or all of them. Perhaps, united in divinity, they were all one. One holy lady, saint, virgin, martyr, mother, goddess, dragon slayer. The statue might be gone, but perhaps the well could still heal.

Angharad dabbled her fingers in the peat-dark water, and stroked her cheek, where the cut, across the bone, a gift from her loving family, still stung. It soothed, whether miracle or no. She said a prayer to the lady, whoever she was – to any saint who would walk with her in the battles yet to come.

High above, out on the hills, she heard the rumble of the herd, the lowing carried on the wind. They were on the move. No time to linger now.

Out on the open moors, the breeze was fresher, blowing in from the sea that sparkled and flashed on the horizon. From this high place, it looked unreal, a fantastical dream of freedom and eternity, but she had touched its surging waves at the borough, and tasted its salt. The seasoning of life. It was lapping on the quays of the borough even now. She shielded her eyes, straining to look for ships, but the flash of the water was too bright. The sun was dipping down into the long summer evening, shadows lengthening on the land, but there were no shadows on the sea. It burned like a thousand diamonds dancing.

A fantasy.

She strode on, towards the black cattle, and the men driving them, preparing to pen them for the night. There were always men attending the cattle these days, standing guard over them. Against wolves, they said. They didn't mean the grey howling beasts that Angharad had heard in her sleep but had never seen in waking life, except as skins nailed to the hall wall. They meant two-legged wolves, and those she had seen in plenty. Quarrels over boundaries with William Lange's steward at Cwrt Isaf had ebbed and flowed over the last year, but mostly flowed. Robert ap Tomos had neither forgotten, nor forgiven, his treatment at the fair. Cattle had been stolen, on both sides. Brawls erupted on the slightest pretext. One man had been killed. The courts were growing weary of them.

Angharad spied Ieuan sitting on a rock, easing his back as he swung his legs. She hailed him, raising the basket to show that she brought him food, and he waved, his solemn face breaking into a wide smile. He was a poor choice for a protector of cattle. He would willingly clasp a crucifix, but there was no urge to wield knife or fists in his young bones. He possessed none of his brothers' belligerence, but such was their father's obsessive distrust of their arrogant neighbour that even Ieuan must take his turn, guarding the herd.

'Thank you, sister.' He studied her as she sat down beside him, stroking the cut on her cheek, so gently that she didn't feel the pain. 'It is healing.'

'Thanks to St Bride, I think. But it is nothing. I am well enough.' She couldn't remember whose fist had done it – her father's or Siencyn's. It was Hywel who had painted the bruises on her arm, she knew that.

'You should not defy them, sister.' Ieuan set to on the bread and cheese she'd brought him.

'I should marry this Madog ap Rhys without a murmur of complaint?'

'Of course.' When had Ieuan ever questioned any orders, from his father or the church? 'You must obey our father. It is commanded. If it is his will—'

'What is your will, Ieuan? That I should be passed across for another man to beat me? That I should be got with child and die like Marged, like our mother?'

'Submission in a woman is a holy virtue, sister. Women must endure and suffer. It is ordained by God, as judgement upon the sin of our first mother. Learn patience. All the trials of this life will be repaid in full in the next. Be like our Blessed Lady, and you will find peace.'

'Perhaps I shall be like you, Ieuan. You desire to become a monk, do you not? To be in the quiet of the cloisters?

Perhaps I shall become a nun.'

'You know our father would never permit it. He would refuse to pay your dower, and no house would take you penniless. Besides, you are not truly bent on it.'

'Am I not?' She foresaw a life in a house of women, with prayer and song. Just women. No roaring. No beating. No birth and blood and screaming death. 'I think I could be a nun.'

'No,' said Ieuan, firmly. 'For a religious must practise obedience gladly, and you do not. When you speak, you do not speak of Jesu, you speak of the world, of distant places, of Johan Hamblyn and the noise and bustle of the fair. That is not the talk of one who seeks submission to God.'

'But I must speak of it no more, since I am forbidden to visit the fair this year.' Again she looked to the glint of the sea, the diamonds gilding now to topazes, as the sun slipped down. Were Johan's sails in sight? Already the borough would be raucous in preparation for the business and bustle that Ieuan so scorned – but this year, it would be denied to her. It wasn't the business and bustle she would miss, it was Johan. The one day of the year when she could embrace her busy merchant sister, and speak of Marged and pirates and pilgrims, of trade in wool and wine and spices, and faraway places. Why must even that one fleeting illusion of freedom be denied? Because they sensed in her the wilful wickedness of an untamed beast that would throw off the halter and flee at the first opportunity. Though they had done their best to beat and burn and starve rebellion out of her, they were convinced that she still sought to flee the latest marriage they were scheming for, now that Maredudd ap Rhys's wife had so miraculously recovered. She was not to be allowed to leave their lands again until she was safe wed and disposed of.

No use complaining to Ieuan. He would only tell her to

210

turn her thoughts from the vanities of this world. She looked away, so that he would not see the tears shining in her eyes. 'Should you be following the cattle?'

Ieuan followed her gaze. 'I should. Guto and Gwion can drive them well enough without my aid, but I must follow.' Reluctantly, he rose, massaging his spine.

'I'll light a candle for your return,' she promised, and kissed him before he ambled off in the wake of the rumbling, black beasts.

She was still hurrying homeward, in the fading dusk, along the stony moorland, when she heard the horses, coming hard behind her, along the track that led up over the hills and down into the valley beyond. She turned to look. Too distant to see the riders' faces, but she knew, in an instant, the red cloak of the leader. Robert ap Tomos and his man.

She ran.

She should not have run. She knew it, even as instinct took over and her legs carried her, leaping like a deer over rock and furze. She should have stood her ground, taken his insults in silent dignity and he'd have contented himself with lewd comments, hustling her unnecessarily out of his way.

She'd thought she could reach the shelter of the steep woods before he caught her, but she was wrong. His horse was swift, sure-footed even on the uneven ground, and he was laughing bitterly as he reached down from the saddle to snatch at her mantle. What red-blooded man could resist the hunt? The blood-churning excitement of pursuit. In fleeing, she had set herself up as his quarry. One helpless dove to his sharp-taloned falcon. His game and his revenge.

She was no dove. She fought. With fists and claws and teeth and every ounce of strength in her, she fought. She had blood in her mouth – his blood, where she bit into the hand

211

that sought to stifle her. It was he who screamed, not her. But he wasn't screaming now, and there was no hand to bite, only folds of his cloak clamped over her face, smothering even as she kicked and clawed against his weight and fury, his ripping of her kirtle, his wrenching of her limbs. She would not surrender. Nothing would make her surrender. But the cloak enveloped her, wool robbing her of air and consciousness. She prayed 'Holy lady, help me,' but for all her will to fight, blackness was closing in.

And all she could think was, 'Johan would think this is very good cloth.'

She's gone. She doesn't breathe... Demon or angel? Who was whispering her death to her? The wind carried the words away.
No, master, I cannot... Then stand guard, fool. I'll do it.

Demons and angels. Fighting over her soul as it drifted. Purgatory – that was where she must be, then. It was a place of pain, just as she'd heard tell, of cold and biting winds, of stabbing, scratching... branches.

Fleetingly, she realised she was still alive. This windy moor was real, and he, Robert ap Tomos, was panting and grunting like the beast he was. Grunting not as he raped her now, but because he carried her. She was bent double, flung over his shoulder. Numb, uncomprehending, she saw her hand, white in the gathering gloom, hanging down, lifeless, blood clogging the nails.

Then all was black again.

Ah!

Again, her soul lurched back into being, as if it raced up from the depths of a well of unconsciousness. Blood was surging through her veins once more, in a great rush, sweeping back the aching, bruising pains to engulf her.

Where she was, or who or why, she didn't know, but there was life in her again, shrieking for salvation. Cruel, gripping hands wrenched her from her perch, heaving her inert form round and she gave a gasp, a groan, as breath rushed back into her.

He roared.

Why did all men roar? Her father. He was nothing but roar. He was Owain…

For a moment, the briefest of moments, there was clarity and understanding. She knew where she was. On the brink of the cliff above St. Bride's well—

And Robert ap Tomos was throwing her.

A wild panic seized her, She grabbed, at something, anything. Fingers closed on leaf, leather, air, but nothing stopped her fall, over, over, striking rock, moss, water.

A long and dying scream.

6

Sinking. Out of life. No struggle left. Let it go. Leave this shattering pain behind and accept oblivion. Angharad was not there. She didn't fight.

Not until the slime closed over her mouth and nose. Then something deep within the battered wreck of her body sparked into one tiny flame.

One thought.

No!

I will not die! I will not, I will not, I will not!

Her futile struggling sucked her deeper, but the deeper she sank, the brighter burned the flame. Her hand hit wood. Her fingers closed around a root and would not let go. Never. She would never let go. Like a forged chain she clung on, and the strength of the still living tree ran down her arm and found her heart.

Lady, be with me, give me strength.

She heaved, with the will and power of all the saints, and her face broke clear, just enough for her to spit foul muck and water from her mouth and draw a precious breath.

But the saints had not yet won. The enemy was fighting back. A demon gripped her other arm. She could feel his wicked fingers winding around hers, dragging her down, sucking her back into the mire.

'No!'

On a mighty surge of fury that roared through her, as great as any roar of Owain ap Elidyr, she wrenched her arm up and it came free, up and out of the swamp. A severed demon's claw clung to it, heavy with the weight of Hell, still seeking to reclaim her, but she would not surrender. No! The fire within her had become a raging tornado of flame. She would live! She gripped the root, spat out more slime, fought and hauled and struggled and, at last, like a mud eel, she slithered free, onto rock and grit and moss.

She hurt.

Sweet Jesus, how she hurt. Now that the first urgent struggle had eased, she could only think of the all-consuming pain. Was it possible that there could be so much agony, in every part of her? The hand that had grasped the root was streaming blood. It scored red grooves through the black filth. A finger ground, broken. How had she gripped anything? What inhuman power had possessed her? Not human at all, but divine. The lady's, it must have been, bearing her in holy arms. But now those arms had released their hold and she had no strength left. She wanted only healing sleep. A death of sorts, without the tortures of Purgatory. Without memories or dreams. Just sleep.

But not here. Not in the place the filthy beast, Robert ap Tomos, had sought to make her tomb. On torn elbows and knees, she crawled out of the dell, over sharp rocks, into the soft embrace of grass and leaf mould. Shivers ran through her, wave upon wave, and nothing would stop them. Blood was seeping, from every inch of skin, it seemed, but she didn't care. All she knew was that she must sleep. Seek the relief of darkness again. As it closed round her, she could hear them, the saints, calling her name.

Angharad! Angharad!

Saints, it must be.

They sounded like Ieuan.

She slept.

Pain.

She woke to an ocean of pain. It gnawed and knifed at

215

every limb, every joint, every muscle, every inch of her innards. Her head throbbed. Her stomach heaved. Her nostrils were still half-clogged with foul-smelling mud. Slime braided her hair. She wore the ragged remnants of a shift that was streaked green and black and crimson. It pricked her as if it were woven of pins. Perhaps it was. Bruised fingers groped for the pricking and found the cause. The brooch of St. Margaret. Its beading bit into her flesh as she lay on it.

A very little pain, that one. A very small pricking. She fixed on it, concentrating all her thoughts on it, so that she would not feel the rest. She raised the brooch to her swollen lips and kissed it. St. Marged, her sister, had pulled her out of the dragon. She loved her sister.

The sun had gone. A half-moon began to glow through the branches of the trees. An owl swept low. Hounds were crying, baying out the sorrow of the world.

Hounds.

She was so used to the sound that, for a while, she gave it no heed. Then it rose, unleashed, and she was jolted into a wider consciousness. Her father's hounds. Her brothers would come looking for her. She had tarried and they were ever watchful for her escape. They were right. She would have fled long ago, except that she knew the hounds were there, ever ready to hunt her down. After all that she had endured this day, still they were hunting her to drag her back down to the homestead, to be beaten and imprisoned and married against her will, to be ripped open in childbirth for their games of gain.

Lady, set me free.

Why would the hounds not cease? Then, like an echo of their song, she heard the drumming of hoofs far above. She felt their beat vibrating like a bell in the ground beneath her.

A voice. High, shouting in angry panic. His voice. Robert

ap Tomos. The beast. 'Ride on, man. Search the track.'

She caught the jingle as he dismounted.

He was coming back for her.

No!

She would not let him find her. Not him or the hounds, or her brothers, or any of them. Never! Anger and determination flared up in her again, setting the fire in her veins once more, driving her to action.

There was an oak branch, low and straight, above her head. She swung herself up, the fire raging now, pouring itself into her limbs, refusing surrender, no matter what the threat or the battleground. She would escape from them all. Up to another branch. Keep climbing, up and out of their reach. Hide among the fresh leaves, bark biting into her raw flesh.

She was so high now she could look down over the rocky divide, into the black glint of the holy well.

A voice murmured in the whispering of the trees, caressing her, commanding her. 'See what I brought you from, to live still. Do not surrender.' St Margaret. Marged. Holy lady.

But now that Angharad was as secure as she could be, the urgency and strength began to seep away again. The flashes of lucidity that had driven her up to safety gave way to a dream-like trance, in which she could only witness.

So she witnessed, and did not altogether understand what she witnessed. What was vision and imagination? What was real?

She heard Robert ap Tomos thrashing about at the top of the cliff, his muttered curses. 'Where is it? Damn her, by Jesu, the bitch, where is it?'

He came slithering down to the well's edge, by the side path, and now she could see him, the flash of pale linen above his leather jerkin. A thrashing of saplings. He'd hacked out a bough and was using it to probe the waters of the well, stabbing into the mud.

'The cursed whore. She-wolf.'

She could see, in the flickering light of fading sunset and glowing moon, the fury and fear on his face, and dried blood from claw marks on his cheek.

Still the hounds were singing, drawing closer. Straight to the well. How did they know where to come? They couldn't be following her scent up the track, because she'd wound her way here in such a tortuous route, in and out through the trees, delayed meandering as she'd savoured her brief dreams of freedom. She hadn't taken the direct path and yet, along the direct path they came, the hounds straining against the leashes gripped by Siencyn and Hywel, and a dozen men with them, savage rage and blood lust on their faces. Straight to her tree and the holy well.

Robert ap Tomos heard them. Perhaps the enclosing walls of the dell deceived him, at first, muffling the sound of their murderous advance in its own echoes, misleading him as to their closeness, because he paused to listen, but he didn't flee. Instead, he bent once more to probe the waters. He realised his danger too late, only as the first hound bounded over the rocky threshold of the dell. He straightened, dropped his bough and ran, clambering up the craggy path.

Too late. The hounds, let loose, were on his heels. Like her, his flight marked him instantly as quarry, before the dumb beasts even had their orders.

'Bring him down!' Hywel shouted.

Siencyn whistled commands as he burst into the dell, sword in hand. Robert rolled back down the slope, trying to fend off snapping teeth, struggling to loose his dagger. A hound's mad growls rose in pitch to a whine, and he almost broke free, but it was too late. Siencyn's men had fanned out through the trees, circling the dell and some were already at the top, blocking the way.

Robert staggered to his feet, attempting to draw his own sword as he faced Siencyn, but the dogs were on him again, tripping and ripping.

Siencyn was hissing and spitting with rage. 'You filthy midden rat! You'd lay a hand on a woman that is ours?'

Robert ap Tomos struggled, as if there were some hope of escape, but men and dogs had him down, and all he could do, as they bound him and kicked and bit, was shriek curses and promises of retribution.

'You touch me, curs, may the crows feast on your entrails. You'll be hunted down...' His voice was stifled by a gag.

She felt again the red wool pressed over her face, stifling her.

'I'll not sully iron on him. String him up!' roared Siencyn.

'Angharad!' Ieuan's breaking voice rose high and piercing over the clamour.

It was the voice she had heard as she'd crawled from the well. Now her heart froze within her, as she heard it again. He must have seen her, in her tree, hiding high above them all. Not Ieuan. Not her only tender brother. Why must he be the one to betray her?

No, she would not let them drag her down. Her bloodied hands gripped the branch, locking round it like forged steel. Let them shoot arrows, if they would, but nothing would bring her down! She would die in this tree.

But no one looked up. Not even Ieuan. He was looking down, instead. Down into the well, hunched, gnawing his fists. 'He threw her over. I saw him. I saw him! I ran and ran, but I was too late. I couldn't find her. She is in there!'

It was clear where she fell – a pool of muddied water, glinting in moonlight, lay shimmering in the midst of the velvety moss and slime. The signs of her fall were there for all to read, but none of them paused to read the signs of her escape.

'So she is gone,' said Siencyn. 'And he will pay.'

'She might live.'

'No, she's finished. And since she has been befouled by this beast, it's as well for her she is dead.'

But the men, at Ieuan's distraught insistence, stopped to search, probing the waters just as her murderer had done, finding nothing, for all the boy's desperation.

Siencyn stood and watched, unmoved.

Hywel, ever more hot-blooded, kicked savagely at the prone man. 'Why waste rope on him? If he drowned our sister in the mire, let's do the same to him!'

The simple justice of it appealed. They dragged Robert, squirming against the ropes that bound him, gurgling round his gag, to the water and pushed his face into mud, pinning him down though he heaved and bucked like a serpent in his struggles.

Ieuan cried, 'He is not shriven!' but they paid him no heed.

'Was our sister shriven?' demanded Siencyn, his boot pushing Robert's face deeper, as the struggles and convulsions weakened, until, finally, they ceased.

They hauled the lifeless corpse back, jerking his hair back to spit in his blackened face, then they hoisted him up and, between them, swung back and forth, back and forth, and heaved him out, onto the mire. The bound and battered remains of Robert ap Tomos landed with a splash and lay motionless for a moment in the wavering light. Then the mud began to close around him, taking possession. The waters soaked into him, softly sucking him down.

His executioners helped, determined that their hand should be on it all. Yelping and whooping, they heaved rocks at the corpse, until it sank from view, and nothing remained but oozing blackness and a few stinking bubbles.

Then at last the men were silent, breathing deeply, thinking on their deed.

Ieuan was on his knees, praying.

Hywel clapped Siencyn on the shoulder. 'It was well done, brother. No filthy cur will soil what is ours and go unpunished. Our father will approve.'

'Yes, he will.' Siencyn had the greater judgement, for all his snarling anger. 'But others will not be so eager to praise us. Back to the hall! Back before the cur's men come looking. They'll take nothing more of ours.'

Battle-blood up again, they loped away, sweeping Ieuan with them.

Voices and howls faded away. Silence fell. After the commotion of fury and murder, the forest resumed its night-watch as if nothing had happened. The owl swooped back.

Angharad lay along the branch of her oak, feeling the soft dew on her skin, hearing the rustle of the leaves, the soft breath of the wind. She remembered that she was alive.

It was summer, but the night was chill, and she was almost naked, shivering. She was wounded, bruised and broken, violated in every way, but she was alive. None of the devils that beset her had conquered her, not Robert ap Tomos, nor her brothers, nor the demon lurking in the mire... that demon, whose hand had snatched at her... that hand that she had wrenched free...

As her senses returned, her mind began to still. She recalled. A devil's fingers had twined in hers, had they not? Dragging her down, until she had fought back. It was not mere delusion, surely.

Gathering her strength and her will power, she raised herself, drew deep breaths, then began to clamber down from her high perch. Dropping the last few feet to the ground with a jarring scream of pain, she returned to the spot where she had come to rest, seeking sleep. A nest of grass and moss.

And there it was, abandoned among tree roots and tangled weeds, the devil's hand. Her fingers must have worked free from its clutch as she slept.

Now, in the white moonlight, she could see that it was not a clawed hand, after all. It was a purse. Soft leather, with a crested clasp. Robert ap Tomos had worn it on his belt – and she must have grabbed at it as she fell, the straps entwining in her fingers, her weight snapping them.

She picked it up. No wonder it had dragged her down. It was heavy. She opened it. Coins. Silver coins. A stream of them, tumbling out. She scrabbled to gather them. There must be five pounds there, or more. No wonder he'd returned, despite the danger, when he found the purse was gone. Whatever business had taken him over the hills that day, be it his own or his master's, he had ridden home carrying more wealth than he could afford to lose. So, finding it gone, he had had no choice but to retrace his steps and look for it.

And it had killed him.

It would have killed her too. Now let it help her live, instead.

She pushed herself onwards, staggering, skirting the black glimmer of the well, stepping over a dead hound, and began to haul herself up the steep slope, out of the trees onto the open moorland, ignoring the screaming of her limbs.

In the eerie, moonlit landscape, drained of colour, she saw red. Fox red? A beast? But it didn't move. She approached. Robert ap Tomos's fine red cloak, abandoned where he sought to smother her. Stained but still good wool. So warming as she pulled it round her. She would not freeze. She would not die! It had come near to killing her. Now it too would be her salvation.

Out across the valley and far woods and fields, silver light glimmered on the black sea.

Two days to Curig's fair. Ships were at anchor in the harbour. Perhaps Johan was already there.

Angharad took a deep breath, forced her muscles into submission, and set off along the hills, towards the sea.

7

'There now, Kat, he'll do.' Johan de Pulteney handed the baby to the waiting nurse and settled back comfortably on her cushions, pulling her chemise back over her ample bosom. 'Perhaps now he'll sleep, the little glutton.'

Angharad watched as the child was carried away, a bubble on his contented lips. 'He will thrive, that one.'

'So he should. He drinks me dry. Now it's my turn.' Johan helped herself to a plate of honeyed dates and almonds. 'Have some. No need for you to subdue the flesh with flogging and fasting just yet.'

Angharad took a nut. 'Not yet.'

'And are you still determined on this thing?' Johan asked, as she had asked a hundred time before, in a wistful tone, but resigned to the answer she knew would come.

'Yes. I am resolved. It is time.'

'Ah well. And nothing will tempt you from it? Not even the excitement of this magnificent fair?'

Angharad laughed. They had come, sailing down the Severn and round the coast, to Curig's fair, and she had seen the Borough for the first time since she had crawled to it, seven years before, broken and bloodied, wrapped in a cloak of red wool, to fall in a swoon at Johan's feet. Only now, seeing it again after having seen the world, did she understand how small and insignificant a thing it was, where once it had been the awesome highlight of her year.

'I shall endure the loss of that excitement.'

'But what of this loss? The loss of me? Your sister?'

'I am not losing you, Johan. We shall be sisters, still, until the end of our days and in Heaven too. You will be first in my prayers, day and night. But our lives are changing. You are married and have a fine, healthy son. It's time for me to seek my own road at last.'

'Oh, very well. I know your stubbornness. You will have your way. Matthew! Thomas! Bring the horses. Time that we were on the road.'

Their men servants, strapping lads who could sing rounds, lift ladies and send insolent men flying with equal ease, had their horses ready at the door of the inn. Rain had cleared away and the sun was riding up a sky of high summer blue. Fold upon fold of oakwood stretched before them.

The smell of oak and black cattle, the high Welsh hills and the wind off the sea – this was the smell of home, a world Angharad had not tasted for seven years. She had seen so much since, travelling with kindly, cunning Nicholas Hamblyn as his second daughter, sharing Johan's duties and pleasures, seeing wonders, enduring sea-sickness, once wrecked and near to drowning. She had walked in the streets of Ghent and Bruges, of Bordeaux and Lisbon, Florence and Messina. She had touched the ruins of the martyrs in Rome. She had walked barefoot to the shrine of St. James. She had learned to read and to write. She had mastered English and spoke enough of low German, French and Latin to pass as a woman of great worldly learning. She knew the quality of wool and wine, and how to read the signs of storms at sea. Her five pounds of silver, given with gratitude to her new father, had become a comfortable fortune, a dowry that could have purchased any husband that she chose, despite her scars, her slight limp and the crooked finger that would never quite straighten, though it had healed well enough, like all her wounds.

She found, to her surprise, that for all the glories and mysteries of the world through which she'd travelled, she had begun to miss the rain-soaked oaks of Wales, the rustle of leaves, the song of the blackbird and the caw of the rooks. But she had no thought of returning to the lands where her father and brothers nursed their petty grievances and roared at the skies. To them she was dead, and it was her great care in life never to place herself within their reach again.

At last, Nicholas Hamblyn had sickened, taking to his bed at his hall in Bristol and he had died, at peace, well shriven, with Johan and Angharad at his side. They had wept as they prepared him for burial, but the book of life had turned a page. Johan thought to wed at last, choosing Philip de Pulteney from the many suitors who panted after her generous curves, her fat purse and her busy ships. Philip was a merchant with ships of his own. It was a wise and profitable match for them both.

Angharad had been happy for her sister, but when Johan's men had gone that year to Curig's Fair, trading for their mistress, she had bid them seek news from Llys y Garn. They knew nothing of her history, thinking of her as Nicholas Hamblyn's daughter. But understanding that she had had some past knowledge of the Borough and the lands around, they had enquired and she had listened intently to their tale on their return.

'It is said there was great havoc and bloodshed, lady. The men of Llys y Garn accused Robert ap Tomos of rape and violence, and the men of Cwrt Isaf claimed their master had been foully murdered. All was riot. Six men were killed, including Siencyn ap Owain, eldest son of the master of Llys y Garn. The Lord Martin's men were hard put to it to restore peace, and not before Owain ap Elidyr's hall was burned to the ground. Hywel ap Owain was taken prisoner, back to the Borough, but while the wise men squabbled over whose court should try him, he escaped and fled. No one knows where. Some say Ireland, some say Jerusalem.'

'And Owain ap Elidyr?'

'An arrow caught him, lady, while he was out hunting. An accident, some say. Other say not, but there were no kin crying for justice.'

'What of his third son. What of Ieuan ap Owain?'

'Lady, we were told that he is now a monk at St. Dogmael's Abbey. The Baron Martin took back the lands of Llys y Garn.'

So. She had retired to her chamber, her comfortable chamber with its fine hangings and cushions and its window looking out on a sweet-scented garden, and she had knelt, dutifully, to pray for the souls of the dead. But she found herself praying for Nicholas Hamblyn, and for Marged and her mother and the babies, her nephew Rhys and her sister Gwenllian and her prayers stopped there. Perhaps, in time, with God's grace, she would find it within her to pray for her father and brothers, and even for the monster Robert ap Tomos. Or perhaps pay others to pray for them. Now, all she could do was thank God and the blessed Lady that they were gone.

The green oak woods were cleansed. She could go home.

She stayed with Johan in the first year of her marriage, by her side, calmly concealing her dread until Johan's son was safely born, with some squeals and good round oaths, but no screams or fever, no frantic visits from the priest. Then she told Johan her mind – to return at last to her own country. Not her own estate. She was a woman and could have no claim to any. But to the hills and woods. She meant to take the veil at the nunnery of Llanllŷr.

Johan sought to dissuade her, but she understood her little Welsh sister's mind, and so they took ship one more time together, to the Borough, for Curig's Fair, and after watching the cattle wading across the wide estuary, and the jugglers and musicians and the wool merchants, they had set off

227

north.

'How do you think you'll like a house full of women?' Johan glanced at her sidelong as they rode.

'I'll like it well enough. Very well indeed,' said Angharad, serenely.

'You know we are just as fallible as men – as petty and malicious and silly in our thoughts.'

'But we do not roar. Or beat, or rape or murder. If my holy sisters are inclined to sullenness or spite, I shall charm them with songs and bewitch them with tales of Avignon and Santiago.'

Johan gave a great belly laugh. 'And so you will. You will be abbess, you know.'

'I seek only to be a humble sister.'

'No, you will be abbess.' Johan yelped. 'Hi there, Matthew, have you found me the laziest horse in the Borough? He trips on every stone. And I thought my rump had cushioning enough for any ride.'

Angharad smiled. 'You should be back in Ashwell Hall, with little Nicholas in his cradle and a stool beneath your feet.'

'Ha! And leave you to ride here alone? I could do no such thing.'

Angharad reached out and clasped her hand.

The trees parted. The track widened. Walls rose above fields of oats and beans. The gateway of the nunnery lay before them.

Matthew and Thomas leaped down to hand the ladies from their placid mounts. Angharad drew the rings from her fingers and handed them to Johan. One jewel she kept – a small enamelled brooch. Then the women embraced, and Johan wept.

Matthew knocked upon the gates, and when the grill

opened, he crossed himself devoutly. 'Here is Margaret, daughter of Nicholas Hamblyn, sister, seeking entry to your house.'

The gate swung open.

She became Abbess. Of course. She lived content among her sisters, cajoling them into good humour and comfortable piety, and no one roared. She survived the great pestilence that swept through the land twenty years later. So did Johan de Pulteney, though it ravaged Bristol and claimed her husband. Johan died wealthy and content, with grandchildren about her.

A grander house was built on the site of Owain ap Elidyr's smoking halls. A house with a hall of stone and a tower and defending walls. Though the blood line of Hywel Groch lingered on at nearby Hendre Hywel, it was forgotten in Llys y Garn.

Devout pilgrims and superstitious girls ceased to visit St. Bride's holy well. It gained darker names. No one dared to probe its depths. They said that demons dwelt there.

Postlude

The rooks of Llys y Garn have seen so much. They have watched, with a nonchalant lack of surprise, the fitful restoration work of new owners, the Elizabethan fayre intended to resurrect the glories of the ancient hall and the hapless archaeological excavations that delved too deep. They observed blazing curtains, cars roaring into darkness, flapping police tape and funeral fires and they didn't bat an eyelid. If rooks have eyelids.

The rooks will still be here when... what? When Llys y Garn becomes a residential nursing home? A film location? An obscure religious retreat? Or perhaps just a burnt-out shell. Whatever becomes of it, the rooks will still be here, along with its secrets and its ghosts.

THE END

If you have enjoyed LONG SHADOWS. try its companion and sequel.

SHADOWS

Kate Lawrence can sense the shadow of violent death, past and present. In her struggle to cope with her unwelcome gift, she has frozen people out of her life. Her marriage is on the rocks, her career is in chaos and she urgently needs to get a grip.

So she decides to start again, by joining her effervescent cousin Sylvia and partner Michael in their mission to restore and revitalise Llys y Garn, a decaying mansion in the wilds of North Pembrokeshire. But as she takes on Sylvia's grandiose schemes, she realises she has come to a place thick with the shadows of past deaths.

The house and grounds are full of mysteries that only she can sense, but she is determined to face them down – so determined that she fails to notice that ancient energies are not the only shadows threatening the seemingly idyllic world of Llys y Garn.

Sylvia's sadistic and manipulative son, Christian arrives – but just how dangerous is he? Once more, Kate senses that a violent death has occurred…

Set in the majestic and magical Welsh countryside, Shadows is a haunting exploration of the dark side of people and landscape.

About the author

THORNE MOORE grew up in Luton, but in the 1980s, she moved to Pembrokeshire in West Wales, which provides a rich source of inspiration for several of her books.

Besides working in libraries and the civil service, she set up a restaurant with her sister, and ran a craft business making miniature furniture. She now writes full-time.

Her genres include crime, family sagas, domestic noir, historical novels and science fiction.

thornemoore.com

Ingram Content Group UK Ltd.
Milton Keynes UK
UKHW041433120423
420044UK00001B/172

9 781788 762816